THE PATRIOT'S WARRIORS

by

John Paltanawick

RoseDog Books
PITTSBURGH, PENNSYLVANIA 15238

RoseDog Books
585 Alpha Drive, Suite 103
Pittsburgh, PA 15238
Visit our website at *www.rosedogbookstore.com*

ISBN: 978-1-63661-047-4
eISBN: 978-1-63661-105-1

INTRODUCTION

John Colton, an ex-Navy Seal, call sign Cobalt, is convinced by an ex-Army Ranger to attend a meeting at a small-town American Legion in the beginning stages of forming a Constitutional Militia. Their purpose: To protect the local citizens from a storm of violence that is moving across America and has already reached their border.

A global pandemic ravages America, News of unjustified police killings of black people angers millions of Americans. Black People Matter (BPM) a Marxist organization exercising First Amendment Rights to peacefully protest sieges an opportunity to change the course of American Democracy. All police departments must be defunded. With the police handcuffed by their Mayors, protests become violent, businesses are destroyed, looting escalates, and a new domestic terrorist group evolves in several major cities, Antifa. John Colton's militia has an enemy.

John Colton is contacted by his former Navy Seal Commander, recently promoted to Admiral, and has accepted a role in President David Travis's Administration in the Department of Defense (DOD). John is offered the position of special operations manager but turns it down. The faithful Christian that he is, can't turn his back on the commitment he made to the militia and will not leave until his State is safe from Antifa.

With the support of the DOD, the militia is supplied with combat gear and recognized as a First Amendment Regulated Militia. Secret missions are assigned by the DOD which takes them to the hot spots across America, from East to West and beyond U.S. Borders.

PROLOGUE

On the roof of the Capitol Building, ex-Navy Seal Chief Petty Officer John Colton and Captain Dutch Swanson, kneeling alongside two Secret Service snipers were gazing over the sea of people extending to the National Monument. The Mall grounds were swarming with haters called Antifa (short for Anti-fascist). "Defund the Police" and "Black People Matter" and "Block the Recount" signs were everywhere. The reason John was there was that the National Security Agency (NSA) had intercepted Internet chatter exposing a large insurrection force whose intentions were to see the White House burning, as in the day when British troops burned it in 1814.

The Department of Defense and the President, in accordance with the Second Amendment, called in the regulated militia, three thousand forty-two strong to prepare for the insurrection. Looking out at the mass of haters, John thought, *"Who are these people? How did we get here? Why are American citizens burning flags, assassinating police officers, and now attempting to attack the White House?"*

Maybe It started when American schools began accepting curriculums like the 1619 Project now indoctrinating students that the United States is and always has been an evil country? Maybe it's because the United States had taken the God of Christianity out of just about everything and has inserted materialism, paganism, and every lust one can imagine in God's place. As Billy Graham was reported to have once said, "If God does not judge America He will have to apologize to Sodom and Gomorrah". The United States is no longer a Christian nation. Now, the American way of life had been and is now being threatened by a hostile and perfect storm from five different directions:

First, was the global outbreak of Corona Virus (COVID-19) affecting the respiratory system. Released from a bio-lab in Wuhan, Hubei province, China. Now at the height of the crisis killing more than 2,000 each day.

The second was an organization called Black People Matter (BPM), a Marxist political and social movement supporting civil disobedience against any justified or unjustified police actions against black people. Their objective is to disrupt_the Western-prescribed nuclear family structure and abolish or defund the police.

John supported the organization after the unjustified death of a black man, but something changed, the organization's speakers began a crusade against all police, even for incidences involving justified police actions against black people. It looked like the organization was making a move to re-form the government starting with the police.

The third was Antifa. The far-left movement was comprised of an array of autonomous groups whose objective was to achieve fear and tyranny through the use of violence, effectively piggybacking on the BPM Protests where masses would gather for peaceful protesting. Fearful of being seen as racist, Democratic mayors and governors held back their police force while Antifa cowardly attacked, looted, and indiscriminately destroyed residential homes and businesses.

Forth, the mouthpiece of the evolving American culture was Big Tech and the Left Winged News Media which flagrantly displayed their bias of politics as one huge campaign ad for the new Democratic Socialist Party. Their social media platforms were abusing the First Amendment by supporting disinformation while redacting anything in favor of the Republicans on the social media of Twitter, Facebook, and Google.

CNN was once considered John's favorite news network but had become so anti-American, John actually thought the Russian's had purchased CNN due to all the propaganda. Instant credibility was given to any anonymous source as long as it was unfavorable about the sitting President. Interviews of political hacks who were the epitome of hatred were cheered by the news anchors. So many times, these networks were proven wrong and never once apologized or rescinded the attacks.

The fifth was the most anti-American, the new Socialist Democratic Party. Never in American history did one political party attempt a coup against the other as many times as this party. Before the election, President Obama conspired with the running presidential candidate Clinton and top echelons of the FBI and CIA. They actually colluded with the Russians for disinformation to impeach the President elect on charges of <u>Russian Collusion</u> of all things.

Despite the Republican landslide win in 2016, the Democrats would not concede the election. They continued to coordinate with the most ruthless and cynical figures in American politics. The Democrat leaders didn't want its citizens to know what they're doing. Their first instinct was to manipulate rather than persuade, they would hide their real beliefs about policies that would negatively affect their own party.

They would say precisely the opposite of what they meant every time. They accuse Americans of the crimes they themselves were committing. Finding middle ground for a much-needed pandemic stimulus package with them was pointless. They didn't believe in the existence of truth or in the fixed meaning of words. They cared only about power.

The 2020 election wasn't over. The media was calling the weak and feeble 78-year-old former Vice President of a divided Democrat/Socialist Party the 46th President. The Big Tech and media propaganda machine were claiming victory. In their search of the truth, Republicans discovered evidence of fraud and cheating in five Democratic battleground States, and Black People Matter and antifa were not happy they might lose.

NSA confirmed that the attack would begin at fourteen hundred hours. John turned to his militia's leader, Captain Dutch Swanson who spoke into his throat mic. "All elements, prepare to execute."

CHAPTER ONE

Earlier that year at an unknown Location, Portland Maine

Looking around with scared eyes, Abdul Kimoni sat at a dining table inside a basement of a closed down restaurant. Abdul was a scarecrow of a man, tall and skinny. An illegal immigrant from the country of Somalia. His hair was short cut, he had bloodshot eyes and rotten teeth. The restaurant they were in had been broken into and ransacked during the riots the week before as rebels stormed the streets. It was the most violent night of the movement in the small city of Portland Maine. The rioters left behind several destroyed businesses and cars, one of the cars being a local police vehicle.

Before Abdul sat two members of the anti-American group called Antifa. The leader, Chuck Nelsen was a large white man who moved to Maine from Philadelphia at the beginning of the uprising. His head was shaved, his body was bulk, once muscular and now unmaintained. His arms were covered in tattoos. He had a teardrop piercing hanging from his left eyebrow. His mission orders came from Mike Durham, operations manager working for BPM.

"Relax Abdul, in America, you're a very special man, not like in Somalia. As a protester for Black People Matter, you can get away with a lot and the cops won't harass you. Maine's governor, Jan Moody, is rolling out the red carpet to the Black People Matter organization and she doesn't want to offend them, so I have an offer you shouldn't refuse" he said. "You proved yourself by torching the police cruiser Friday night. We decided to bring you into our organization.

We want to help you to be equal to the whites in this county. We want you to have the same rights. Do you want my organization to help you become a citizen of America? We can help you receive more government money, more than you're getting already. Helping you succeed is the main purpose of the Antifa movement. But it will take dedication and loyalty in our organization and your commitment to following all orders".

"Yessur I'd be vadie good fo Amadica!" Abdul replied in broken English. "Working with us, you will eat better, dress better and you will be a leader in the Antifa branch of Maine.But you must never, I mean NEVER mention you work for Antifa and never mention Antifa to anyone!! You work for Black People Matter, get it?" Chuck asked. "Yessur" Abdul replied. "I am assigning you to my lieutenant here, his name is Carl. He will train you on how to shoot a pistol and use a knife for your protection. If you're arrested and thrown in jail, don't worry, we will get you out."

"A queshun I have fo you missur Chuck?" Abdul asked. "I have Somalian friends who able to fight too." Carl, a dark-skinned, hawk-faced man, black hair with black eyes and a crescent moon tattooed on his neck said, "If you train and perform well, we will give you your own group and you can bring in some friends."

After Abdul left, Chuck Nelsen spoke, "Carl, Antifa just submitted a standing order. I want you to find someone affected by the Wuhan Flu and use them to affect others. Spread them throughout Maine to affect as many as possible. Mix them into the protesters, on beaches, in department stores. We will destroy capitalism by shutting down businesses to make room for the Marxist agenda, Infect Abdul, I don't care. Just be careful, I don't want my best lieutenant sick. Another thing, we will be scheduling a protest next weekend.

I want you to go business to business in Portland, around Congress Street, and collect a protection fee. If they decide not to pay the fee, we will destroy that business. Keep 20% of what you collect. Finally, recruit more Antifa soldiers. I am planning a massive event that will shake America."

Black People Matter (BPM) headquarters, Philadelphia

We disrupt the Western-prescribed nuclear family structure requirement by supporting each other as extended families and "villages" that collectively care for one another, especially our children. And by wealth distribution, we will make mothers, parents, and children comfortable. We will make our spaces family-friendly and enable parents to fully participate with their children. We dismantle the patriarchal practice that requires mothers to work "double shifts" so that they can mother in private even as they participate in public justice work. **Black People Matter website 20 March 2020.**

Marxism is a political and economic way of organizing society, where the workers own the means of production. Socialism is a way of organizing a society in which the means of production are owned and controlled by the working class. ... Communism is the theoretical classless, stateless society that Marx proposed would arise after Socialism. **Marxism - Wikipedia**

Rasha Tossa sat behind her desk in the fifth-floor duplex office suit. Rasha, a slender 30 something woman with light brown skin, shoulder blade length dread locks, was looking down at her files while her next appointment sat outside in the lobby. The Ukrainian Immigrant, Nationalist, writer, strategist, and community organizer who co-founded the Black People Matter Movement continued to flip through the files while sipping the gourmet Star-Bucks Cappuccino.

Rasha was vital in the re-organizing of the BPM movement which became a popular political project in the wake of the shooting of black man (eight years ago). in Sanford, Florida. When a Hispanic man (a neighborhood watchman) fatally shot The 17-year-old African-American high school student during a struggle and was acquitted at his trial after claiming self-defense. The incident was reviewed by the Department of Justice for potential civil rights violations, but no additional charges were filed, citing insufficient evidence, which gave Black People Matter their opening to aggressively protest.

Later, instead of using his popularity as the first black President to unite America, Democratic President, Barack Obama fanned the flames of the case and promoted systemic racism in America. Now, only two months ago, the new unjustified death of black man looms as a black cloud which BPM began the cause of reverse discrimination blaming all police in America for the bad mistake of one officer.

Another problem that faces America and helps BPM is how the media searches for every case which involves the shooting of a black man. The media offers no coverage at all of any shootings of white men. The media also promoted BPM Protesters chanting "Pigs in a blanket, fry them like beacon" which has led to multiple police assassinations. The success of BPM has tributed to the "Cancel Culture" (the elimination of anything resembling racist by BPM's definition). Canceling TV shows, pulling down historical statues, changing the names of sports teams, etc.

"Send in my next appointment," Rasha spoke into her intercom. Sara Roseberg stepped in. She was the BPM Co-fundraiser, Sara was a medium size, white women with gray peppered afro style hair and glasses. Vice chair of a California-based charity that handles fundraising for Black People Matter. She was a veteran of the May 1980 Communist movement that carried out a bombing campaign. Rosenberg landed on the FBI most wanted list and was arrested with stolen explosives in 1984. The terrorist drew 58 years but served only 16 because in 2001 President Bill Clinton commuted Rosenberg's sentence.

"What are your strategies on this latest death of Lloyd? Rasha asked. "I have already spoken to Lloyd's partner and she was almost relieved Lloyd is dead. He constantly abused her and his daughter while under the influence of drugs. The parents are sad over his death and would like to go on record to try to prevent others from making the same mistakes as Fred.

I offered each member of the family a stipend of $5000 if they would present Lloyd as a wonderful and kind man. I made it clear what I was aiming for and they agreed. I also offer to open a 'go-fund-me-page' which would cover all funeral arrangements. I believe we'll get what we need from them," Sara reported. "What about the parents wanting to go on record concerning drugs?" Rasha asked. "They won't even mention drugs now," Sara answered.

"What about public opinion concerning the violence in protest rallies?" "Nobody likes the violence except antifa, but the media is doing a great job ignoring the violence and is labeling the protests as peaceful," Sara could not help chuckling after she said it. "I'm sorry,

4

moving on, lawmakers in the Democrat cities are moving towards defunding the police. Minneapolis has let twenty officers go. The President wants to send in the National Guard to stop the violence, but governors are standing up to him.

As for Fox News, they're continuing to report on Antifa and black on black murders in Chicago, including the deaths of black children" Sara stated. "Chicago is not ours to worry about, and we have every network, except for Fox stifling the reports out of Chicago," Rasha said. "Just continue our narrative about 'white supremacy' in the Fox network. Thanks for the update. Will you ask Mike to come in when you leave?" Rasha asked

Mike Durham walked in and making himself comfortable, sat on the leather couch across from Rasha. He was the operations specialist. A big black man with an athletic toned body, an ex-marine who served in Iraq as a military police officer, dishonorably discharged for the shooting of a civilian. It had come out in the court martial that Sgt. Durham was also involved in gun running in the black market but without solid proof, the court couldn't convict him for it.

"What have you got Mike?" Rasha asked. "BMP is affecting major policy changes with police departments in twenty-five large cities thirty small cities and multiple townships," he reported. "But the violence is not helping. Antifa is indiscriminately attacking people and businesses of all political parties.   Now rumors are pointing to the rise of some militia groups around the country."

Rasha got up and paced her office thinking to herself and finally said, "Mike, get the word out to as many left wing news networks as possible and spread the story that these so called militia groups are merely President Dave Travis's racist support based. Call'em white supremacists, white privileged, survivalists, link them to that Proud Boys group, I don't care, but stress they are committing violence against peaceful protesters. See if you can plant some evidence on them, I don't know, be creative. Update me in one week."

Yard sale: Colton residence, Kennebunk, Maine, May 31st

It was a sunny day with a hint of salt mist drifting in the cool air off the ocean. John Colton and his wife Leah sat on their porch deck watching over their yard sale property. An ex-Navy Seal, John Colton, call sign,

Cobalt, was retired after twenty years served with Seal Team Four stationed at the Little Creek Amphibious Naval Base in Virginia Beach. John's position was the sniper of his Seal Team and whenever deployed into the danger zone, the team knew one of the best was on overwatch.

Plagued by numerous deployments and kills in his military service, John would fantasize about living the quiet life with his wife in the little town atmosphere. Now that he was retired, he found himself unrestful and edgy especially in America's current situation. Thanks to John's wife, a math teacher who married John late into his navy career, had led John to his faith in Jesus Christ. That faith enabled him to make friends with the ghosts and make sense of the crumbling morality in the world.

Their house sat on a medium travelled side road, one mile from a popular beach in Kennebunk Maine. John and Leah didn't need the money, they just wanted to simplify and get rid of the excess accumulation of the past years. Occasionally a passer-byer would stop by the yard sale to shop for a deal, of their unwanted property.

John observed the double cab Ford F-250 pulled off the road across the street. He actually remembered seeing that truck around town with stickers of the American Flag, NRA and that 'Don't Tread on Me stickers. A six-foot man exited. He wore his hair close to the scalp, had a muscular toned body, maybe a jogger. He was wearing green cargo shorts and a "Keep America Strong" tee-shirt. John Colton stepped off the porch deck to meet him as he approached the merchandise.

His name was Richard Bloomer and he had his eye on John's Toro Lawn Mower. "How much" he said. Well, it is a Toro, I just had it tuned up, oil changed, blade sharpened and starts on the first pull. I'm looking for $150." John replied. "If the Toro is so great, why sell it?" Rich asked. "Last May she ran really rough, not cutting well and I called a bunch of small engine repair shops. The earliest appointment I could get was late June. We needed a lawn mower now, so I bought a new mower. I never canceled the appointment for the Toro.

Richard squatted down, lifted the mower, checking the blade. Then he pulled out the oil dip stick. "Nice and clean," he said. Straightening up he said, "Hey, did you hear about the riot in Portland Maine last week?" "Yea, I saw it on the news." "The news? The news didn't report what really happened. Did you know three cars got torched, including one cruiser?" "Really? But the news called it a peaceful protest." "How peaceful is three destroyed businesses." "Wait a minute. As far as I know, there's been no police abuse in Portland, has there?" "No, but there was one case in Portland Oregon."

"So, why are they rioting in Portland Maine?" "Brother, I haven't figured that one out yet."

After introductions and for the next 45 minutes, John & Richard talked about politics, the successes of the President's economy, the Black People Matter movement, antifa and the violence in democratic cities, the Chinese Wuhan COVID-19 Flu pandemic. So entrenched in conversation, they had to be told to move aside by John's wife while people stopped by to barter.

"So, you look like someone who served in the military," Rich said. "I guess you could say that, I'm a retired Seal" replied John. "I'm an ex-Ranger, eight years and four tours." Answered Rich. Really? Where'd you serve?" John asked. "Ramadi, Mosul, Basrah and Kabul" answered Rich. "Looks like we played in the same sandboxes," John stated.

Richard then mentioned, "You know the American Legion is starting a militia to replace the Kennebunk police if abolished. Hell, the Kennebunkport police is already gone, you'd be a prime candidate." John laughed, "You think riots could happen to a little town like Kennebunk?" Richard got really serious and said, "Rumors are, Antifa organized the riot in Portland, and they want ALL Police Departments either defunded or shut-down. So, an ex-Marine Captain and I convinced the local American Legion to bring it to a vote. Now we are forming our own militia. You want in?"

John thought for a minute and said, "Richard, I'm not a Seal anymore, I'm 45 years old and haven't been in the shit for ten years. My last four years in the Navy Seals were in the States." "Look John, you won't have to dig foxholes, and run twenty miles with a sixty-pound pack. All we're doing right now is organizing and attending meetings. Your input as a Seal could be crucial. What are the chances we would be called upon by the government anyway? Meeting's this Thursday at nineteen hundred." After contemplating John said, I'll need to clear it with the wife." "Outstanding! Give me your cell number, I'll text you the info." They traded numbers and John said, "I'll take $125 for the Toro." "Deal!" Richard said.

Later that evening during dinner, Leah smiled at John and said, "I saw you exchange phone numbers with that gentleman, seems you've got a new friend." John explained, "Name's Richard, he's an ex-ranger who served in the Gulf. We've got a lot in common. He's forming the Kennebunk Militia and wants me to join." Laughing, Leah said, "What are you going to do, storm the beaches of Wells Maine? "Leah, you've seen the news, there's chaos everywhere in America. We're just being pro-active." "Sounds like you've ready joined." Leah said. "Nope. Not without your support. You've been through a lot while I was on all those deployments, some which I still can't talk to you about. I just want to be open with you." "As long as you don't have to deploy in Iraq." Leah replied, John immediately called Richard.

American Legion Facility, Kennebunkport, Thursday June 4th

Fifteen minutes before the meeting began, John entered what could have once been a warehouse. To the right was an open kitchen behind a twelve-foot serving bar. Behind the bar a full kitchen with two refers and three stoves. A men's bathroom on the left of the kitchen and women on the right. From there it was an open space, larger than the size of a high school gym. Along the back wall were a couple of offices. The meeting hall had twelve eight-foot plastic folding tables set up in a large square with chairs. There were twenty men and women already there and more parking their cars.

Richard approached John as he entered and led him to a chair next to him. "Good to see you Squid" Rich said. "Same here, you Grunt." Replied John. Looking around, John said, "Nice place for a Legion hall, is it big enough?! What are the dues, fifty a person?" "Nope, this use to be a furniture storage facility. It was legally left behind along with an enormous Trust Fund for annual taxes, including electrical and insurance for the Legion by James Gilenski a WWII Vet. All free and clear. You ought'a see downstairs, I'll give you the tour later," Rich answered. "Sign me up" John said, they laughed and shook hands.

At eighteen hundred hours the hall was full, twenty-eight out of thirty-two chairs were occupied. Conversation and laughter echoed throughout the building. Then a man stood and extending his arms forward palms up asking for order. He was a medium size man, standing five feet nine inches, 180 pounds, with sandy brown short hair. He wore a green tee-shirt and beige cargo pants. His appearance screamed Marine. "My name is Captain Dutch Sawnson, I served as a marine twelve years. Spent time in the Gulf leading combat divisions, qualified with most weapons that shoot including mortars.

Welcome to the second meeting of the Maine Militia. We are not a survivalist group. We are not a white supremist group. We are not a Republican or a Democratic group. We ARE Constitutionalists. We will defend the Constitution, protect all American citizens, and support the police.

I see a lot of new faces tonight. If your new here, I assume you've been thoroughly vetted by the person who invited you. If you were not invited and somehow found out about this meeting, I want you to check in with Gunny Wilson sitting here to my left after this meeting. If you check out, you will not be rejected.

Looks like we have eight new bodies, I would like you to stand, starting with you." Pointing to a man next to Gunny Wilson. "Tell us who you are, what branch of service, what your MOS was and any specialties you were trained in and let's move around the square clockwise."

When it came to Joh Colton, standing six feet three inches, 220 pounds, with a surfer's body. "John Colton, Chief Petty Officer retired Navy Seal. Qualified diver, HALO jumping, SAW M249 machine gun, pistol expert, Sniper and close combat training," then he sat back down. Richard turned to John and all he said was "Jeeze!"

As people stood and gave their backgrounds, one female stood who caught everyone's attention. She was black, maybe late forties, 130 pounds, solidly in good condition and a attractive face. "My name is 1st Sargent Ruth Taylor USAF, retired, I was a pilot, UAV (Unmanned Aerial Vehicle) drones. I can't get into a lot of detail as most missions were Top Secret. My hobby is playing with several classes of remote-control aircraft, helicopters and drones."

One other person caught John's attention. John knew him. He stood five six, 150 pounds and in a police uniform. "I just got off shift and rushed over here. I am Sargent Steve Paris, Wells Police Department, qualified in communications, Shot guns, Remington 700 sniper rifle, and pistols." After the last person finished, Captain

Dutch stood and his first comment was "Thank you for wearing the uniform Sarge, most men & women consider you a hero here just for wearing it.

People, every meeting is going to begin with the Pledge of Allegiance, so let's all stand, face the flag and I will lead the Pledge. After the Pledge of Allegiance, Captain Dutch spoke, "There are a few people I want to introduce who were key to the idea of a militia, Sargent Richard Bloomer, US Rangers, he is my second in command, Drill Sargent Bob Simpson who will do the majority of your training." When Bob stood, he was straight as a board, a typical poster marine. "and Gunny Sargent Ann Wilson the Administrator." She was a strong looking female, black hair, Five feet four maybe, 160 and what looked to be all muscle. She projected authority with an attractive face.

Dutch continued. "You will give Gunny all your pertinent information where you live, work, the hours you work, blood type and much more, which will be entered into your new service records. Your service record will be kept in a top quality safe in an undisclosed location when not in use. And If you accept that, we will commence training soon after. Once organized you will be assigned to a unit with a Team Leader. You will train together until you know how each other think. Gunny Wilson owns some twenty acres in North Berwick which has a pistol range and a sniper range. She has several buildings on the property where we will conduct training on clearing, stalking, attack formations, and two-man team patrols. Once we become sufficient units, we can begin to deploy into the communities."

A woman raised her hand and stood. "My name is Ester Ames, I was a corporal in the Green Berets. What exactly will be expected of us in the community?" Captain Dutch replied, "Good question, I would like to see POV patrols, (Private Owned Vehicle) teams of two at 4 hour rotation, how often, depends on how many volunteers we get from the communities of Kennebunk, Kennebunkport and Wells. I am asking all of you to find and interview new potential members and bring them with you for the next meeting, Qualification for the militia is they MUST be Patriots. A military background is not required.

The more members we get, the easier to patrol. I already spoke with the Kennebunk Chief of Police about our plans of establishing a militia and our intentions of patrolling the communities, so there's no surprise. He suggested we act as a crime watch. When on patrol, if you spot a crime in progress, you will call 911 first, assess situation and take command or back-up the police if required. If worse comes to worse, they will call upon us for back-up.

If you are ex-military, your final rank will be respected, but your starting over and your level in this militia will have to be proven. When ready, we will eventually choose Team leaders in units of eight. Any more questions?....No?...Gunny will be passing out forms that we want you to fill out. Your addresses will be considered top secret, and nobody will have access unless you give it to someone personally. When you are done, we have beer and soda downstairs. One beer only!! Right Sargent Paris?"

The meeting ended with the echoes of conversation and laughter filled the hall. John greeted Sargent Paris and talked about last week's church service. First Sargent Taylor (The UAV pilot) approached John and said, "Wouldn't you know it, I've always wanted to scuba dive. "That's funny" John replied, "I've always wanted to play with remote controls" A Navy Petty Officer walk up to them and asked, "1st Sgt Taylor, my name is Harry Hodge, I specialized in EOD in the Navy, and was wondering, could your drone carry a bomb? Maybe the weight of a grenade?" Ruth replied, "No problem, you'd just have to configure a release mechanism under the fuselage." "Cool." He said and walked away.

CHAPTER TWO

One Month Later: Training Camp, North Berwick, July 30th

Captain Dutch Swanson and Sargent Rich Bloomer were standing on a knoll overlooking at least forty tents in the South fields of Gunny Sargent's property. "It's good to have you back Sarge. Did your coordination attempts work out with the other Maine Militia?" Cpt Dutch asked. Richard replied, "Excellent! They're all just getting started like us and seem to be in good hands with well qualified leaders. I found them in Sanford, Biddeford and York Maine. It seems current events have really concerned our Mainers."

As they looked to the west side of the property, they could see the out-buildings where Drill Sargent Bob Simpson was evaluating building clearing. Dutch said, "Your friend Chief Colton is giving Bob a hand. He's got a lot of experience. An excellent sniper. seems our range of one thousand yards is too small for him. We have some real talent In the North Woods, a Mike Ackroff has two units training in stalking attack formations with paint guns."

Suddenly there was an explosion in the east field. A blossom ball of fire rose up and Richard Bloomer shouted, "What the hell was that?" "That's our UAV pilot, Ruth Taylor who's been training with EOD Hodge, they're configuring her drones to carry a bomb, that was their first live drop." While Rich was watching, he noticed a small dot in the sky approaching, as it flew by, it sounded like a mosquito bussing round his head. Then it circled and landed no more than ten feet from them. Looking back east, they watched Harry and Ruth walking up the hill, when they got closer, Harry said, "Shit hot, that was great!!" "Well that could come in handy in a jam." Dutch said. "Rich, I want all groups at the fire pit after chow at 6pm" "Yes sir" Richard replied.

North Berwick Training Camp Fire Circle

"Quiet down people." Dutch said with his arms extended. "I want to read the latest highlights from Today's Fox News. The Covid-19 pandemic is spiking throughout the nation. They are recording 100% increases in most states. The CDC is even confused by the spikes. Riots causing unrest. Every corner of the country is left with charred and shattered businesses in dozens of American cities. More than a dozen U.S. cities are still reeling from grim nights of violence. Curfews are not recognized. Efforts have failed to mitigate the worst destruction and looting cities have seen. Thousands of people were arrested Saturday night alone after demonstrations turned into violence and in some cases deadly. The next day, rioters are released. Meanwhile, President Travis have the National Guard ready to deploy in at least fifteen states, but Democratic Governors and Mayors are refusing any Federal help despite the mayhem, chaos and wreckage.

Attorney General William Barr said in a statement Sunday that as the rioting spreads in cities across the country, "voices of peaceful and legitimate protests have been hijacked by violent radical elements and that they are working to pursue their own separate, violent, and extremist agenda." Multiple Governors nation-wide are feeling the pressure including our own Jan Moody, she is talking about reducing police departments beginning with smaller quieter towns like ours while maintaining departments in cities like Portland, Augusta, Lewiston/Auburn and Bangor. That way she can show substantial defunding dollars."

"Excuse me sir" someone spoke up, "Who's going to respond to 911 calls?" "Good question, the plan is to replace the police with Social Workers. One social worker for every three police officers.

Moody says she will keep the State Police intact. The State's Republicans are fighting Moody, but the Democrats own the House and Senate."

Someone else spoke, "Wait a minute, you mean if I'm getting robbed, a social worker's going to show up and what? Talk the robber out of it!?" Dutch answered, "We don't know any future specific plans. The police are being downsized as I speak, so we should be getting ready for the worse.

I was thinking police scanners would work well for our patrols, but if there are no police patrols. We might have nothing to listen to. We may have to pass out flyers to all our neighbors with our Command Central's phone number. If they call with a problem, then central will call our closest patrol in that area and we will react."

Militia Patrol, Drug Bust, August 3rd

Lester and Max had been on the road for two days straight, driving North on Interstate 95 from Florida, stopping only for gas and fast food. It was Max's turn to drive and after completing one hundred fifty miles he was ready for a break. Five miles past exit nineteen he noticed the needle on the gas gauge was right on empty.

"Max! Wake up! I've got to pull over for gas and have a piss call, and there's a service station up ahead." Stirring awake, a groggy Max rubbed his eyes and looked up at the neon sign with the gas prices. "Shit man! Don't stop here dude, look at the gas prices! We're cutting into our profits! Aren't we ahead of schedule? I hate these food malls with all the bright lights and crowds.

"Okay, why don't we stop in this little town here, Kennebunk?" Lester suggested. "I don't know, we only have about fifty miles left to Lewiston and the sooner we drop this load the better" Com'on Max, we're almost out of gas! let's get off the interstate, I need a stretch and a sit-down meal without the Interstate service station Hoob-la." Damn it Lester! Are you gon'na wine about this all night?" "Yes I am, look, I'll just take that service road right there, we'll get in and back out on the Interstate in no time." Max gave in. He always gave in. So, they drove down the service road and turned onto Fletcher Street.

They passed a High School and with no stores in sight. Max complained, "This is a mistake, this is a one-horse town. Probably

15

rolls up the side-walks at six o'clock." "Just a little further Max, They've got to have a gas station in this town!" They drove around a little rotary and took a right continuing down Fletcher Street. They could see a traffic light up ahead when they heard the engine begin to choke from the lack of gas. "Damn it Lester, this is all your fault! Now what do we do?!" Lester managed to pull into a Bank's empty parking lot and turned off the 72 Buick Skylark's engine.

Richard Bloomer and Dean Tron were patrolling Southbound on route one as they approached a red traffic light in front of the Library at the intersection of Fletcher Street. They could see the Kennebunk Savings Bank parking lot and one lone car with two people involved in what looked like an argument. "Check that out Dean."

Dean looked over and said, "Looks like two citizens in distress, want to check them out?" "Yea, let's go have a look-see" The traffic light turned green and Richard drove his truck into the parking lot. "Hmm, Pennsylvania plates." Richard said. As his headlights lit up the two males. Dean noticed the look of surprise and fear on both faces. "Stay alert Rich, they don't look so happy we're here." "Okay Dean I'll talk to them from inside." Richard maneuvered the truck, so the driver's side was facing the two strangers and rolled down his window.

"You guys okay? Need any help?" "Ah, yea I guess we do. we ran out of gas looking for a damn filling station. Do you have one in this town?" Lester said. Richard smiled and said, "Yea, we've got a few of them. You have a gas can?" "No, we don't have a can," Max answered with a sarcastic tone. "Well, I have one, you can use mine. I can drive one of you over to the station, you'll be able to get enough gas to drive back and top off your tank." "That would be great." Lester said.

Richard got out of the truck and opened the tool chest in the truck's bed and retrieve his three-gallon gas can. While getting the can, the two strangers jostled over who would stay behind, neither wanted to go for the gas. Finally, Max relented to go with Richard. While they were arguing, Richard got a peek inside the back seat. *"Looks like a couple of AK-47s,"* he thought.

He invited Max to get in the back and drove him to the Irvings gas station less than a mile away. Max got out, places the gas can by the pump and went into the store to pay cash and have the pump turned on. While Max was in the store, Richard turned to Dean and whispered. These guys are carrying an arsenal in the back seat." "Yea? Did you notice the bulges in their pants? They're carrying personal weapons too," Dean added.

"The way I see it, we have two options, let them go and call 911, or we search them ourselves," Richard suggested. Dean answered, "The problem with option one is the Police will have no probable cause. Carrying guns is legal in Maine. Problem with option two is we could get shot taking down what could be hardened criminals.

"Come on Dean, we're trained for this, we'll have the element of surprise. We pull our weapons first, show confidence and don't show panic or fear. I'll do all the commands; we zip tie them and have a look in the trunk." If their innocent, we apologize and say we thought they were someone else and they can be on their way. I'll take Max and you take the other guy. When I say, *what year is the Buick*, we execute on Buick."

Max finished pumping $5.00 of gas into the can. He placed the can in the bed of the truck and got back in. "You all set?" Dean asked. "Thanks, I'm all set" replied Max. The ride back was spent making small talk. They arrived at the parking lot and they all got out. Both Richard and Dean got into position, Max was pouring the gas and Lester was focused on Max. Then Richard Spoke, "what year is the Buick?"

Richard and Dean had their pistols out before Max could answer the question. "Don't move!" Richard commanded. Shocked, Max and Lester's language got loud and explicit, but they complied. Richard and Dean had them spread eagle against the car, disarmed sat them down and zip tied in no time. Dean grabbed the keys out of the ignition. Lester growled. "Let us go and live, open that trunk and you will die." Richard flipped the blanket in the back seat and discovered four AK-47's and a Remington 16 gauge shot-gun. Dean popped the trunk and discovered bags of white powder and several pounds of marijuana. "I guess we don't have to apologize." Dean said and pulled out his cell phone and called 911.

Richard knelt next to Lester and said, "Your biggest mistake tonight was stopping in our little town. Just about all of our citizens belong to a militia and are armed to the teeth. You want to kill me? Take your best shot, but you wouldn't get one hundred feet of me without someone monitoring your every move." Minutes later a cruiser pulled in and

Dean said "hands up Rich, they're here" Richard and Dean faced the spotlight that shone on them and raised their hands.

The officer got out and approached them with his hand on his unsnapped holster. You two the militia who called 911? "Yes sir, and those two are the bad guys." Dean said pointing. "Sargent Stewart Casman," the officer said with a hand extended. After introductions, the officer asked, "What do you have here?" Richard announced, "weapons in the back seat and drugs in the trunk." That night Richard and Dean were wondering if it was worth it. They were interviewed by the State Police criticized by some Drug Agency, and they went two hours past their shift.

They were able to call the Militia Command Central, and Dutch showed up. Dean turned to Rich and asked, "What was all that about back there. Every citizen in this town is militia?" "I was just discouraging him from doing something stupid." Rich answered. "You mean like killing you?"

The next morning the Seacoast Journal reported a couple of local citizens foiled a sizeable drug shipment passing through the town of Kennebunk. The State police reported the seizure of 2,800 grams of fentanyl, 501.9 grams of cocaine, 17 pounds of marijuana, four AK-47s, a 16-gauge shot-gun and $8,000 in cash. Street value of the drugs: One million two hundred fifty thousand dollars.

BPM Protest, Kennebunk Town Hall, August 7th

At least one hundred BPM protesters were gathered in front of the Town hall which was also in front of the Police Department and Fire Department. The protesters were blocking traffic on Route one and Summer street. There were only six police officers in riot gear. But there were militia soldiers incognito surrounding the protesters. The police were aware of the militia's presence. Dutch Swanson had established the call sign "Friendly" with the Police Chief, which would be used by the militia if things got confrontational. The militia surrounded the protest with fifty men and women. Wearing normal civilian clothes, blending in well, wearing masks and carrying signs. The militia wore loose shirts and jackets concealing their pistols.

John Colton was sitting on the steps of the Police Station and Richard was sitting on the steps of the Town Hall across the street.

Between those two vantage points they had the best view of all the protesters. After one hour the chanting was getting louder, John & Rich were watching for the instigators in the group, John called Richard's cellphone and pointed out three suspect instigators moving around stirring up the protesters. Richard had a couple picks of his own.

Some of the protestors had cell phones on long handles. John wondered if they were assigned to film the event or just trying to get their film on the six o'clock news. The protesters held their hands up in surrender as they crowded the police line. They were being encouraged by the instigators trying to stimulate a police reaction so the News media could use any violence to report police brutality. but the police showed excellent professionalism for small town cops, they held the line and kept their mouths shut. Attempting to argue with a twenty something protester is like trying to get a baby with soiled dippers to stop crying.

To avoid a stalemate, one of the instigators stormed the Police Station trying to incite violence. He carried a four-foot long 2X4. John stood with his hands up in a stopping request motion, but the guy continued. When he reached John, he took a baseball homerun swing at John's mid-section, but John jumped back, and the instigator hit air. Then he came back with a chopping swing and John dodged left of the arc and when the 2x4 hit bottom of the arc, the instigator committed a big mistake and left his face exposed. John shot a lightening quick kick and the instigator almost did a back-flip from the impact. He didn't get up, he just laid there moaning.

None of the police saw anything with the protesters in their faces. Across the street Richard observed John knelling down talking to the instigator and then notice another instigator approaching from John's flank. "You know dude, you're standing up for the wrong things. There's a spiritual power more special in this world, more special than anything in life. You should learn about Jesus Christ" John preached. Suddenly, a body dropped next to John's instigator and when John looked up, standing there was Richard. "Were you just preaching to that scum? Here's another one for you!" Richard said, pointing at the new groaning body.

One of the militia named Jason ran up to John & Richard and reported. "Sir, you better come see this." They followed Jason to a corner of the cement wall between Town Hall and Fire Department. There stood Ruth Taylor with her foot on a black rioter, pinning him on the ground. The black man was sweating profusely and coughing.

Ruth put pressure on the man's chest and said, "Go ahead asshole, tell them what you told me." "Two day ago, a man pay me $100 to kiss a girl who had flu, he also bot me dee nice clothes for protest, then he toad me go to all protest, hug everybody because I am happy dat dey protest fo me, but I think I dying now, please help me." Abdul said.

"Jason, go get a paramedic from the fire department, let them know he's got COVID. Ruth, take your foot off the idiot. What is your name?" Richard ordered. "My name Abdul Kimoni" "Abdul, who was the man who paid you the money, what did he look like?" Richard asked. "Him a block man name Carl. Dat all I know." Abdul pointed at Ruth, "that block woman kick me and put her foot on me…very big insult!" Ruth shouted "You better be thankful you're not dead. Rich, he pulled a frigging knife on me."

"Ruth, use your cell phone and get some pictures of his face, don't let the paramedics take him until you know where he met Carl, what Carl looks like and which protests did he worked." Rich ordered. Later, the protest began to fizzle out and by twenty hundred that night, after six hours of protest, traffic began to flow again. John and Richard returned to the American Legion.

As voted, the American Legion name was changed to the Militia Command Center. Dutch was working as dispatcher at the command center when John and Richard arrived, "We've got a Sitrep for you on the Kennebunk Protest." Richard said as they entered the room. When they explained everything that happen, Dutch asked, "so the protest disbanded, your people took down five instigators, nobody's dead and we may have discovered a link to some bad people? Great job! What do we know about this Abdul character?" "We know he's Somalian, got recruited by some guy named Carl who we assume is African American mixed ethnicity. We're waiting for Ruth Taylor; she took his picture and will fill us in with more details. How goes the rest of the war?" Richard asked.

"The Networks are reporting that protesters have taken a city block in Seattle. They're calling it the CHOP zone short for, Capitol Hill Organized Protest Zone. Two police assassinations in Portland

Oregon. Media aren't connecting the dots and are still calling the protests peaceful. but it all seems organized. In our own state, violent protesting in Bangor, riots and two police shot in Lewiston, A few stores B&Eed (Broken & Entered) in Portland.

Here's some interesting news, half a dozen protesters were wounded in Rumford, the protesters were outnumbered by anti-protesters. That's all in one day. It boggles my mind, 90% of all the protester are white. All these people are mostly jobless due to the State being shut down by the pandemic and now we have all these idle kids with nothing better to do." Dutch answered. John laughed, "I grew up in Rumford. It doesn't surprise me that the protesters took a beating there."

John looked outside and noticed the militia assigned to the protest were returning. Ruth and Jason walked in the door and said, "the Somalian gave me descriptions of two Antifa bad guys." "Let's have it" Dutch asked. We have Carl, he's a lieutenant with Antifa, he's dark-skinned, thin man, black hair with evil eyes and a crescent moon tattooed on his neck.

His boss's name is Chuck. A white man, bald, muscular body, his arms are covered in tattoos and he has a piercing attached to his left eyebrow." I'll get Gunny Wilson to type up BOLOs (Be On the Look Out) on these two and disperse copies to all our militia, Richard, you should dispense BOLOs out to all your militia Commander contacts in the State. And definitely get these BOLOs to our roving patrols tonight."

"What do we have out patrolling tonight?" John asked. Proudly Dutch answered, "We have TEN patrols, two in each POV (privately owned vehicles). One of our newest militia is a civilian lawyer, Helen Knowles. She briefed our patrols on how to make a citizen's arrest and I briefed them on Rules of Engagement before they left at twenty hundred hours. The patrols will cruise their assigned area provided by Gunny Wilson until zero hundred hours (midnight), Then ten more POVs will take over until zero four hundred hours. Gunny issued maps for their assigned patrol areas so there's no overlapping, and she's provided command central with the same, so we'll know the patrol's approximate locations at any given hour.

We will also have five rotating militia in the Command Central throughout the night. Because our numbers have grown, tomorrow night will be all new people. Also, I'm getting a lot of requests for more training from our people who have no military background. Most of those people don't even own a gun. Thanks to Drill Sargent Simpson and John here, their training got them proficient, but they want accuracy and personal improvement.

Most of them who can afford it are buying guns for the first time. So, I put word out that the gun range will be open at our training camp and Gunny will be assigning our experienced people with military backgrounds to train them." "Wow! Our militia is really coming together! I'll help out this weekend, but the wife and I have plans next weekend." John said. "Excellent, Sgt Simpson volunteered too," Dutch added.

"One problem that concerns me," Dutch said. "The weapons we're using are nowhere standard. I mean, I've seen every rifle from AR-15s to a damn a flint lock and every pistol from an antique 22 revolver to Clint Eastwood's 44 magnum! I was thinking of collecting dues so we could begin to stock an armory here."

Jason, who was still standing there spoke up. "Not a good idea, many of these people are just volunteers who are out of work and I believe we would lose a bunch when we start collecting dues."

"What about collecting donations from the local establishments?" Richard asked, "I don't think so, "Dutch answered. "The establishments are suffering enough with all the governor's shut down policies, and that would look too much like embezzling money for protection."

"This country's first militia was organized in 1787 and were essential in kicking professional British soldier's asses in the American Revolution and they started out with hunting rifles and pitchforks," John commented "Nice history lesson." Rich said. "Let me give it some more thought, we're ok for now, it's not like we're fighting a major war." Dutch ended the conversation and sat back down at his desk.

Some serious questions

Richard turned to John and asked, "Let's go downstairs for a cold one John." "I don't drink anymore." "Ok, I'll buy you a soda." As they arrived at the unmanned bar, Richard went behind the bar and served himself a Budweiser and slid a Coke over to John and asked, "What was that shit back at the protest? Why were you trying to save that rebel from hell where he belongs? John answered, "Jesus doesn't look at a man and compare him one to another, we are all equally sinners and in desperate need for salvation."

"Are you saying I'm equal to murderous drug dealing scum?! "What Jesus said, is we're all subject to the Ten Commandments and nobody's able to keep them. For example, do you consider yourself to be a good person?" John asked. "Yes, I do." Richard responded. "The Bible says, 'the LORD does not see as man sees; for man looks at the outward appearance, but the LORD looks at the heart.' 1 Samuel 16:7

So, I may see myself as a saint when I compare myself to Hitler, but to God, I'm still a sinner." John stated. "But doesn't God give me credit for at least trying?" Richard asked. "Let me give you a little test and see how you're doing. Have you ever told lies?" "Yes," Richard answered. "So, what would you call yourself for telling lies?" "Ah... human?" "If I told you a bunch of lies, what would you call me?" "A liar." Richard answered.

"Have you ever stolen?" "Yes," Richard answered. "What do you call someone who steels?" "Ok, I'll bite, a thief, right?" "Yes." John answered. "How about using God's name or the name of Jesus as a cuss word?" "Guilty." Richard answered. "That's called blasphemy."

"Here's one that got me! Jesus said, 'You have heard that it was said, you shall not commit adultery. but I tell you that anyone who looks at a woman lustfully has already committed adultery with her in his heart.' Matt 5:27-28 Have you ever looked at a woman in lust? Don't leave out porn." "Ok, I'm guilty on that too." Richard admitted.

"Dude, by your own omission, you're a lying, blaspheming thief and an adulterer at heart and that's just four of the Ten Commandments. If you died right now and faced God and He judges you on the Ten Commandments, would you be guilty or innocent?" "Oh, come on! What happened to; God is Love! Doesn't He forgive us?" I'll get to that, but first, let's look at THIS world's justice. If a man rapes and murders your mother, are you going to let him go free? No, you're going to ask for life in prison or capital punishment.

Would you consider a judge good if he lets the killer go free? Where's the justice in that? When people claim that God is love, they're forgetting that He's a JUST God too. So, if God is JUST, would you be innocent or guilty? "I guess I'd be guilty." Richard surrendered.

"Would you go to heaven or hell?" "Now, I've got to challenge that John! You're saying, I get born into this shitty world, I'm given ten commandments that are impossible to follow, die, and now I go to hell? Who qualifies for heaven, some monk in the Alps?"

"Let me explain it this way Richard, Let's suppose you're that killer who committed rape, you're in court and the judge is about to sentence you to capital punishment, all of a sudden, somebody walks into the court-room and says, I'll take Richard's sentence upon myself and the Judge agrees."

"That would be crazy John!" "Well Richard, that's what Jesus did for you and me! That's your get out of jail free card! Even though we were yet sinners, Jesus Christ died for us. John 3:16, that's the Bible verse that says, 'God loved the world so much, that He sent his Only son Jesus to die for us, and whoever believes in Him will have eternal life in heaven.'

God IS Love Richard, and He sent His son to die on the cross so we CAN be qualified for heaven." "So, that's the bottom line? Just believe in Jesus?" Richard asked. "If you read the New Testament in the Bible, you'll see belief in Jesus means having "Faith" in Jesus. It's like on paper, you believe a parachute will work when you pull the rip cord right? but when you're thirty thousand feet up in a crashing plane, you're going to have faith in that parachute before you jump. God wants to wash your slate clean, but first you need to have faith in Jesus to receive God's forgiveness." Richard started thinking and finally said, "I need to think about it. This is all very compelling you know." John replied, "Don't think too long, we play with weapons of war and you can get hurt and die before you commit."

Next morning John & Leah's residence, August 8th

John and Leah were sitting on their porch deck enjoying the year's last months of decent Maine weather having coffee and reading their Bibles. Leah put her Bible down on the table and spoke. "John, the women from my Bible study group are getting concerned with where America is moving. With the protesting, pandemic, the violence, right is wrong and wrong is right, then there's the election with the socialist vice president Joe Black, who's raising more money and has the Polls in his favor, it's just scary!"

You know Leah, I believe we are at the beginning stages of the Great Tribulation period written about in the book of Revelation." It's the job of every Christian to fight the coming evil at every front until the day of the Lord. "Yes John, and I agree with you 100%, but as we approach that day, should we expect some terrible days before our Lord Jesus returns for the church?"

Then John said, "yes, and we can now see the evidence.

torms are more violent. Hurricanes, tornado, flooding and fires, Satan has power over storms. You can see evil is more prevalent in the world. God is losing popularity and the Name of Jesus is offensive to people, and evil is gaining ground" Then the Colton's prayed for the country, the president, their families, the church, Richard's salvation and all the militia, the weapon situation of the militia and much more and after they stopped praying, they returned inside.

John was getting ready to leave for militia command center when his phone buzzed in his pocket. He observed the ID Caller and thought to himself, *D.C.?* "Hello?" "Is this John Colton?" He heard a voice he quickly remembered. "Captain Palton? How are you sir, how'd you get this number?" "Well John, It's Admiral now. I got out of Navy Seal Team Four, shortly after my promotion." "Congratulations Admiral, you got out?" John asked. "I got out because I was offered a job in the Travis Administration as Deputy Secretary of Defense which is the second-highest-ranking official in the Department of Defense, and I have some authority over the NSA. They got your number for me." Admiral Palton said. "That's hilarious, and your still active duty?" "I am," The Admiral said with a smile in his voice.

"I thought you had to be retired seven years before commissioned for that job" John claimed. "You ever hear of a waiver?" The Admiral replied. "Wow, DOD! Congratulations, I think." "What do you mean, you think?" The Admiral asked. "Do you know, how long will that job last, how long will there be another Travis Administration? Joe Black is winning every Poll" John said. "Mark my words John, America is not that far gone yet."

"Wow, DOD? So why is the Deputy Secretary of Defense calling me?" John Asked. "Well Chief, in all of my Thirty years, you were my most impressive team-member, plus it's nice to reconnect, don't you think?" "I am sensing a second point in this conversation Admiral."

John hinted "You are right again Chief; I want you to come work for me as an operations specialist." There was silence.

"You ok Chief?" "First of all, I am honored sir, Yes I'm fine, it's just that I've got myself into something up here in Maine." "What kind of something John, anything I can do?" "Well sir, with everything happening in the U.S. and locally, we're organizing a militia." "Chief, that's amazing and exactly the reason I want you down here, I need your strategic skills, although I'm not starting a militia in D.C. but I'd like someone with your training and foresight to help oppose all evil intents against the United States. Think of the affect you can have with the support I can offer here. Helping with the situation here will help with the situation there. Besides, how big a commitment are we talking about, how big is your militia?"

Well sir, between the current affairs in American, downsizing of the police, and so many lost jobs, thanks to the pandemic, we are growing. Plus, we made the news last week by nailing a couple of dealers with 1.2 million dollars in drugs, weapons and cash. We're growing pretty fast. We have a compliment of over one hundred people. We're also advising many more militia groups throughout the State. In our command, 60% have military backgrounds, We have a real squared away commander, Captain Dutch Swanson, he's an Airborne Ranger, we've got a twenty acre training camp, equipped with long & short gun ranges, out-buildings for clearing practice and lots of forest, we even have an aerial recon/bomber drone with one hell of a UAV pilot, a 1st Sargent Ruth Taylor, USAF.

One other thing Admiral, we took down a group of instigators last night at a protest and one of them admitted to being a soldier with Antifa. He was affected with COVID and had orders to spread the disease. After a mild interrogation he gave us one of Antifa's lieutenants and a leader's description. We issued BOLOs to all police and militia commands in the State." "That's very interesting Chief! But I'm looking at your State and Maine is a low danger State, your efforts are reasonable, but your skillset is overqualified there. I know it's your home State and I don't want to be insensitive, but what will it take to get you on my staff. You can better serve your State and Country from here.

I was planning on stationing you at Naval Air Test Center in Pax River, You and the wife loved being stationed there before! Besides, that's where we have some heavy tech support" "I'll talk to Leah Admiral, but my decision is to first help our militia accomplish a satisfactory sufficiency at best and capture the antifa leadership. But, I need to find a way to get their weapons up to a reasonable standard. We've got some very dedicated brothers and sisters here who deserve better, especially the wounded Vets. I don't want to let them down."

"Ok Chief, get it done, how can I help you to transfer here within say, eight months?" After speaking with the Admiral and submitting a wish list, John was amazed how quickly God responded to his and Leah's prayer.

Militia Command Center Meeting, The Armory, Saturday, August 15th

During the meeting, one of the members, Paul Grant, stood to introduce a potential new member, "Militia, this is Elijah Goffstien. Elijah was recently sworn in as an American Citizen. Elijah received an applause from the assembled militia. He is a financial consultant in Wells Maine." Elijah stood. "I was impressed about the how the militia had taken down some of the instigators at the Protest last month. I would like to offer free lessons in Krav Maga combat, used by the Israeli Special Forces."

Dutch interrupted, "I'm sorry, but what is Krav Maga?" "It's a military self-defense and fighting system developed for the Israel Defense Forces (IDF) and Israeli security forces. It is simple and very easy to learn quickly. It is derived from a combination of techniques sourced from Aikido, Boxing, Wrestling, Judo, and Karate." Elijah explained, "I would be happy to offer free lessons three times a week at the command center."

Dutch exclaimed, "We are honored and grateful Elijah. This is outstanding, we accept your offer. Get with Gunny and he will work with you to provide sign-up rosters and scheduling."

As the meeting continued one of the militia asked about the possibility of assisting a smaller militia in Maine's capitol city of Augusta with the protest violence there. "I will agree to send only volunteers since we have so many in our alliance. But we have a long way to grow. Between starting our community patrols, learning legal procedures with Miss Knowles and now our own Krav Maga training schedules, we need to concentrate perfecting our own proficiencies." Dutch explained. Another militia asked about weapon.

John stood up to the surprise of Dutch and Richard. "I have a handle on that issue, in fact, we're going to need a work detail, loaders and carpenters after this meeting, we have a shipment arriving at fifteen hundred." Rich, sitting next to John turned and said, "What gives you squid?" John looked at his watch and said, "surprise, surprise, our armory will be delivered soon."

After the meeting, Dutch and the volunteer carpenters and work detail walked over to John and Dutch asked, "What's going on John?" John replied, "You're not going to believe the resource we have in high places." As the last few cars were leaving the parking lot, an eighteen-foot cargo truck pulled in. John went out and directed it where to back in the truck. The driver got out and asked for Chief Petty Officer Colton and when John stepped up to the driver, he was handed a clipboard. The driver showed John where to signed and commenced with opening the cargo doors. The driver operated an elevator and jumped on. "I'll need two bodies chief" Two volunteers immediately jumped on without being asked.

Off-loading began with sections of a portable armory. The sections had steal plated self-attaching latches, double plated doors with an internal combination lock plus back-up cylinder lock. The portable armory had racks for rifles, hooks, shelves drawers and a closet with heavy metal hangers.   They carried the parts down a thirty-foot dirt path to the basement side door to the American Legion. The front part of the finished basement was a large saloon complete with a "U" shaped bar, back mirror, assorted liquors, coolers under the bar for beer and soda. The room had two pool tables two dart throwing boards and about forty small round tables with four chairs each. The location for the proposed armory location was decided upon, picked out by Dutch.

The carpenters had the assembly instructions laid out on a pool table and were busy putting the armory together as the parts came in. When the last part of the armory was off-loaded, one of the volunteers shouted from the back of the cargo hole, "Hey what are all these boxes." The truck driver yelled back, "get-em off-loaded boys" then he turned the page on his clipboard and started to inventory the rest of the cargo's contents as they came off.

"Twenty Heckler & Koch HK416 rifles, Twenty 9mm SIG Sauer P226 offensive handguns with suppressors and laser-aiming modules, twenty compartment belts with holsters, one Heckler & Koch M110A1 compact semi-automatic Sniper System (CSASS), one satellite dish, Twenty L-3/EOTECH Insight GPNVG-18 Ground Panoramic Night Vision/thermal Goggles. Twenty Kevlar vests, twenty Special Operations Peculiar Modification Ballistic Helmets (SOPMOP2), several cases of 9mm hollow point, 4 cases of 7.62×51mm NATO rifle cartridge for the HK416s and CSASS sniper rifle and finally Twenty throat mic radios.

Dutch turned to John and said, "Two questions, "who the hell do you know? Is it all above board and what's the dish for?" John answered, "That's three questions boss, and don't worry, it's all legit, legal, above board and completely free, no charge, no favors. But the who is for your ears only Dutch." Together they walked out into the parking lot until they were alone. "This is Top Secret Dutch okay? Dutch agreed. "Everything is from my last seal commander, Admiral James Palton. He is now the Deputy Secretary of Defense of the United States and wants to remain anonymous." "Are you shitting me?!? The Deputy Secretary of the DOD!? Why us, these weapons could be used in a lot of places, why Maine??" John explained all the details and about the eight month deal he made with Admiral Palton.

"We need to get our militia patrols proficient by yesterday and I want the Antifa leader Chuck before I leave." "So, this Admiral wants you this bad? Dutch asked. "Actually yes, but the Admiral is also familiar with you too. He know these weapons will be it the right hands. As for the dish, Part two be arriving here soon, he's a little late. He should have arrived with the truck." "What, is he, an assassin?' Dutch asked. Then a lime green ford mustang pulled into the parking lot. John waved at it and it pulled right up to where John & Dutch stood.

A man stepped out of the car. He was five feet four, one hundred twenty pounds, thirty something, straight shoulder length, jet black hair, a mustache and goatee and was wearing faded blue jeans and

"Hack the World" sweatshirt. "Man, if it wasn't for GPS, I never would have found this hole in the wall. Hi John, long time dude, who's your friend?" He asked.

"Rene I'd like to introduce you to Captain Dutch Swanson. Dutch, this is Rene Cyr, the reason for the dish." "I'm a global-communications gathering expert." Rene said. "He's a hacker" John added. "Rene is on loan to me. He will assist us in taking down the Antifa leader the Somalian gave up." Rene interrupted, "Come on John, please use my professional title!" John chuckled and said, "He came up with that title," "I always wanted to visit Maine, If you don't mind, I would like to get started with installing the dish, is there a place where I can set up my station?" "You can use my office; we have two desks in there, we'll get more." Dutch said. "We should enlarge that space and set up our central communications there too." John suggested.

CHAPTER THREE

Militia Command Center, Organized Patrols, August 18,

Twenty men and women were sitting at the tables in the saloon of the Command Center. Some were seeing the armory for the first time. Gunny Wilson and Lawyer Helen Knowles was once more explaining the Rules of Engagement and Citizen's Arrest procedures. Each car was assigned a captain and partner. The call sign for Command Center would be militia-Zero, the cars would be militia One thru Ten. Each person would have a call signs. Patrols were issued maps of patrol routes. Everybody's weapons kit would be signed for and ammo counted.

Gunny went over special instructions for the throat mics and night vision goggles. Everybody got a Kevlar vest, belt with 9mm pistols & ammo, throat mic, and night vision. Each car was only issued one HK416 rifle with ammo, because Dutch thought two HK416s were too much firepower and unnecessary. The remaining ten HK416's would be used to back-up patrols. Everything would be inventoried when passed to the next patrol and the next patrol would fill out the same paperwork.

It was also decided there would be no patrols during daylight hours between zero four hundred and twenty hundred because it was an unnecessary burden and there were always several people hanging around the center ready to deploy. A Command Communications Center duty roster was also created. Eight personnel rotated during patrol hours, so the Command Center was manned 24/7. At twenty hundred hours, the patrols were on their way.

Militia Six Patrol, The robbery, August 19th

Senior Chief Brown answered the phone, "Command center, Ronald speaking, how can I help you." A female voice answered in a whisper, "there's someone in my house, I hear him moving around downstairs…please help me!" "What's your address ma'am" Ron requested. "I'm at 28 Marifield Street, please hurry!" "Ma'am, get under your bed or get in a closet, help is on the way, and keep me on your phone." Ron turned to his radio and spoke "Anyone in the area of Kennebunk Merrifield street respond."

Patrolling northbound on route one was Militia Six. Militia Six-two, who was sitting in the shotgun seat, was immediately checking his cell phone GPS. "Hey Mike, we're about two miles from Merrifield Street!!" Using his throat mic, Mike called; Militia Zero, this is Militia Six, we're two mikes away, ETA three minutes." "Copy Militia Six possible robbery in progress," Ron responded. Ron then turned in his chair, and on another phone, dialed 911.

The police dispatch informed Ronald a patrol was thirty minutes out due to their downsized department by Governor Moody. "Militia Six, the police are thirty mikes out. You're on your own." Ron informed. "Roger Zero," Militia-Six answered.

Militia Six-two's name was Dick Vinaldo, owner of a Seafood Restaurant in Wells, he was a rugged man pressing fifty years old who never served in the military but loved reading police and combat novels. Militia Six-one, Mike Ackroff, a corporal who served four years in Afghanistan, now a schoolteacher at Biddeford High School. At five-six 140 pounds, you'd never know by his demeanor that he served. He never talked about it. Approaching the house. Mike turned off their headlights and stopped out front. "Militia-zero, Militia-six, we're outside, assessing and preparing to engage." Ronald Brown informed the victim that militia people were there.

Mike's side of the car was facing the house, so he got out, took cover behind the passenger side hood of the car and flipped down his

Night vision/thermal googles. Dick was doing the same. "I can see his thermal image in a room to the right of the house Mike, these googles are great!" "I see him Dick. Make your way around the left side of the house and cover the back so he doesn't escape. See if you can see how he got in." Mike ordered.

"Militia-zero, perp is still here," Mike informed. Dick moved around the house and got into position on a back porch and immediately saw the welcome mat flipped back. He quietly tried the doorknob and noticed the key in the knob. "Mike, he came in this way and the door is open." Dick whispered into his mic. "Front door is locked." Informed Mike. "Hold there, I'm coming around, we'll breach together."

When Mike arrived, Dick slowly turned the knob and opened the door, it didn't squeak. With pistols drawn, they entered a hallway which led down to the front door, dividing the house. The house lights were off which gave the militia an unfair advantage. They could see the thermal image of the robber still in the left room and could hear what sounded like silverware being dumped into a bag. The perp was either very stupid or very bold.

A stairway was on the right at the front of the house which led to the bedrooms, a study was at their immediate right. Dick stuck his head and pistol into the study clearing the room of any possible threats. He could see all drawers to a desk were open.

Mike gave a signal to Dick to take the hall down to an entrance to the dining room where the prep was working while Mike advanced through an open concept kitchen on the left. This would position the perp between them. As dick moved down the hall, he observed all the drawers opened on a bureau half-way down. Mike started into the kitchen and saw the perp working the room with a flashlight.

Just as Dick was maneuvering around the corner to the dining room, the perp was leaving the room heading for the hallway. Dick found himself face to face with the perp. With a knee-jerk reaction, Dick smashed his pistol into the perp's face dropping him right there. Without looking up, Dick felt the wall for a switch and found it. "Goggles up Mike, lights coming on."

The warning was essential, lighting a room while wearing night vision could temporarily blind you. He flipped his goggles up and flipped the switch, and there laid the perp, moaning and bleeding from the nose. They zip tied the perp's hands behind his back and Six-one radioed the Command Center. "Militia-zero, Militia-six, target down and house is clear." "Roger Militia-six, I'll inform the KPD.

Militia six would stay there until the police arrive then turn custody of the perp to the police. Ronald informed the female victim in the house that the robber was in custody and she was safe to come out. "Thank you, thank you so much!" and hung up her phone. Ronald then called 911 and informed dispatch. Meanwhile, Dick grabbed the perp by the back of his collar and dragged him into the frame of the front door. "Ouch you muther, this is abuse!!" The perp said with a Jamaican accent. "So sorry sir." Dick said, "If we were cops, you might be right."

Then Dick commenced to dragging the perp like a sack of dirt out the door and dropping him on the front lawn. "Who the hell are you guys!" the perp asked. "We are concerned citizens and are placing you under citizen's arrest." Mike said. The perp was a black man, tall, skinny in short dreadlocks. Mike was frisking him and took small .22 rugger pistol out of his pocked handling it with his thumb and index fingers and dropped it into a large plastic freezer bag which he removed from one of the belt's compartment pouches.

He continued his search and removed a leather wallet, pulling out a Massachusetts driver's license. "John Smith? Is that a common name in Jamaica?" Dick asked. "I'm gun'na find out your names and kill you and your families." The Jamaican said. "Get a picture of this guy's face and we'll let Rene sort this out," Mike ordered.

While Dick was snapping pictures with his cell phone, Mike could see the police cruiser coming up the street. "Dick, the police are here, holster your pistol and kneel down and raise your hands." They both got into that position and watched as the cruiser stop and switch on the blue lights. A woman got out with pistol drawn. She pointed the weapon towards the ground and called out, "Are you the militia?" "Yes Ma'am" Mike responded. She walked up to them and holstered her weapon. "They abused me! Arrest them you pig!" "That attitude will not go far we me asshole" she snapped back. "We were able to cold cock him without a shot officer, when he fell, he hit his head." Mike said. "That's not true!!" He yelled.

I'm Mike Ackroff and this is Dick Vinaldo" "I'm Captain Tee Parker," she said and commenced in reading the perp his rights. "I searched him, and he had this gun on him." Dick picked up the bagged weapon from the front stoop and handed it to the officer. "Mike noticed the captain bars and said, "they have Captains patrolling now?" He asked. "I may wear the captain bars, but I only get Sargent's pay. Everybody below Sargent were cut from the department. Even the Chief of Police patrols now. If all your militia responds like you two did tonight, I'm relieved," she said. "We'll help you get him in the cruiser." Mike said. Mike then radioed in and let Ronald know the police took custody. They would have to fill out a report when they got back.

The Police Captain interviewed them for her report she also interviewed the housewife of the home. Her husband was working a graveyard shift and was racing home for the emergency. Captain Tee looked the two militia over and said, "I hope all your gear is legal, I mean, Kevlar vests? Military issued SIG Sauer P226's? Night vision?" "With thermal imaging," Dick said proudly. "With thermal imaging too?" she asked. "All I can tell you is everything is legit, I don't know who our supporters are, but our Commander can answer that question." Mike answered. "Well, I'm going to send my chief to your command center and check things out." Captain Tee said.

"Captain, will you be taking the bad guy to jail?" Dick asked. "He will, and by Zero eight hundred this morning, a couple of social workers are going to try and understand his feelings, psychoanalyze him and try to get him to change his ways. Then after he stands before our liberal judge, he will get a trial date and be set free without bail, thanks to our governor." "I'm sorry, but that sucks!!" Mike sadly replied. The husband's car was pulling into the driveway. The captain stayed to fill him in, and militia-six returned on patrol. The whole event took one hour. Militia-six still had a few hours left to their shift.

KPD Chief visit, August 19th

John Colton stuck his head inside a newly renovated communication office on the far-left side of the warehouse-style building. "So, this is the militia command center." Dutch and Richard were sitting at the communication center's desk, Dutch was reading from a folder and

Rene Cyr had three desks with a computer on each and was typing away. Rene decided this was the best place for his station would be because the satellite dish had the best open view of the sky on this side of the building.

"Morning gents," John said and then held out a tray of four large cups of coffee. Rene immediately stopped typing and grabbed a cup, stirred in four sugar packs, took a sip, and said, "Ummm! This is way better than the would-be coffee from that forty-cup pot in the kitchen. I think you guys need fresher grounds."

John passed a cup to Dutch, Richard, and kept one for himself. Dutch took a sip and handed John the folder and said, "You've got to read this report from last night!" John took the folder and sat in a chair and started reading. "Wow this IS good coffee, where did you buy it?" Dutch asked. "A place called Mornings in Paris, they're in the Lower Village." After a while, John looked at Dutch and said, "My goodness, are these guys ex-cops? This is a text-book takedown!" "That's exactly what I thought," Dutch replied. "I've met these guys during their new member interview, I'm scheduled for another meeting with them and I'm going to shake their hands!"

Looking at the file John said, "I'm sure I've met them too, I do remember Ronald Brown was assigned to communications, but since we started assigning the militia into units, the only time I get to socialize with them is on the range. The unit leaders are going to know them best. To tell you the truth, it's going to take a while to get to know all one hundred twenty members, I'm thankful we started to use service files on everybody.

Ackroff told me he served at Cobra FOB in 2002." Richard said. "Oh man, he was in some real shit! I got deployed there back in 2001 because they were about to be overrun. Twenty years in the Seals and I got most of my kills at that FOB," John said. "The real tragedy at Cobra FOB in 2002, was so many of our brothers were wounded by IEDs. Rumors were going around about another massive attack a month before it happened. The Base Commander continued to send out probes into the village," Richard recalled. "I tried to get his story about his experiences there but he's not talking about it. In time, as he bonds here, he will," Dutch said.

"So, I see Rene has made himself comfortable. Trust me gentlemen, this office to Rene is like an M1 Abrams Tank to the

Army," John claimed. "Thanks John, never been called a tank before, but I'm checking facial recognition to see who our robber is. I'll bag him. John Smith can't be his real name. This scumbag has got to have a police record somewhere! Rene promised. "All this talk about FOBs brings up something I've been thinking about," Dutch said. "Richard, you've been to more than one FOB. If the center was a FOB, how would you evaluate it's security?" "You mean the minimum one hundred yards of nothing?" Richard answered. "Not exactly, a secure buffer zone." The more enemies we make the more threatening our FOB is. We have over a hundred militia all in one building at one time."

"Ok Dutch, I see where you're going with this. If someday we get hit during a meeting, we could suffer some major casualties." Exactly John, during our meetings, we should be setting up a protective perimeter, maybe ten militia with HK416s"

"I've bagged him guys!" Rene shouted. "John Smith is really Marley Kilroy. He is a known follower of Sara Roseberg and has got quite a rap sheet. Lots of convictions but has never spent any time in prison. He was a suspect in the bombing of a Wall Street Bank in 2015 but it didn't stick." Whose Sara Roseberg?" John asked. "She's the Accountant and Vice-Chair of a major fundraising organization for Black People Matter. Do you remember the bombings back in the early 1980s? That was Rosenberg. She landed on the FBI's most-wanted list and was arrested with stolen explosives in 1984. She was sentenced to 58 years but served only 16 because President Bill Clinton commuted her sentence in 2001," Rene explained. "Let's pass that on to the KPD," John said.

"Looks like we don't have to call the police, they're here," Rene said pointing out the window to the parking lot. "Captain Tee Parker did say she was sending the Chief of Police here, last night," Dutch said. "Let's go meet him," John said. "Oh, by the way, Rene, are you making headway on our Antifa Leader Chuck?" "I'm all over it boss. I've been hacking into every CVTV camera in Portland looking for Abdul entering a busted-up restaurant. When I find the restaurant, I'll find our Chuck.

Facial recognition technology has changed the man-hunting process immensely, by creating a blueprint of a face. This is done by taking an image with a camera and then measuring distances on a face, known as nodal points, including between eyes and the width of noses. Using

Automatic teller machines to a gas station to store security feeds, cameras are always active. The intelligence community can scan millions of images obtained every second from the tens of millions of security cameras in the USA alone.

"When my program identifies Chuck, a cyber-bell will ring on this PC," Pointing at the center computer. "And the target's location will be identified, then I follow him when he passes other cameras" Rene explained. "Amazing Rene! I guess my privacy just flew out the window! keep up the good work."

John turned and caught up to Dutch as he was opening the door for the Chief. The Chief stuck his hand out as he entered, "Chief of Police Ned Camron." He glanced around and noticed about a dozen men and women practicing some sort of combat training in the spacious room. He noticed the office space on the other end of the building. After the introductions were out of the way, the Chief started.

"Let me cut to the chase gents, when an outfit in my area is better supplied than my department, I'd be a fool not to check them out. Regardless of what your outfit did last night! I will have no problem confiscating illegal weapons." "Don't worry Chief, you won't find any automatic weapons." Dutch said.

"I'd appreciate a tour, but what I want to know right now is, where did you get all your expensive equipment like the vests and NGV goggles?" "Look Chief, how we got our gear is legal and we want very much to be open, but we must demand that you keep our source secret. My men don't even know where the gear comes from. Will you consider keeping our source secret?" Dutch asked. "No promises, but if its legal and checks out, you'll get my word." The Chief replied.

Dutch paused and pointed to John, "He served as a Navy Seal for twenty years, his boss, (pointing at John), is a Rear Admiral, who got promoted to a very high-end job in the DOD. The Admiral wants John here to join his staff, but John won't go until we capture the Leader of Maine's Antifa." Dutch then explained how the militia got the type of equipment including a computer expert from the NSA. They showed the Chief the communications office where he met Rene and then they proceeded downstairs. When they walked in, they found twenty-four men and women sitting at tables with notebooks and two people standing at a whiteboard, giving instructions.

The Chief recognized the two instructors. Sargent Scott Paris of the Wells PD and Helen Knowles, who is a defense lawyer in Kennebunk. "Well, at least I know why your two people did such a good job last night." The Kennebunk Chief said. Sargent Paris stopped his training lecture and said, "Take fifteen people." Chief Camron walked up to the instructors with John & Dutch in tow. Two militia captains rose from their seats and approached the group. So, Sargent Paris and miss Knowles, you train this militia?" "Yes Chief, we instruct all units and their captains. Let me introduce Sargent Bloomer and Senior Chief Brown, who was the communications officer last night during the B&E." Sargent Paris said. The chief shook their hands and told Senior Chief Brown, "good job! So, where's all that nice gear I heard about?" Chief Camron asked. Chief Petty Officer Colton stepped forward and said, "I'll give you a look. I'm in charge of the armory." "An armory huh? where do you keep that." Asked Chief Camron. John walked behind the whiteboard, and Ronald Brown rolled the whiteboard to the side while John was opening the doors.

"Ho-ly-shit" was all the Kennebunk Police Chief said. Then he turned to Dutch and said, "I'm NOT going to find any automatic weapons in there am I?" Militia or not, they're illegal in Maine." "No sir," said Dutch. "You may examine them if you want, but soldier to soldier, I'm telling you, they're all semi-auto." When the Chief took a closer look he pointed and said, "You have an M249 SAW? Is that semi-auto too?" "Unfortunately, yes," said John. "It came from my personal collection."

After Chief Cameron examined each weapon, they locked up the doors of the armory, the class resumed, and they went back upstairs. Once upstairs the Police Chief turned to Commander Dutch. "So, your militia are out there every day, patrolling Kennebunk?" Dutch answered. "Our patrols cover Kennebunk, Wells, and Kennebunkport. We NOW have ten roving patrols on four-hour shifts from twenty hundred to zero eight hundred. Each militia is on a four-day rotation. The Command Center has militia on standby if something happens in the daylight hours. Those people upstairs and downstairs may be training, but they are on standby. If we keep growing the way we have been, we'll be roving patrols 24/7.

This militia is all-volunteer, and the current political environment in America is our best recruiter." "Listen Dutch this is a fair warning, if your people step out of line, I will arrest them. I understand Chief. If you do, I'll back you up. I see you're also training your people in some kind of karate?" "It's called Krav Maga," Dutch answered, "It's a military self-defense fighting system developed by the Israel Defense Forces, our trainer is now instructing day & night classes because everybody wants the training."

"There were five men put in the hospital during the protest. They all complained to being attacked and beat up. Was that your men? Dutch answered with a smile, "Sorry Chief, I wasn't there, and my people know nothing about it. I will confess to taking down Abdul." Dutch continued to explain, "Abdul confessed he had orders from Antifa to infect as many as possible with the Wu-Han virus. He gave descriptions of two leaders" Dutch handed the Chief ten copies of the BOLO.

The Chief of Police informed Dutch he was receiving updates on Abdul and that he had been moved to Portland's Maine Medical Center where he remained in bad shape on a ventilator. Before the Chief left, Dutch also handed out the militia's procedures for when citizens call the Command Center for help. They all shook hands and the Chief of Police left satisfied with the professionalism, and that the militia had his back.

Marley Kilroy is free, August 21st

John Colton was manning the communication desk when the call came in from the Kennebunk Police. "This is Captain Tee Parker of the Kennebunk Police department, to whom am I speaking with?" Hello Captain, this is John Colton, how can I help you." "I would like to speak to the militia leader, Dutch?" "Sorry Ma'am, he's not in, I am second in command of the militia."

Chief Cameron asked me to give you a courtesy call concerning Marley Kilroy, AKA John Smith." Yes, I am familiar with the would-be burglar." Well John, the district judge has seen him, has set a date for his trial and since the Bale Bond system has been done away with, Marley will be set free later this afternoon."

"What do you mean the Bale Bond system has been done away with?" John asked. "It was determined by the Maine Circuit Judge that since only rich people can make Bale, and poor people stay in jail until their day in court, the Bale system has been waived." Captain Parker explained. "Unbelievable! [pause]." You still with me John?" "Has he made any calls, what time will he walk?" "He's made no calls, and it's now thirteen hundred so he'll be out by seventeen hundred."

"The holding cells are at the York County Jail in Alfred right?" "That's right John." "Thanks for the heads-up Captain Parker and thank the Chief for me." John immediately called Dutch. "Dutch, where are you right now?" "I just turned onto School Street; I'll be there in three minutes. What's wrong." "We'll talk when you get in." John turned to Rene, "Stop what you're doing and see what you can find on Marley Kilroy from the FBI database. Also, who his associates are and I need it yesterday!"

"Boss!" "Not now Rene, get to work on that please!" "Boss!" "What Rene!?" "I already have a complete sheet on him, and I also tapped all his cell phone contacts." What? But how, I mean, he didn't have a cell phone on him when he got busted." "You'll have to thank Dick Vinaldo for that. He's right into those Special Ops Thriller novels you know." "He stole evidence? John asked. "I don't know if I'm going to reprimand him or take him out to Billy's Chowder House for a seafood platter." "You can't do that Boss." "Why not?" "He owns the Chowder House."

Marley stepped out of the correctional facility cussing up a storm. He lost his phone which had all his contacts. He couldn't remember anybody's number because there were all on speed dial. They told him he was in Alfred and Kennebunk was that way. *THAT WAY? What the f**k! One thing I'm going to do is to find and terrorize those two who popped me and probably stole my phone,*" he thought.

He watched a Jeep Wrangler drive right up and stop in front of him with a hot babe driving. "Are you Marley Kilroy?" "Yes, I am, who are you honey" "I'm Lisa, Marcus Lacky sent me to pick you up." "Marcus? How'd he know I was here." "When you didn't call, he checked around and found out you got arrested." "Who are you again?" "I'm Lisa, I work for the Southern Maine Black People Matter Charter. I'm going to give you a ride to wherever you want to go, inside the State of Maine that is." Marley got in. "Kennebunk," he said sternly.

John and Dutch were taking a chance. Rene found that the most frequent calls Marley received were from Marcus Lackey. Rene found that he and Marley had been busted before in Philadelphia and this little militia plan, although a long shot, could end up being a treasure trove.

Lisa volunteered to pick Marley up because she enjoyed the thrill. Richard picked Lisa for this mission because he thought, no heterosexual male would be able to resist the cute turned-up nose, pouty lips, and long neck.

"So, what were you in for?" Lisa asked. "I was trying to rob a house in a high-end neighborhood and got ambushed by six neighborhood crime watch guys with guns," Marley lied. "That's too bad. I bet those rich folks needed to be rob! Hey, wanna smoke a joint?" "Music to my ears Lisa." Lisa stuck her hand into her purse and pulled out a nice fat rolled joint.

Dutch had to send someone into Biddeford to a legal marijuana store, The Pot House, Maine's first State legal marijuana store. When they bought the marijuana, they asked for the highest potency marijuana in the house and paid dearly for it. Then they had to find somebody back at the Command Center who knew how to roll it.

Marley took a long pull, held it down, and past her the joint. "No, not while I'm driving my baby Jeepy." So, he smoked it down to a sizable roach and put it out using his tongue to smother it. Suddenly, Lisa pulled over and stopped the Jeep, "Look at that rich bitches house." While he was looking away, she jabbed his arm with a syringe containing Propofol, an Anesthesia drug. She jumped out of the Jeep to avoid any last second violent reaction before he went to sleep. He tried to get out, but something was holding him back? The seatbelt....That was the first of two laws the militia broke. Kidnapping and the illegal use of Propofol. The militia also had a volunteer veteran surgeon.

The Interrogation

When Marley woke up, he was hooded, his arms were zip-tied to the armrests of a chair, his legs were zip-tied to the chair's legs and he was naked. Around his hood were bright lights. He could hear whispers, maybe three people were in the room with him, he heard an engine running outside in the distance. The room was cold and smelled like a basement. Something under his feet, is that plastic?

Marley began to scream at the top of lungs, curses filled the room, and then they pulled off his hood. He was bombarded with bright spotlights, three maybe six of them. He tried to scream louder and urinated all over himself. He screamed until his voice was giving out. Between breaths, someone would say his name "Marley, Marley, Marley, are you done? You are so far out in the boondocks my friend; the nearest house couldn't hear a grenade go off outside. It's time to pay attention."

"What'd ya want from me?!?" "We just want a little talk about some of your friends and their hobbies" "I gut nutin to say!" "Oh, I hope not. Because I'm offering you only two options, Option one: If you don't talk, we're going to start drilling." Someone pulled the trigger of a drill gun behind Marley, "Then we'll chop stuff off, some special stuff. That's why you have no clothes. Get the picture?" Option two: You answer my questions, we inform your boss that you sang, and we drop you off somewhere out of State with $300 in your pocket and you're free."

Marley got very serious and said, "Kill me if you must but don't tell them I ratted. PLEASE, I'll take option two, just don't tell them I'm alive. They are evil and sacrifice animals and drink blood! I will tell you what you want. I can't identify anybody here." "Okay, but we'll know if you're not telling the truth. Those nice crime watch people gave us your phone and we tapped all your contacts. We just want some, you know, inside stuff."

CHAPTER FOUR

Antifa's Shipyard Attack Plan, Tuesday, August 25th

The meeting began at zero eight hundred sharp. Dutch, John, Rene, and all twenty-four militia unit leaders were there. John spoke first "I want to know if Marley's alive! I've seen plenty of interrogation time in the sandbox that still gives me nightmares and it's one thing to be under the cover of orders, but it's another giving the orders. I'm telling you all now, the militia needs to stay within the law and kidnapping should not part of the militia agenda." John said.

One of the unit leaders Scott Major spoke, I was a Police Officer and got cut after eight years on the force because my rank was one promotion under Sargent. As far as I'm concerned, he was not kidnapped, he got stoned, taken to a party and he left unharmed."

Bob Simpson (the Drill Sargent) spoke. "Great point of view Scott, but I agree with John, we need to seriously consider any movement approaching the thin blue line of the law. But, as Scott said, Marley Kilroy is free and $300 richer.

What about the girl? Somebody asked. For your information, the unknown female who lured him was in disguise and drove a rental jeep with fake license plates. She dropped him off on a back road. Out of twenty or more men and women, three inexperienced interrogators were picked out of a hat using a number system so even I had no idea who they were.

After our stoned Marley got dropped off, the partiers" he said bending two fingers in the air, "picked him up and brought him to a deep woods hunting camp where only the owner and our partiers, now know about. The camp owner had spotlights there, they brought a couple of power tools and used John's script to get Marley to talk. He chose option two and is now somewhere in rural Vermont. Vermont can have him." Richard Bloomer spoke next, "Everybody has deniability then, except me, the female and maybe the camp owner, who better be quiet because I believe they're illegally spotting deer up there." Everybody got a laugh about that.

Dutch spoke next. "Our partiers, recorded, the questions and answers using the script and asked a few of their own. Last night, somebody left an envelope on Rene's desk containing a sim card with the interview video. The voices were masked and unidentifiable. Here's the intel we got from him:

Marley Kilroy was supposed to meet some other low-level Antifa soldiers in Portland about recruitment for a big event this Sunday. He had some free time before the meeting, so he thought he'd come to Kennebunk for some easy pickings, knowing our police department has been cut. We did get very lucky using one of his contacts, Marcus Lacky, the name we used to lure him into the Jeep. Interestedly, Lacky sent an anonymous tip of a big scoop to CNN & MSNBC. We also uncovered from his cell the leader of his group, Curtis Foley.

We ran Foley's name and found he is a drug and weapons runner who has ties to a very relentless Mexican Drug Cartel, the Los'Cartos family. The FBI is certain they are supplying America with drugs and weapons. Foley's presence can only mean weapons will be used at this big scoop event. Foley's phone is encrypted and Rene is trying to break it, but Kilroy gave us the big fish, Mike Durham, who the low level's call the General of the Black Flame Warriors, a VERY evil bad guy. Kilroy says he worships the Biblical Satan and has weapons for war.

We ran Mike Durham's name and found he is an ex-marine Sargent who served in Iraq as a military police officer, dishonorably discharged for the shooting of a twelve-year-old Muslim boy. Testimonies from some of his unit's soldiers claimed that he enjoyed killing too much. Some speculation revealed in the court-marshal suggested Durham was also involved in; guess what, black market gun running, but the prosecutor didn't have enough proof of the actual crime. Kilroy says they're going to attack the Portsmouth Naval Shipyard."

All the unit leaders were shocked and began talking over each other, upset about the gall of such a move. John spoke in a raised voice to get over the grumbling of the unit leaders. "Hold it down people. Let's hear the rest." Dutch continued. "According to Marley Kilroy, a bunch of cars and buses will meet at a parking lot off Traip Ave. They will dismount, gather, and peacefully walk down Wentworth to Stoddard Street to the main gate. CNN and MSNBC will be there to televise the event. Antifa will bring mortars, grenade launchers, and AK47s"

One of the unit leaders commented, "So, what's security supposed to do against those weapons? They would look disgusting to the world, shooting peaceful demonstrators." Dutch continued, "So the protesters will storm the gate, walk to the piers with the probable intent of something destructive, the weapons will probably be hidden in back-packs and maybe baby carriages." "Can they hide mortars in backpacks?" Someone said with a laugh.

John spoke, "During the Gulf war, I've seen a three-man team of insurgents carry a mortar system in back-packs. One carries the bipod & sights, another carries the tube and base plate, the other carries the explosive shells capable of launching a high-arcing ballistic trajectory which will cause substantial damage to a ship. They can hide Anti-tank rocket-propelled grenade launchers too." "Richard Bloomer spoke, "We need to notify the Base Commander! The question is will they even listen to us?" John answered, "They will. Let me handle it. I'll make an appointment." Dutch smiled knowing John would contact his source in Washington, the Deputy Secretary of the DOD.

Meeting the CIC, Portsmouth Naval Shipyard, Wednesday, August 26th

Dutch and John made their announcement to the OOD (Officer on Deck) and took a seat. They heard the Base Commander's voice over the intercom, "Send them in." They got up and passed through the solid oak door with the Base Commander's titled rank and saw four people, two in uniform, and a man in civilian clothes.

The officer behind the large cherry wood desk rose with a hand extended, "Good afternoon gentlemen, "I am Base Commander, Captain Donald Connely," and shook their hands. "I'd like you to meet my XO, Commander Clint Shaw, this is Commander Beverly Page, she is the military side of base security detachment and this is Jon Anderson, civilian security. As you all know, this is Chief Petty Officer John Colton, a retired Navy Seal, and Captain Dutch Swanson former Unit Commander, Airborne Rangers, Have a seat.

Admiral Palton sends his regards and tells me you two were invaluable in the Gulf War and we all would like to thank you for your service. That's not all, it seems you two have been busy forming another branch of service that hasn't been used since the 1800s. The Militia of Maine.

Now, Admiral Palton informs me you two have uncovered HUMIT (human intelligence) that suggests that this base will shortly come under attack from aggressors hiding behind Black People Matter protesters. Admiral also persuaded me to hear you out, and I hope it will not be a waste of our time."

Dutch spoke, "Thank you Commander for giving us an audience." Dutch withdrew a copy of the sim card complete with a written report and asked, please promise to destroy these after this weekend. We will deny any wrongdoing, the informant is free and doing better than before the meeting in this video, and good luck trying to prove anything. Also, THIS meeting is concerning action against a domestic terror attack against THIS military installation and must be kept Top Secret"

Mr. Anderson took it smiling and said, "Okay, but YOU'RE setting terms?" After the surprised looks faded, Dutch explained all of the evidence and the identity of the two major gun-running players involved. "So," the base commander started. "you're claiming, a low-level HUMIT revealed plans that domestic terrorists are going to storm the base. But to what end? What's the purpose? It would be suicide!" It was John's turn to speak,

"On any given Sunday, your base is down to one duty section right?" Commander Page spoke, "If the day's threat level is low, yes, one duty section after Noon." "So, how would you respond to the gathering of peaceful protesters at the Stoddard Street Main Gate, and from within some of the unknowingly innocent protesters, you receive mortar fire and RPGs (Rocket Propelled Grenades). While your gunning down the threat, CNN & MSNBC will televise it all for America to see.

The Media would be a tool of the terrorist discrediting the military. You know they will edit out the mortar launches, or heavy weapons used against your base, televising only the Armed Forces mowing down innocent people. The BAD news is the BEST news that will improve their ratings. For the terrorist, that's just the diversional front. Another attack will come from the back gate on Wyman Street, by only aggressors, again using heavy weapons. The final attack will come from the Piscataquis River, maybe from two to three small boats with launchers and mortar fire. Their end game is to inflict damage to the world's most respected power.

The players are psychotic and are expecting losses, and if successful, they claim two major victories if they can damage any ship. It will be a big incentive for the recruitment of the Marxist movement against the United States." Commander Connely interrupted, "Admiral Palton said you were exceptional when it came to analyzing big enemy plans with sketchy intel, but shit John, this is all very thin!" Dutch took over,

"Commander, Admiral loaned us an operative from NSA. We took a phone off our HUMIT and our NSA Tech tapped the informant's cell contacts. One of those contacts, Mike Durham, his phone was encrypted, and yesterday we just broke it. He's been speaking in code to his lieutenants who are very undisciplined and speaking vaguely in the open. We've picked up bits and pieces with references to back gate bombs, pirated, yachts, launchers, and hostages.

One other thing, Sargent Durham was stationed on FOB (Forward Operating Base) Viper in Fallujah 2002. They were attacked in the same way. Hidden mortars, RPGs behind the shield of civilians. We lost a lot of good men, and we perpetrated a lot of civilian damage which gave us a real bloody nose thanks to the media. Durham is taking this attack right out the enemy's playbook!" [Silence].

The XO asked, "What about the FBI, shouldn't they be handling this? John answered, When I asked, they explained that all of our evidence had been obtained illegally. The agent I spoke to said, the worst part of the job is the fact that the FBI is not prepared to prevent crime. No police agency can do that. They investigate crimes after they happen, and they do their best to put the perps away. They're janitors, not operators.

I asked Admiral Palton to do something and all he could do was guarantee the FBI will be here. They will be used in the arrests and clean-up." Commander Connely spoke, "Gentlemen, I'm familiar with that Viper tragedy. Would you be so kind as to wait outside while we talk behind your backs?" Dutch and John walked out into the front office and sat for forty minutes. They both agreed the coffee was pretty good.

When they were called back into the office, they found the CO, XO and both Security leaders gathered around a large map of the Naval Base and surrounding Piscataquis River, which was pulled down from the wall, like a curtain. Commander Page turn to them as they walked in and asked, "I'm assuming you already have a plan?"

John and Dutch walk up to the map. Dutch explained, "The shipyard only has two access roads, Stoddard Street and Wyman Ave. We're sure the insurgents will attack from both. when you see the protesters beginning their walk down Wentworth, pull your gate guards back behind a blockade you set up on Stoddard Street using whatever you have for Armored Vehicles. DO NOT blockade until their march starts."

The XO, Commander Shaw asked, "and how do you suggest we respond to RPG and Mortar?" "You leave that up to the militia. We will use a little trick we learned from the FOB Viper attack. If the militia does it right, and we will, you shouldn't see a single rocket or mortar." "And if your wrong?" the XO asked. "I guarantee success." Dutch claimed, then began to explain his plan pointing to the back gate. "Use spotters to monitor the attacking surge and for the element of surprise, wait until you see the aggressor commit to crossing the channel, then blockade the road on the far side. Put your best shooters on the blockade and take out anyone with a weapon. When they see the bodies dropping, expect a retreat.

When they retreat across the channel, stop shooting, the militia will be on the other side waiting to finish them off. John continued the plan pointing towards the piers. We'll counter the attackers who might be pirating local yachts and hostages with snipers. They don't know we are aware of their plans. We will have the advantage.

I offer my service as one of those snipers, but we'll need more." Mr. Anderson spoke up. "I can supply a dozen." John apologized, "No offense Mr. Anderson, These snippers will need to be able to hit a six-inch head-shot at one thousand yards and move quickly to the next target to take another shot to protect any hostages. I can get my old command Seal Team Four here before Sunday."

Mr. Anderson put his hand up in a stop signal. "Chief Colton, I've got a couple of snipers who you probably know from Team Four, plus the rifles we use are top of the line, much better than what was available to you. I'll guarantee twelve people capable of accurate fire at one thousand yards." John asked, "Who do you have from Team Four?" Mr. Anderson answered, "Do you remember Racoon and Reaper? I'll get them on the horn for a meet & greet before you leave."

Defense, Portsmouth Naval Shipyard, Sunday, August 30th

Portsmouth Naval Shipyard (PSN) is on Seavey Island in the middle of the Piscataquis River which flows between the borders of Kittery Maine on one side and Portsmouth, New Hampshire on the other. PNS is tasked with the overhaul, repair, and modernization of US Navy submarines. Currently, PNS has three subs under modification and maintenance, two attack subs, and one ballistic missile submarine. Ballistic missile submarines have the single strategic mission of carrying nuclear submarine-launched ballistic missiles. They are the biggest and the slowest of the US Subs and most likely the target of the attack.

Since all three subs are on the western side of the Island, the sniper teams would have the North-west, West, and South-west of the Island to defend. After the meeting, as promised, Mr. Anderson reunited John Colton, Reaper, and Racoon. All three Ex-Seals had analyzed the possibilities of an attack from three hundred sixty-degrees.

The three concluded that having several Coast Guard Cutters or smaller ships patrolling the river would be nice, but the Coast Guard Commander explained it was not going to happen based on a hunch. So, they requested a single Coast Guard Boat to coordinate with Base

Commander. A single Cutter Class Boat was approved, which is where they placed John Colton's position.

The area of water where the Piscataquis River enters the Atlantic Ocean is so vast, expecting to find one of several enemy vessels with one Coast Guard Cutter is like finding a needle in a haystack. Police searching for hijackers along the miles of coastline and thousands of marinas and boat docks on the mainland of Portsmouth and Kittery was impossible. So, the snipers set-up a defense perimeter around Seavey Island. Each sniper had a spotter whose scope had a wider view covering more river area.

Their call sign numbers followed Hunter which was appropriate for the mission. Hunter-Base was command headquarters. Hunter-zero (Reaper) was covering the back gate. Hunter-one (John Colton) was on the Coast Guard Cutter which slowly patrolled between the submarine piers and Shapleigh Island State Park.

Hunter-two was on the Northside of Seavey Island at the narrows of the Island's Parker Point and Bowen Road Point Maine where the river was only one hundred feet wide. Hunter-three (Racoon) was five stories high on a Chapel Street gentry crane overlooking the narrows between Seavey and Clarks Islands.

Hunter-four was in a lighthouse on Clarks Island covering a three hundred and sixty degrees of river view including commercial shipping. Hunter-five was overlooking the one thousand-foot narrows to Shapleigh Island. Hunter-six is on the Ballistic Submarine's Island bridge and Hunter seven has overwatch towards Badger Island. All snipers and spotters were set up, radios checked, and were watching by Noon.

Main Gate, Portsmouth Naval Shipyard, Thirteen forty-five

Eight school buses arrived by convoy and parked at the already full Wentworth parking lot, parking anywhere room was available. Cars in parking spots were blocked in. Buses blocked access roads into the parking lot as people disembarked and organized their march. Each bus contained at least 25 people including the signs and back-packs.

Marcus Lackey got out of a bus and started quickly coordinating the unaware peaceful protester towards the front to lead the march and the rest intermingled in with his Antifa rebels who had linked up with their assigned teammates. The three-man mortar team, each carried one part of a destructive mortar that when assembled would rain down havoc on whatever important target they could get close to, The two-man RPG team was one man with the launcher and one man carrying the rockets. The ultimate target would be a submarine.

When questions were asked by the peaceful protesters why the heavy backpacks, the insurgents answered they were carrying rocks for throwing. Finally, the march exited the parking lot, entering Wentworth Street southbound, and was moving toward the intersecting Stoddard Street when Marcus noticed another marching group northbound and was about to join his group.

This smaller group had maybe eighty and were all wearing black balaclavas over their faces carrying banners with red and orange flames. The signs they were carrying were radically anti-military. Marcus trotted ahead of his group before the two groups combined and was met by their leader who convinced him they were Black Flame Warriors dispatched by General Mike Durham and together they marched towards the main gate.

As the marchers approached, they witnessed the two guards at the main gate abandon their post and begin running across the channel bridge towards two armored troop carriers. "Shit!" When he saw it, it dawned on Marcus putting two and two together. They're expecting us and Marley Kilroy is missing. He's a rat! That's okay, nothing a couple of RPGs can't take care of. Besides, Marley missed the most important part of the meeting, the plans for the other attacks.

The maximum range of an RPG is two-hundred meters, but Marcus wanted to be sure that the RPGs were launched at an optimum range, so he figured twenty-five meters would be effective. Never having served in the Armed Forces or seen the effects of an RPG, Marcus had no idea that his front line would be wiped out by the shrapnel and heat explosions from that distance.

Marcus halted the group, started stirring them up, and encouraging them to begin chanting. As he returned into the thick of the crowd. He noticed the news media was bringing up the rear of the protest. He stopped to look over the bridge's guardrail. The tide was high. Plenty of depth to jump into for when the military troops open fire on the crowd. Smiling as he thought to himself that these overeducated richy-rich followers had no idea, they were only sacrificial lambs for the Marxist cause and CNN's cameras.

The troop leader in the armored vehicle was observing the crowd with his binoculars. He saw the Antifa insurgents bend over to retrieve the RPG launchers out of their backpacks while others were pulling the rockets out of theirs. "I hope this Seal Chief knows what he's doing." But just in case, he gave the command to aim and prepare to fire. Suddenly a ruckus began in the middle of the crowd.

The people in the black masks began to fight the men with the weapons. It looked like some kind of Bruce Lee Ninja scene. The insurgents were dropping like flies. He saw most were taken down with a single blow to the nose and others crippled by a single kick to the knees. The women began screaming and were retreating to the buses, leaving behind dozens of bodies squirming and moaning in the street and fifty men with black masks sorting through the backpacks.

As if waiting for it to be over, Federal Police and three Federal Prison busses arrived along with medical personnel. They began rendering aid to the injured insurgents and escorting them into the busses. Meanwhile, the retreated protesters arrived back to their busses only to find the police barricading off the parking lot and tow trucks hooking up to the illegally parked busses. Six masked men carried the packs over to the CNN and MSNBC cameras. The crew emptied the bags in front of the reporters. One of them stepped over for an interview. He kept his mask on.

Back Gate, Portsmouth Naval Shipyard, Thirteen forty-six

On the fifth floor of an engineering facility with a good view of the Shipyard's back gate, a lone man on a pillowed conference table laid out his Multi-Role Adaptive Design (MRAD) bolt-action, bi-pod sniper rifle. The rifle's scope had a prototype computerize Argos BTR optic sightings. The right user could bullseye a quarter from one thousand yards away. Reggie Austin (The Reaper) was one of those users. Reaper was the best sniper on Seal Team Four, and after eight years of serving his country, Reaper got out for a bigger paycheck and calm the ghosts.

In his scope, he spotted two approaching SUVs with insurgents hanging out of the sunroofs holding RPGs and two pick-up trucks behind with riders in the back beds holding AK-47's over the roof of the cab. Reaper spoke into his voice-activated mic, "Hunter-base, Hunter-zero, I have a convey of four approaching the back gate, four tangos each, two mikes out, RPGs and heavy weapons, stand by." "Hunter-zero this is Hunter-base read you five by five." Thirty seconds later. "Gatekeeper, Hunter-zero, I suggest you evac."

Reaper watched as two gate guards jumped on a motorcycle and raced across the channel. "Hunter-Base, Hunter-zero, Intent hostile, targets just took out the guard shack with an RPG" "Hunter-zero, Hunter-Base, you are clear to fire, weapons hot."

As the four-vehicle column passed the guard shack, Reaper fired his MRAD rifle and took out the insurgent hanging out of the sunroof of the leading SUV. Three seconds later the driver of the leading SUV's head snapped back obscuring the inside windshield with blood and brains.

The SUV veered off the road and crashed into the guard rail. At the same time, two armored troop carriers blocked the road on the base side of the channel. The second SUV slammed on his brakes to avoid running into the leading SUV and managed to drive around it. The insurgent in the sunroof got tossed around during the maneuvering but hung on to his RPG. In a mist of red, the body slumped down inside the second SUV's sunroof with a partial head as his RPG tumbled down the road.

Both pick-up trucks let loose with undisciplined spray and pray method, firing their bullets in the general direction of the troop carriers without aiming, but the troop carrier's shooters were sighting their MK 416's accurately and peppered all incoming vehicles with 7.62×51mm rounds. The attack was over in two minutes. Nobody retreated. Curtis Foley, drug and gun runner for the Mexican Cartel Los'Cartos family was not among the dead.

Earlier: Portsmouth Marina, Thirteen twenty

Curtis Foley finally arrived in the stolen Ford van at Portsmouth Marina having once taken the wrong road searching for Route 1B. He illegally parked near the boat ramp not expecting to be there for very long. He got out of the van, stood, and examined the docks and forests of masts swaying in the gentle waves. He was there to find the right candidate.

Having spent time in South Side Chicago, he learned carjacking required patience, waiting for that one driver to stop at his traffic light and pulling a gun on them. He was going to steal a boat using the same method and all he had to do is find that driver.

After five minutes of searching his hopes were quickly fading, not seeing a single person out there. Suddenly, out of the corner of his eye, he caught a man climbing out of the cabin of a small cabin cruiser that would suit his needs. So, all Curtis had to do is walk down the dock, jump in the boat, show his gun, and wave for his partners to join him for a short luxury ride of raining hell on his target.

But the man jumped out of the boat and started walking away on the dock. Curtis wasn't quick on decision making. Should he meet the man and pull his gun out on the dock? *What? He's coming right towards me and the van*, Curtis thought. So, Curtis waited until the man was passing by and jabbed the gun into his back. The Van door slid opened and Curtis shoved him in. "Tie him up and gage him, but first, the keys if you want to stay alive." The man relented and gave his keys away. "I'll be standing right outside, so If you make noise, I'll have to knock you out cold," one of the hijackers said.

With keys in hand and his partners in tow carrying two heavy duffle bags, Curtis jumped into his prize. They were losing time. All of the hijacked fleets were supposed to converge on the target at 2:00 pm. "Untie us and start assembling the mortar while I figure out how to start the boat," Curtis ordered. *How hard can it be, just turn the key and hit the gas?* He thought

After several tries, he noticed the word "Idle" next to the throttles, so he set the throttles to idle and it started. He moved the throttles forward too quickly and turned the wheel away from their parking spot. The engines roared, the bow came up in the air, they were closing in on another boat tied up to the dock. Curtis reversed the wheel hard and barely escaped ramming the neighboring vessel broadside, instead, they scraped along the vessel leaving fiberglass and paint in their wake. They were on their way.

Hunter-two, North Side Seavey Island, Thirteen fifty

Everything was quiet on the Northside of the Island and were not expecting any rebels to invade from that side of the sub's birthing piers. Buster & Boy Scout both heard the horn blast from one of the yachts on the river and Buster (the spotter) said, "appears we have an Ensign Parker." "What do you mean by Ensign Parker?" Boy Scout asked. "You ever watch McHale's Navy? Ensign Parker was a bumbling idiot who always screwed things up, so the Coast Guard applied the term when a boat's captain does a dip-shit or amateur move."

"What did he do wrong," Boy Scout asked. "When two boats are sailing on a collision course, the law is to turn to starboard. When both boats turn to starboard, they just pass by and continue to wherever they're going. That idiot turned to port and got the horn and a bunch of middle fingers from that other yacht." After Buster explained, it dawned on them at the same time, Eagle and Boy Scout both simultaneously focused on the dip shit's yacht bridge.

"Two people," Buster said. "Looks like the one standing behind is pressing something into the skipper's back, possible gun. The skipper went to port on purpose," Boy Scout added. "Their crew is doing something on the deck [pause]. They're assembling a mortar on the deck! It's a bogey Boy Scout!" "Hunter-Base, this is Hunter-two over." "Hunter-two, Hunter-Base, read you five-by-five." "I have a bogey turning to course one eight zero, towards Clarks Island, registration ME-2701. Three tangos and one hostage, mortar on deck. He'll be passing between the lighthouse and the Shipyard." Hunter-Base, Hunter Four, I've got him." Hunter-Base, Hunter three, I've got him too." Hunter four, disengage and continue searching the commercial shipping lanes, Hunter-three, confirm hostel intent, weapons free, watch-out for the hostage."

Hunter-Three, Gentry Crain, East Seavey Island, Thirteen fifty-one

The yacht was approaching Hunter-Three's (Racoon's) position head-on. The Navy Seal Racoon got his name when training on a Marine sniper range. Someone from the Marine unit put ink around his scope and after knocking the jarhead out, the name Racoon stuck. Racoon only had a half-head shot behind the hostage through the bridge window. "No joy," he said to the spotter Eagle. Eagle responded, "If they stay on this course, you'll have a perfect shot as they pass by the lighthouse." Just as Eagle said, the yacht would be broadside in a minute. "Eagle, my tango's head is full in my scope, what is the crew doing?" "One is sighting the mortar and the other just pulled two RPGs out of a duffle bag and laying them down on the deck."

"Eagle, can he reach a sub from this distance?" "Sure, but he'd be shooting blind, he can't possibly see any subs from here." Shit! he's loading a mortar round! Thuuud Round away! He's shooting at the Coast Guard Cutter! Racoon didn't waste a second more, he fired, and the bullet entered the kidnapper's brain through the temple dropping the kidnapper like a sack of dirt. Blood and brain splattered all over the cabin window and the hostage, but at least the hostage was alive.

Racoon moved to the next target, his weapon of choice was the Heckler & Koch M110A1 automatic Sniper System (CSASS) he selected the single-shot selector and took out another tango, when he shifted to the next target, the tango was convulsing from bullets peppering his body. The yacht was so close that Eagle made the kill with his MK 416 machine gun.

They both looked up from their scopes to where the mortar exploded and it had exploded some fifty feet aft of the Cutter, so he called John Colton, "Hunter-one, Hunter-three, mortar weapon is neutralized." They re-focused on the hostage. He looked shocked and didn't know what to do as his yacht aimlessly floated in the currents. Eagle and Racoon waved him over to the lighthouse boat dock.

Hunter-one, Coast Guard Cutter, Thirteen fifty-five

John "Cobalt" Colton laid on the roof of the Coast Guard Cutter monitoring Hunter-three's encounter with the pirated yacht. He was tempted to move his scope in their direction but knew Racoon had everything in hand. John Colton had his own search grid to deal with. There was a small cabin cruiser he kept coming back to in his scope, nothing unusual, one skipper and two men lounging on the deck, but when he came back to it a third time, the loungers were working on something.

John zoomed his scope and could identify parts of a mortar and a couple of RPGs sticking out of a duffle bag. "Captain, we've got a cabin cruiser at your twelve-o'clock heading course two seven zero just off Shapleigh Park, three tangos, two deckhands setting up a mortar." The Coast Guard Cutter's skipper was monitoring Hunter-three when John broke in with his threat. Lieutenant Commander Debbie Brown spotted the subject threat, ordered General Quarters, and turned her boat in pursuit to intercept.   Suddenly an explosion off the starboard stern shocked the Coast Guard's skipper but she heard over the radio that the threat was neutralized. The explosion also alerted Curtis Foley and as he turned aft to locate the explosion, he noticed a Coast Guard Cutter turning in his direction. He pointed and shouted "Shoot that boat! RPGs shoot'em now!" John saw that the deckhands were scrambling to arm their weapons so he picked the deckhand who was most prepared. John sent his 7.62×51mm round which entered the rebel's forehead creating a third eye.

The second rebel made the mistake of glancing down at his fallen buddy and never steadied his aim. His rocket shot went wide of the Cutter and exploded in the water. Realizing his efforts were squashed, he dropped his spent RPG onto the deck and raised his hands in surrender. Curtis Foley picked up his AK-47, shot his partner in the back, and began firing at the Cutter.

His bullets were hitting the steel hull of the ship harmlessly making panging sounds. John Colton was lining up his next shot when he heard Lt. Cdr. Brown give the order to open fire. The ship's gunner was already sighted in and began firing the fifty-caliper mounted on the bow. Firing for only two seconds, the gunner severed Curtis Foley's body in half and chewed most of the bridge up into wood and fiberglass splinters. Curtis died gazing at the bottom half of his body that laid next to him.

Earlier: Parker's Piscataqua River Marina, Thirteen fifty-five

Alejandro & Orlando Azul were cousins in the Mexican Cartel's Los'Cartos family assigned to help Chuck Mason's and Curtis Foley's assault on America's society. The Los'Cartos family was the most prominent family in Mexico. They manufactured and distributed more drugs, traded more weapons, and more human traffic to their worldwide customers in and out of the country. With the billions made from the products sold, they paid higher bribes and had more military and police assets than any other organization.

The brothers were ruthless killers and strategists sent to help Curtis execute the task of reducing the police force which would enable a constant surge of drugs into America. If the plans of Chuck Mason, BPM's operations manager worked, Alejandro & Orlando would make millions as the Los'Cartos New England Drug Cartel. Today's task was simple. So simple, the brothers wanted a piece of the action. While on a lazy Sunday afternoon, with the protesters and rebels storming the gates to the base, the brothers would blind-side an unexpected, world power with this attack.

Just destroy a few submarines and escape on America's great highway Ninety-Five, how had could that be? When they found a marina on the river, they decided to storm the base in class. Instead of pirating a vessel, they rented two speedboats with cash.

"Hunter-Base, Hunter-six, two speed boats just cleared Route One Bridge, closing fast with two tangos each. RPGs are shoulder ready to fire" "Hunter-seven confirms the same." "Hunter-five is targeting." "All Hunters insight of bogeys, clear to engage! Weapons hot!" The brothers were traveling over fifty miles an hour. Both brothers have used RPGs before, in fact, these weapons came from the Los'Cartos family's arsenal, so when the brothers came within range of the RPGs they wasted no time and fired on the closest and most exposed attack submarine. One rocket exploded as it hit the submarine's pier and the other hit the submarine. The Coast Guard Cutter was four hundred yards down river and moving towards the threat.

John Colton was monitoring the radio when he saw the rocket hit the sub. He searched with his scope to assess and report the damage to the base, he was amazed. The attackers were using lightweight rockets, which were merely rocket-propelled grenades. A grenade rocket launched at a soft target had the potential of a lot of damage and life but launched at a steal hull just left dings and gun powder residue.

If the attackers had chosen a heavier projectile with a C4 liquid core, the launch distance would have to be closer, but the explosion was far more damaging. Both brothers ordered their drivers to circle for another run when the bullets from the snipers started hitting their boats and raining down in the water. Mr. Anderson's security was not all professional snipers like Cobalt, Reaper, and Racoon. The security personnel were proficient on a gun range, but not experience at moving targets.

Orlando signaled to his brother the direction of the incoming fire and as each finished reloading their RPGs fired their weapons at the mussel blasts of the sniper's rifles. Hunter-five was high up on a Gentry Crain when one of the rockets struck directly beneath his catwalk, rattling his body to its core. Realizing he was still alive, he refocused on the threats below and continued firing.

Hunter-seven was shooting from a window of an administration building when the RPG passed through the window he was shooting from and impacted the office wall behind him. He was severely wounded by the shrapnel but survived. The best of the three was Hunter-six nestled on the Ballistic Submarine's Island bridge. Securely sheltered by the walls of the membrane coated steel, he took his time on target. He put his crosshairs on the tip of Alejandro's nose figuring the speed, leading his shot, and fired. He was rewarded with seeing his target somersaulting across the water behind the speed boat. If the shot didn't kill him the broken bones probably did.

Seeing this cousin's body disseminated in the water, Orlando's temper flared to temporary insanity, and instead of running, he ordered his driver to charge avenging his cousin's death. He threw down his RPG and grabbed a heavy explosive rocket for the already set-up mortar launcher and was about to drop it in the barrel when his body spilled overboard performing its acrobatic bone-crushing stunt.

With the loss of each boat's offensive attackers and the threat of dying with their buddies, the drivers pulled back the throttles and surrendered. "Nice shooting Hunter six! Two moving target kills!" radioed Hunter-five. "The first one was mine, but who killed the other target, was that you Cobalt?" Hunter-six responded. Colton zoomed his scope towards the engineering facility building across the base and saw Reaper smiling from the windowsill holding his snipper weapon waving at Colton. Colton radioed, "Hunter-one to Hunter-zero, one hell of a shot brother!" "Holy shit!" Shouted Hunter-five "Reaper made that shot!? That's a moving target at two thousand yards!!"

Sunday, August 30th, Evening News with CNN

The News Anchor reported: *"A quiet Sunday erupted in a different kind of battle at a Black People Matter protest today at the Portsmouth Naval Shipyard in New Hampshire. Janis Dickson is there with some footage* and an interview with one of the soldiers who disrupted an organized attack on the Shipyard. What do you have Janis?"

Janis stood with a microphone in her hand while the TV screen was split showing the footage of the militia in black balaclavas taking down the rebels. "*CNN received an anonymous tip this morning promising "a big scoop" of the devastation of military might, and what we captured was indeed devastation, but not of the military, but against the attackers.*" The cameraman panned down to show the backpacks opened and the mortar parts, rockets, and RPG launchers. Then the camera focused back on Janis and a man in a black balaclava standing next to her.

Janis: "I have one of the men here who was in that battle. Who are you and why are you masked for this interview?"

Militia: "We are the Militia, Americans, every one of us. Democrats and Republicans fighting against tyranny. We can't stand by watching our American cities and flags burning while the Jihadists watch on satisfied with our self-destruction, and I am masked because I fear the rebels would seek me out to destroy me and my family."

Janis: "Tyranny? Can you explain your idea of tyranny?"

Militia: "Rioters in countless cities forcing their opinions by violence and governments bowing to their knees relenting to their demands. The media, which should be neutral, are taking sides and suppressing opposing political opinions, trashing the 1st Amendment of the Constitution."

Janis: "So, are you declaring war against American Citizens?"

Militia: "How can you explain the large swaths of citizenry declaring warfare on law enforcement officers using violence to further their cause and the shocking *number of politicians flocking to the defense of the real killers? WE ARE Americans! And I believe the majority of us are fed up with neighborhood parties, office spaces, social media, and millions of Americans demonizing fellow neighbors, co-workers who hold dissonant political beliefs. Cancel culture is taking away our freedom of speech, eliminating our history while Americans are being called racist because they were born with white skin."*

Janis: *"How do you accomplish the redirection of America?"*

Militia: *"Our victory will come in the form of the popularity of the turning tides. What started as twenty volunteer militia has grown exponentially in a couple of months. This country will take notice when they see more militia popping everywhere in the USA."*

Janis: *"So, are you against the Democratic Party?"*

Militia: *"I AM a Democrat! My Party has been hi-jacked by Socialists and a Marxist media who have only one agenda, destroy the current President and all the good he's done. They're fixated on him and Americans don't matter. I am personally sickened whenever our Majority Leader of the House of Representatives speaks!"*

Janis: *"Are you affiliated with President Travis?"*

Militia: *"What part of we are Americans, didn't you understand?"* The masked man started to walk away but stopped and returned to the mic. *"There's a lot of us who served in the military. Some served under both Democratic and Republican presidents. Our country's strength is demonstrated by these UNITED States and our Commander-and-Chief. What do you think Russia, China, North Korea, and Iran think about all this hate within our*

Capitol? Within our borders?" With that, the masked man walked away and join his comrades as they left for home. The camera turned back to the reporter as she passed the report back to the anchorman.

CHAPTER FIVE

Back home and growing, September 3rd zero seven hundred hours

After the success of defeating the attacks at the shipyard, John, Dutch, Commander Beverly Page, and Mr. Anderson all flew in style to Washington D.C. and met with Vice President Penn, Admiral Palton the Deputy Secretary of the DOD, and Jeffery Cummings Director of the FBI for a debrief. The militia got its due notoriety and promised to extend support. Although only a single day affair, it was full of meeting political figures shaking hands, and tours.

Now, returning after only four days, as John pulled into the Command Center's parking lot, the first thing he noticed was a single-wide trailer near the entrance of the command center along newly painted parking spaces outside the trailer. John got out of his car and walked up the new stairs to the trailer's door and knocked. The door opened and a gentleman opened the door. "Chief John Colton, I am honored! My name is Michael Bird, please come in.

John entered and saw six office desks all with their own computers and partitioned spaces. "What is this Mr. Bird? Is this some kind of mobile office building?" "Let me explain Chief, when I arrive here to join the militia there was a long line. I found Sargent Richard Bloomer and volunteered to fix the problem. Money used to purchase this trailer, furnished the computers and office furniture is from a community fund, Richard suggested this placement of the trailer. I hope you agree."

Interrupted by a knock on the door, Dutch popped his head inside and noticed John. "John, what is this!? "Mr. Bird here was just explaining how this was all funded and what long line are you talking about?" John asked. Mr. Bird continued "This building and all the furnishings are donated by me and the Parson's Beach Homes Association. In return, we would like to have the road accessing the Parson's beach homes included in your patrols. As for the long lines, ever since your victory at Portsmouth Shipyard, and the coverage you got on Fox News, CNN, and many other networks, everybody wants to be a militia member. Gunny Wilson was swamped! But now, she has plenty of administrative volunteers to handle the influx of Service Records on every militia member."

Interrupted again, Gunny Wilson walked in. "John, Dutch, happy to see you're back! I see you met Michael. Let's go to my office." Gunny led the way to what would be expected as the master bedroom. Both John & Dutch noticed the nameplate on the door: Ann Wilson, Administration Manager. Gunny led the way inside to a spacious office, complete with a large oak desk a bookshelf, and two comfortable leather wing chairs in front of her desk. She moved around the desk and sat in a high back padded office chair. With a smile, she said, "sit down gentlemen."

Dutch spoke with a smile. "Gunny, we've only been gone four days, so please excuse the shock." Gunny replied, "Richard wanted it to be a surprise. Guys! We have grown to just over three hundred people and they're still arriving! I've decided to start Service Records just like the military on every member. Ex-military need their DD-Form-214's, and civilians need to fill out questionnaires of current qualifications.

Then there's training records of Krav Maga Combat training, Rifle and pistol training, procedure training and what about insurance, and much more. THERE'S NO WAY I could handle all the new applicants alone. Michael Bird was God sent" John asked, "who has the second bedroom?" "That's Helen Knowles's office, it's a satellite office for her Lawyer's firm while she works part-time for us, and the spare room is for her assistant, a retired Navy JAG (Judge Advocate General), Commander Clinton Davis."

Dutch looked at his watch and said, "You'll have to give John and me the tour real soon, we need to relieve the Communication's officer. Let's go John." John and Dutch arrived at the Command Communications Center (CCC). Richard Bloomer was there to meet them. "Welcome back, how was the trip?" Very political," Dutch replied. "You've been a very busy man while we were gone," John said.

As they walked into the warehouse area, they saw thirty to forty people stretching before Krav Maga classes, Elijah the instructor waved at them. "I hope you're okay with where I parked the Admin trailer." "Works fine with me," Dutch answered

"Was that you who gave the interview to CNN at the shipyard?" John asked. "Yea, I hope you approve, I was pretty hyped and had to say something." "I thought you were Republican." John asked. "I am, but if I was a Democrat, that's how I'd feel!" "I think we just found our spokesman," Dutch said with a smile.

They all entered the CCC office five minutes before shift change to find Staff Sargent Paul Grant at the communications desk and Rene Cyr at his computer typing away. John offered, but Paul refused to leave his shift early. As a wounded Vet, Paul had begun to feel worth, which hadn't been felt for a long time.

"Any issues last night?" Paul looked at the three and said, last night, militia-two stopped and made a cell phone recording of a couple of fighting aged males walking on Brown Street at zero three ten hundred hours. They met some resistance and got a little physical. No bruises. They confiscated a can of red spray paint from them. They ID'ed and recorded the names, then let them go. Otherwise, it was very quiet." Replied Paul. "Why don't you call the Kennebunk Police and let them know what we found this morning Paul. If any citizens find red-painted artwork, we'll know who did it," Dutch suggested.

Discovering Maine's Antifa

Then Rene swiveled in his chair to face John and Dutch, and with a smile said, "I found our two wanted Antifa!" John grabbed a chair and observed the new fifty-two-inch screen hanging on the wall. Rene pointed his thumb towards the flat screen television and said, "Turn that on, remote is on your desk. "When did that get here," John asked.

"The Admiral gave me a Federal Debit card; I also bought a twenty-foot antenna. We will be able to communicate to our people fifty miles away." "Love that Admiral," John said and turned on the TV.

A street with several pedestrians walking on the sidewalk appeared. "What are we looking at Rene." Rene zoomed in on the left corner of the screen and said, "That's our boy Abdul walking south on Congress Street in Portland." John had worked with Rene many times while a Navy Seals and knew Rene had much more to offer. "I first picked him up in front of a Children's Museum's security camera and picked him up again at Starbuck's. He continues down Congress and we pick him up at a funky stocking store. Who sells just stockings anyway?!? And after Oak street, he disappears." Which means he either went left or right on Oak Street." John offered. "That's right, Oak street has less foot traffic, so it was easy to re-establish him.

To the left down Oak Street is an Asian restaurant, Abdul didn't go that way. Take a right down Oak and I picked him up in front of a Taco place. He stops and looks both ways, and he's gone. A few stores down from there and no more Abdul. I figured he went inside the Taco place. That my Seal friend is A LOT of hacking."

"Let's stop here for a minute and unpack what you just said," Dutch asked. "How can you hack into ten different store's security cameras? How do you even know those stores have cameras in the first place?" Dutch said confused. "What I'm about to tell you can get me into big trouble. Top secret guys, okay? NSA has agents in the top ten security camera companies. They have back-doors to the wi-fi frequencies. All I need are the frequencies and I just look for the security camera signals," Rene explained.

"I know you didn't stop there." John said. "You know me boss! Rene chuckled, "I went back two hours in the footage history, and this is who I find." "That's our Antifa leader!" John Concluded. "But hold on boss, fifteen minutes prior I find his lieutenant breaking & entering into the restaurant, where their meeting took place. Later, after the meeting, Abdul leaves and twenty minutes later, Chucky and Carl leave. I followed Chuck into a parking garage and when he drives out, and look what I got" "License plates?" John questioned. "Don't celebrate yet" Rene said. "the car is registered to a Katie Morgan, and her address is a dead end. It's a half-burned and condemned apartment building in Portland.

I put him in NSA's and the FBI's Facial Recognition Programs, and Chuck's a wanted domestic terrorist by the FBI. Apparently, the FBI has his fingerprints and DNA on the bomb residues that were used to blow up the US Census Bureau and the US Economic Development Administration in Philadelphia. Here, I printed a headshot of our terrorist for you. I'll give you the pleasure of calling It into the FBI."

"You are awesome Rene. What about Carl?" I lost him, but he was last seen heading down Spring Street. A lot of expensive homes on Spring Street. If he's got a place there, he must be staying with someone. I'll need to find and hack into a private home's security camera in the area." Here's a copy of his face, which I am running in facial recognition." "Outstanding work Rene, keep trying to find that camera! I'll pass on your outstanding work to the Admiral, I'll contact the FBI"

Rene asked Dutch, "Are you going to apprehend these guys?" "We'll have to see how much info you can get. I have no problem sending a snatch & Grab team to Portland and capture Chuck and Carl but right now our search grid is too big. Maybe the FBI nab Chuck." Rubbing his hands together and then cracking his knuckles, Rene said, "well Dutch, I'll just have to narrow your search grid to a couple of blocks or pinpoint their asses!"

Suddenly, Rene's computer dinged and Rene began typing. "Facial recognition has just fingered a Carl Nelson. He's from New York City and comes with an arm's length rap sheet. He's listed as a member of MS-13 and is wanted by the New York City Police for assault, kidnapping, and rape. Also, there's a $10,000 reward posted by the rape victim's father. You've got to wonder how these two model citizens found each other."

"Get me that search grid Rene," Dutch commanded, "I want a snatch & grab team in Portland ASAP! We have a militia unit meeting on the schedule this Saturday and I want to be able to ask for volunteers to apprehend this Carl asshole!!"

Mission Brief, Monday, September 7th, Sixteen hundred hours

As promised, Rene Cyr narrowed the search grid by writing a computer program that would tap into security cameras throughout the Portland area close to Park Street simultaneously. Once running,

Rene just sat back and waited. The program was based on facial recognition. Once a security camera picked up Carl Nelson as he walked by, Rene's computer would ping. After several pings, Rene would begin to establish a pattern of travel. After completing the program on Saturday, Rene had his first ping capturing Carl at Deering Oaks Park at sixteen hundred hours with a group of twenty or so people. Carl appeared to be hosting a meeting. Luckily, Carl didn't accept a ride home but chose to walk with a woman.

Rene ran the woman's face and found she was none other than Katie Morgan, (the woman who was letting the Antifa Leader, Chuck Mason, drive her car). A few pings later Carl was proceeding towards Park Street with the woman and once they entered Park Street no more pings occurred. The next day, his movements were easily picked up in the area of Park Street. *"He is staying within the two-block area,"* Rene thought.

The pings started up again at ten hundred fifteen hours as he walked alone South on Congress. He visited several stores and had lunch at an outside café because of social distancing. After lunch, he began walking northbound on the other side of Congress Street. He continued entering more stores and finally turned down a side street heading towards the waterfront. Although he visited some twelve or more different stores, he carried no shopping bags. Rene called Dutch, "I picked him entering an outside café bar at fifteen thirty-five called Mel's and is still there at this time.

Dutch reviewed the plan they previously plotted with the 'snatch and grab' team. "Militia-Three will be Dean Tron and Ethan Tucker. You will station on the west end of Park Street in the van. Militia Four, Ruth Taylor, and George York, you will be stationed on the east end of Park Street. I will be Militia-Zero on the Roof of 15 Park Street and coordinate from there. I will cover Congress, Park, and Spring Streets.

Militia-One, John Colton will be in the alley of 15 Park Street and will perform the 'Snatch & Grab'.

Mike Ackroff will drop Lisa & Richard off at the bar where Carl is. Lisa will be Militia-BATE. She will try to bate him into taking her to his place. Lisa will have an I-Pod that Rene has rigged so she will be able to listen to music or communicate to us and we will be able to hear her. Richard Bloomer will be Militia-Shadow, he will watch over Lisa.

If Carl is with another woman, Lisa and Richard will shadow them and keep us informed. Our mission is to take Carl (the package) before he enters his apartment. If he's with Katie, John will approach and tase them both. We'll leave the girl and stuff the package into the van. John will accompany the package, gag, zip tie, and hood him. Lisa will be picked up by George and Ruth. Rich will ride home with me. Any question?"

George York raised his hand. "Is this legal, are we kidnapping Carl Nelson?" "Very good question," Dutch said, Carl has a bounty of $10,000 on his head, so we would be acting as bounty hunters. Mike Ackroff asked, "What do we do with him when we take custody?" John took that question, "Kennebunkport PD was disbanded due to the governor's cuts, Since the KPPD is right across the street, Chief of Police of the KPD, gave us the key, but for only two days.

We will have to bring Carl to New York City's 20th Precinct to collect the bounty. It will be dangerous because he's MS-13 and if word gets out, there's a good chance his gang will try to help him escape. New York Law does not allow citizens to carry weapons, so my source in D.C. is trying to fix it so we can. Gunny has assigned people to guard the perp until we can arrange his transfer." Then John stood, "Let's mount up people, we'll convoy to Portland."

Antifa Package Snatch & Grab

"You heard me right!" raising his voice. "You either pay me $300.00 now or you'll have to pay your insurance company a lot more as deductible, plus you'll be out business for repairs. This coming protest is going to be three times as large as the last one. But this time you will have our protection. Antifa will be right out front with guns instead of Molotov cocktails." Carl said as he pointed towards the store's picture windows.

Fifteen minutes later, Carl walked out of that store a happy man as he flipped through the twenties. He walked a little further and made a left on Keel Street and began walking towards the waterfront. Two blocks later, Carl walked into Mel's outside Bar.

He pulled up a barstool and ordered Shipyard Ale. He tried to do the math in his head but needed a calculator that he borrowed from the bartender. He punched in 20% of $3600.00 and got $720.00.

"Damn!!" he said out loud which got a few looks, but that didn't bother Carl because everybody kept their distance from him. That 20% was his cut from today's work. He doubted that Antifa was going to protect all the stores he collected money from, but Carl didn't care. What he did care about was whether Katie would show tonight or maybe some other hot babe he can spend some money on.

He looked at the clock. It was five o'clock, still early, so he ordered another Ale and a fish sandwich with fries. By six-thirty, daylight was fading and the Christmas lights around the perimeter of the outside bar were turned on, and after his fifth beer, no Katie, But there was a hot babe on the other side of the bar he caught eyeing him.

First thing Carl noticed was her face. A cute turned-up nose, pouty lips, and a long neck with pink earbuds that just didn't match her attire. Maybe mid to late twenties and her legs, *Nice!* He thought. Her legs had muscles like a bike rider. She wore spike heels and not some weird biker shoes. He dismounted his stool, found his balance, and tried to saunter over to her.

"Hi their honey, whas your name?" "I'm Lisa, what's yours?" "I'm Carl. You alone here?" "Actually, I came with a friend and her boyfriend, but you know, I'm the third wheel. They dropped me off here and are eating at that floating restaurant on the wharf.

Can I ask you something?" "Anything you want baby." Carl answered. "Are you a bad boy? I mean you have all those tattoos." "You're not afraid of me are you." "Oh no, I can handle myself." She said. "So, you can rough me up?" Carl asked. "Only if you want me too." She answered with an innocent smile. "I think I'm in love." Carl drooled. He bought Lisa a few drinks, they traded more sexy talk, slow danced with her and he even kissed. Richard was nearby and thought it was a deep throat French kiss. Lisa's performance was excellent. Almost like she enjoyed it.

Lisa couldn't handle it anymore she decided to make her move. It was getting late, twenty-two hundred hours. "Do you have a place Carl?" "Man, I was going to ask you if you wanted to move to my place. You're a little fast, but I love it. I'm a few blocks up that way Park street." He pointed. "Let's go, you alright with walking?" "I need to call my girlfriend."

She dialed Ruth Taylor's number who in one of the surveillance cars. "Hi Ruth, call me before you head back home okay?"

"Be careful Lisa" Ruth answered. Carl chuckled and said, "I hope two hours is enough time." "Don't worry Carl, we'll skip the foreplay." As they walked, they traded phone numbers and Lisa's address, all the information Lisa gave was fake.

Lisa was relieved as they passed Dean Tron's van. Up the street, she saw John, who was staggering like he was drunk. Carl paid no attention. He was too busy bragging about his rap sheet. As John got closer, she heard the van behind them start. She let go of Carl's hand to prevent her from being shocked by the taser. Carl looked at John with wide eyes as John hit him with 50,000 volts.

The van's door slid open and both John and Carl were gone. Militia Four with Ruth Taylor and George York arrived as the van drove away. Lisa jumped in and was waving her hands in front of her face like she just ate something hot. Oooooh! I need a shower and mouthwash! Does anybody have some gum?" and they rode off laughing. Richard waited at a corner until the car next to him beeped and the locks popped open. He took a seat on the passenger side as Dutch walk over and got in. "Total success Richard." Richard pulled his cell phone and called Rene. "Mission complete. We have the package. all elements are returning to base.

CHAPTER SIX

Transfer Nelson to NYPD 20th Precinct September 9th

It took two days for Admiral Palton to solve the by-pass the New York gun carry laws. John had to submit the eight names of those who would escort Carl Nelson to the New York City Police Department. When the package arrived by First Class registered mail, John and Dutch stared with dropped jaws after unpacking eight FBI Agent credentials. "Well," John said, "New York's law says only active and retired police officers are allowed to carry. We couldn't exactly expect permission slips could we?" "We need to brief our escorts on the plan soon and kit up for the trip," Dutch replied.

"Okay, I'll call them in and tell them to pack for at least one overnight," John answered. The escort team had assembled and after kitting up with everything but NGV, they went over the travel plans for 120 West Eighty-Second Street, Manhattan, New York. With a map of Manhattan laid out, Dutch explained, "The reason for the FBI credentials is we're expecting an ambush as a worst-case scenario.

Looking at the travel route, I would ambush either along 79th Street or Amsterdam Ave. Opinions?" Police Sargent Scott Paris added, "I agree, the bad guys could easily set-up choke points on either street. I suggest putting Carl Nelson in my Hummer, taking the lead. It's got more armor than any vehicle made today, and I had bulletproof glass installed." Dick Vinaldo spoke next, "And the second vehicle should lag back about a half-mile. I wouldn't be expecting two vehicles. We would have the element of surprise. The Calvary saves the day."

Richard asked, "Ruth, are you able to fly your drone while moving inside a vehicle?" "It's a little tricky because the base isn't consistent, but it can be done. I hope I don't get involved with the firefight because when I let go of the controls, the drone won't return and hover over an unstable base."

John finalized the plans, "I suggest we launch the drone on 79th Street at the intersections of West End Ave, and Broadway then again on Amsterdam at intersections of 80th and 81st Streets, to watch for trucks big enough to block our travel routes. The 20 Precinct knows we're coming but not the specific time, if they have a leak, MS-13 will have to set-up watches to identify us." "Let's mount up and get moving!" Mike Ackroff suggested.   In the Hummer, Scott Paris driving, Richard Bloomer rode shotgun, Mike Ackroff, and Drill Sargent Bob Simpson were guarding Carl Nelson. The second vehicle had Dick Vinaldo driving his Chevy Suburban, John Colton shotgun, Dutch Swanson, and Ruth Taylor in back.   Each of the militia were issued Kevlar helmets vests with multiple chest rigs holding extra mags for their HK 416 rifles, gun belts with extra ammo for their SIG Sauer P226 pistols.

After over two hundred miles and ninety to go, the conversations covered just about every subject. Ruth from the backseat asked, "John, why do you find a book that was written and copied by thousands of people throughout the centuries valid?" John thought about it and said, "Ruth, I have so many reasons, so I'll give you only a few. First, Thirty-nine books in the Old Testament point to an all-powerful creator of heaven and earth. If that is true, then God is powerful enough to guard His communication (His word) throughout the centuries so we can know God.

Second, those same thirty-nine books point to a coming Messiah in the form of prophecy. Every prophecy written about the Messiah in the Old Testament was one hundred percent fulfilled when Jesus walked onto the scene in 6 BC. By-the-way, Christ is not his last name. Christ is Arabic for Messiah. Then you have twenty-seven books of the New Testament. The first four books were written by four different authors and documented the life and the words of Jesus. The four books are called Gospels.

My third point is Jesus who performed some incredible miracles. So many explained the miracles saying Jesus was merely a good man or a prophet. The Bible is very strict and says a real prophet can't lie. Documented in the Gospels, Jesus said He was God in the flesh. So, He was either telling the truth or He was a complete lunatic.

My last point is experience. I was skeptical just like you and was weighing all the evidence. Then one day when I jumped out of a perfectly good airplane in a HALO (High Altitude Low Opening) jump and it hit me. It's one thing to read about the equipment I was about to use in my HALO jump, the parachute, oxygen, and mask, it's another thing to trust the equipment and make the jump. You can read about Jesus, but until you trust Him as your savior, you'll never really make the jump. Once you do, you'll understand what it's like to have His Spirit living inside you. Incredible!!" Dick interrupted the conversation and said, "approaching 79th Street."

In the other car, Carl had to have his mouth taped a couple of times because he wouldn't shut up about how he was going to kill any militia survivors. Mike Ackroff gave stuck an elbow in his face once while faking a yawn. When the convoy turned onto 79th Street, Dick Vinaldo slowed his SUV allowing space between them and the lead Hummer, then Ruth would launch the drone through the Suburban's moon window.

Before the launch, Ruth announced she was going to VOX which was voice-activated radio, that way she didn't need to press a button to speak. "Launch is away and proceeding east down West End Ave. Broadway approaching. Minimum pedestrian traffic….a couple of vans parallel parked…no suspects. I'm at the intersection of Broadway….I'm going to get higher to view North and Southbound traffic on Broadway. Light traffic, nothing large insight that will intersect our crossing of Broadway. Proceeding past Broadway and approaching the Amsterdam turn. Uh-oh! I've found a possible suspect with a phone on the right corner. He's watching us approach and is talking on a cell phone. A very, very shady character."

As the convoy approached Broadway, Ruth's drone was turning onto Amsterdam. "The drone is making the turn onto Amsterdam. Zero foot traffic, except for two shady characters walking quickly down to 80th Street. One of them is crossing the street.....hold it. Wait a minute. We have a garbage truck parked on 80th. The truck has an unobstructed path to pull out and block Amsterdam," Ruth announced.

"I'm checking the surrounding buildings and I have...one, two, three, four tangos with weapons in windows, two apartment buildings right before the intersection of 80th Street. Two tangos on the second floor on the right and two on the third floor on the left, plus two on the street at the intersection," Ruth reported. Dutch spoke, "Great job Ruth! Dick, catch up now, we're about to go active! Scott, stop your Hummer at my command, we don't want to get into their cross-fire.

The militia convoy was fifty feet from the intersection of Amsterdam and 80th when Dutch started giving commands. "When we stop, Scott, take the left shooter on the ground, Richard, the right shooter on the ground. Watch the driver of the garbage truck, he could also be a shooter. Mike, take the left furthest shooter on the second floor, Bob, the right furthest on the third floor. Dick, take the left closest shooter on the second floor, John you take the right closest on the third floor. Ruth, you watch the rear, I'll call 911 and help out whoever didn't put down their shooter."

Dutch wanted perfect timing for the approach. "Execute on my command, three, two, one, execute!! Both vehicles stop one behind the other. All doors opened at the same time and all militia were out and aiming at their assigned ambushers. The ambushers were completely caught off guard. They were not expecting this move at all. The militia convoy had already stopped before the garbage truck had even moved to block the road.

The MS-13 ambushers were just beginning to aim when the militia began firing. The left shooter on the street took a knee and got a couple of rounds off before Scott put two bullets into his chest. Scott then shifted his aim to the truck just as the driver began wildly shooting from inside the cab. Scott didn't have a clear shot, so he put four rounds into the cab door, and the shooter dropped his pistol.

The right street shooter ducked into the front entryway of the apartment building, out of the line of fire. Richard settled his IR laser sight at a point where he expected the shooter would expose his head.

As the shooter's head appeared out of the entryway, Richard sent a bullet through his brain.

Suddenly, a lucky bullet from the truck driver went through the car door Richard was standing behind and hit Richard just below his sternum. The Kevlar stopped the bullet, but it felt like getting hit by a wild pitch in baseball. Richard held his chest and dropped to a knee. "Man down" Scott shouted as he ran to the aide of Richard. "I'm Okay, it hurts like hell though." Richard mumbled.

Dick Vinaldo searched, swing his aim right and left before he found the shooter's arm out the window shooting blindly. The shooter's bullets whizzed by to nowhere. Dick didn't panic and didn't shoot but waited. Dick knew he was exposed, trusting all the other militia to do their jobs. His shooter realized no one was shooting at him and chanced a peek. Dick had his sight receptacle waiting and sent a 5.56-millimeter round through the shooter's forehead.

Bob's shooter was crazy, hanging out the window, firing multiple times, and emptying his pistol without a single hit. It was a panic shooting. He was not using his sights. His bullets made a lot of buzzing as they passed by. A couple of bullets hit the top of the Hummer, but Bob accurately scored three hits. Two in the chest and one in the throat.

John's shooter was blindly shooting from the third floor and got lucky. Three of his shot hit the Suburban, one in the roof and two in the door that John was standing behind. John aimed his CSASS sniper rifle and fired five 7.62-millimeter bullets through the wooden wall just below the window where the shooter should be squatting. John was rewarded when the shooter's pistol fell from the third floor.

All MS-13 shooters were down in less than 3 minutes. Police sirens could be heard in the distance. Ruth called out, "man hit." Everybody looked in her direction and saw she was looking inside the Hummer. One of the bullets that had gone through the roof hit Carl Nelson in the shoulder. "THEY'RE TRYING TO KILL ME!!" Ruth grabbed a First Aid Kit and began applying pressure. He would live. Scott was upset because his wife was sure to see the bloodstains.

The police arrived and saw all our weapons on the ground and all the militia's hands in the air. One of the first officers to arrive said, "please, put your hands down and pick up those weapons! I hope you all have something that says you can carry these weapons?" All the militia were happy to flip out their FBI credentials. The officer laughing said, "I've never seen this many Feebees in one place at one time!"

Carl Nelson was slinging out a string of explicative language screaming, "they're not FBI!!" Another officer asked, "Did you bring any masking tape for his mouth?" Nobody questioned the FBI credentials. The NYPD was happy to have Carl in custody along with five dead and two wounded MS-13 gang members. The militia team collected the $10,000 in bounty money and were on their way home.

After leaving New York, and calling their loved ones, Dutch radioed the team and asked if they wanted to stop overnight. They all just wanted to get home. By the time the team hit Southbridge Massachusetts, they were all exhausted. Being in a firefight is both physically and mentally testing. The team stopped at a Motel Six, checked in, found a restaurant, and ate a rewarding steak dinner. After breakfast early the next morning they were back on the road and arrived at the command center where most of the militia members were waiting for a warm welcome.

Returned to Homebase Kennebunk September 10th

John's wife Leah met him at the door with a tight hug and long kiss. "I was so worried about you and so glad you and the team are okay. How is Richard doing? His wife Cheryl was devastated when she found out he'd been shot." John answered, "He's fine thanks to the Kevlar vest. He's a little bruised. He didn't even need any bandages." Leah hugged John again and gave him a long kiss and said, "I hope you don't mind, but I invited Pastor Dalton over. He's in the living room right now."

John lowered his voice and said, "Jeeze honey, that wasn't necessary, I was hoping for a little alone time with you." Leah responded, "We have all day, I asked him to stay only a little while, come on." Leah led her husband into the living room where Pastor Micah Dalton stood. He was average in size, trim, short salt & pepper hair. His eyes were a combination of intelligence and compassion. A Veteran of eight years in the Air Force got out under the GI Bill and became an ordained minister and Senior Pastor of John & Leah's evangelical church.

John walked to him and they hugged. "Good to see you Pastor," John said. "Good to see you John, the Lord's Angels were busy protecting your team yesterday." "No doubt," John replied. "The Lord has also blessed Dutch Swanson with the gift of wisdom and leadership." "The Lord is great," Pastor Micah declared. "Why don't we all have a seat and give thanks for your team's safe return," Pastor Micah suggested. Pastor Micah led John & Leah in prayer. When the pastor prayed it was like he was speaking to Jesus Himself right there in the room. There were no puffy words, but humble words with authority.

When he finished, it was like being cleansed, washed by the love of God himself. Leah started, "Thank you for that prayer pastor, it was so appropriate to my concerns. Allow me to make it clear, I didn't invite you here for our counsel, Our marriage is great! It's for my counsel and here's why. John and I spoke about getting involved with the militia, it was okay when the purpose of the militia was to be a Crime Watch, supporting the reduced size of the police force here in Kennebunk. He had my full support, but now it's become firefights and bloodshed.

I know it's beginning to sound like I'm ambushing John with this but hear me out. John is a Navy Seal, he calls himself an Ex-Seal, but that's not true, he's a trained killer just as much today as he was while on active duty. And now, the militia is morphing beyond Kennebunk and is responsible for killing people. I feel like, by my support, I am unleashing his skills of death upon Americans.

Pastor Micah turned to John and asked, "How do you feel about that John?" "I suppose Leah has a point. The militia was only supposed to be local, and then we get drawn into this assignment to New York. There could be another fight coming with the apprehension of a very evil man named Chuck Mason. He's the Antifa leader in Maine. We had sightings of him in Portland, but we haven't seen him since.

When I came home after fighting in the Gulf War, all I could think about was living a quiet life. Instead, I come home to find evil is on a fast track in America." I find abortions are handed out like aspirin, or how people become violent over a difference of a political opinion. People kneeling in protest when the National Anthem is played. People burning the American flag and pulling down historical statues. Violence is rampant in America and looting is a fad. Churches and synagogues are being attacked.

I don't want to sound prideful, but my skillsets were critical in the Navy. I became a little confused when I put my faith in Jesus Christ. I became guilty for all the blood I had on my hands. I was a very good sniper. It wasn't until the Navy Chaplin explained the responsibility wasn't mind. I was a tool of our government, used to battle evil abroad.

But now, the fight against tyranny, corruption, and evil is right here in America."

Micah weighed what John said and begun to speak. "Many in the U.S. think that America is a Christian nation and that God will not allow any major judgment to come to her. That theory fails for a couple of reasons. The United States is not a Christian nation. The United States has taken the God of Christianity out of just about everything and has inserted materialism, paganism and every lust anyone can imagine in His place. As Billy Graham was reported to have once said, "If God does not judge America He will have to apologize to Sodom and Gomorrah".

"Leah, your support of John is justifiable. By supporting John, you participate in a spiritual battle of good and evil. Those MS-13 people in New York are the epidemy of evil. They kill people for fun. The militias were defending themselves and Carl Nelson. Good people are under attack by these Antifa and the militia stands in their way.

I fear evil is everywhere in society, but the Bible speaks about a Restrainer in the world, which is God's Holy Spirit in us, the church. We, the church are holding back society from completely turning evil, *'For the mystery of lawlessness is already at work.'* The Bible also speaks of: *'any barrier that sets itself up against God will be torn down.'*

Could God be using your skillset and the militia to fight evil? Yes, it's possible. Just be sure and ask God and He will answer your prayer. Why don't we ask right now?" So, Pastor Dalton led them again in a prayer to open their eyes to where God wants them. After the prayer, they all hugged.

Pastor Dalton spoke more with them to ensure they were okay, and other needs of prayer and the pastor left. While John and Leah were discussing each other's feelings, John's phone vibrated in his pocket. He looked to see who he was about to disconnect. "Honey, this call is from Admiral Palton, I should take it."

More Support from the DOD

"John, we all heard about your skirmish with MS-13 and we're all impressed, including President Travis." "Thanks Admiral, one of the team took a bullet to the Kevlar vest you gave us that I am still grateful for." John replied. "Which is the reason for my call. I want to send your militia more sets of everything I've sent you so far, up to eighty more sets," the Admiral offered. *"Is this God's answer already?"* John thought. "You still there?"

"Admiral, what do we need one hundred rifles and equipment kits for? Besides, the armory isn't large enough. I guess we could build a bigger one, but why are you doing this? John asked. "I'll send you more parts to your armory that will connect to your existing one. If you want to know why, I have something you need to discuss with Captain Swanson," and the Admiral filled John in.

When he got off the phone, John called Dutch and asked for a lunch meeting. They didn't have to return to the command center until Monday the 14th. They met at a restaurant in town which was large enough to be seated inside and maintain social distancing. There was an empty booth in the far corner of the dining area that they requested and once seated, they waited until the waitress took their drink order.

John explained the Admiral had a mission for the militia. He had a map and opened it up for Dutch. "Minneapolis, Minnesota? Are you serious? What does your Admiral want us to do there?" "He wants us to rescue the 5th Precinct Police Department under siege and clear out the CHOP (Capitol Hill Organized Protest) Zone they just created and stop the looting. They can't send the military, and the police hands are tied by the governor. As militia, we can do what the police can't do." John explained.

"Minneapolis has a CHOP Zone?" Dutch asked. "Yes, just like Portland Oregon's. The Administration is tired of it and wants to send a message. The Admiral will fly as many of us as we need with all the equipment to accomplish the mission. He'll fly us from Portsmouth New Hampshire to an Air Force Reserve base south of

Minneapolis. We'll fly military in a C-17 Globemaster III, to by-pass customs. Then bus us to the location of our choice near the 5th Precinct Police Department.

The 3rd Precinct has already been sacked by Antifa which is now abandoned, and the Administration does not want a repeat. He'd like to see what kind of plan we can propose. Dutch didn't have to think long, "We can't post anywhere near the CHOP Zone or the Precinct. We would have to put the troops up in a facility on a military base as a staging area, and then send a surveillance team to spy on the area."

"So, you think we should accept the mission?" John asked. "I didn't say that. Think of the logistics. We would need <u>volunteers only</u>, Nobody over fifty. Then we would require the Admiral to pull strings for the staging area. Time to accomplish the possible goal is two days minimum, any more than that risks leaks. They folded up the map when their food arrived. "We need to meet with all Unit Leaders," Dutch suggested.

The militia had grown to twenty-seven units with twelve militia per unit, so John would phone call fourteen Unit Leaders and Dutch would call thirteen. They would schedule the meeting for Saturday the 12th of September. So much for a long weekend off.

All the unit leaders filed into the saloon basement of the command center, where the armory was located. John also invited Helen Knowles, the militia lawyer, Elijah Goffstien, the Krav Maga combat instructor, Ruth Nelson, the UAV pilot. Ruth brought a guest with her. Finally, Rene Cyr would use a fifty-two-inch screen to project the map of Minneapolis. Helen Knowles stood and looked around the room. "Listen closely! Whatever you're planning must remain TOP SECRET! If you go through with any plan, you must not be identified and you need solid ROE (Rules of Engagement). I suggest you bring our surgeon to patch up any injuries. Believe me, the socialist will turn over every rock looking for you. That's all I'm going to say.

I can't hear any more of this, I must leave now." And she got up and walked out. Dutch stepped next to the map projection with a laser pointer and explained the mission's goal. John confirmed the staging area would be the Army base called Snelling Fort a few miles south of the landing zone. Two military barracks had been reserved. All volunteers will need to submit clothes size for special ops cammies.

Richard Bloomer suggested. "We shouldn't deploy any troops from the base until we have gathered intel for the plan. We should add Ruth Nelson and her drones to the surveillance team. Her drone's video could be crucial to our planning." Mike Ackroff spoke next as he pointed to the map. "I would have a look at those apartment buildings and the Albright Townhomes, Antifa needs to sleep somewhere."

Ruth Taylor stood. "I'm on board with that and I would like to bring my guest here, Scott Hammel, who is also drone pilot." John asked, "Where did you serve Scott?" Scott was a handsome medium size Caucasian with a close-cropped beard and glasses. He answered. I never served in the military. I met Ruth at the Sanford Airport at a remote-control exhibition," Scott said. "He kicked my ass in a bi-plane dogfight," Ruth added. John commented, "I suppose that's a proven qualification if I ever heard one." Then John asked, "Elijah, can you provide me with a list of your best combat fighters? "Yes. I'll send you a copy to your phone. I would also like to volunteer when you're ready to move the troops."

CHAPTER SEVEN

Minneapolis Militia Mission, Monday, September 14th

Late Monday morning, the militia landed at the Air Base, A bus met them at the tarmac and shuttled them to their barracks. They found three large boxes of cammies. Each set had a strip of tape with the new owner's name. They all moved into their rooms and were told that units must room together except for the women. They unpacked and met at the barracks parking lot.

After the unit leaders mustered their unit and called all present, John handed out special IDs and told them the Base Commander knows you're here, but the base troops don't. When asked, who you are or who you're with, you answer 'your special ops, base-hopping to a secret destination.' Tell them, 'the rest is above your paygrade.' Until we provide you with our plan to deploy, you're welcome to use the base chow hall and the Army exchange, but you must travel in a minimum of four people.

John had a rental delivered to the base at thirteen hundred hours. Ruth & Scott loaded large briefcases with their drone equipment inside. "Let's start with the parking garage on W 32nd Street for an overlook," They parked their SUV to hide the team as John suggested. From the top parking lot, using high-powered binoculars they had a good view of the Police station and the surrounding area.

Looking out they could see blockades on all roads entering the area of the 5th Police Precinct. They could see police officers guarding all entryways into the building. The Chop Zone was guarded but they couldn't see any weapons.

Inside the blockades, people were moving around holding "Defund the Police" signs. Some businesses were open, but their storefronts were covered with graffiti, many were all boarded up providing a plywood canvas' for "BPM" or "Police are Pigs". They could not see any sign of Antifa or any violence. John said. "Let's not waste this light. Ruth, fly your drone along those apartment complexes beyond Highway 35 West. Scott fly your drone around the Albright Townhomes.

During the drone flights, they had discovered a couple of buildings with what looked like low-level guards out front. They IDed those entryways for further analysis. They returned to their hotel where they met in Dutch's room to replay the video from the drones. Pointing at the laptop Dutch asked to zoom in on one of the apartments. "Those are definitely guards. Looks like they're armed with AR-15's." John pointed at Scott's computer and said, "yes and I have guards at one of the townhouses on Scott's video. We'll need to return before sunset to watch the traffic from those buildings" Dutch ordered "We need to get some sleep before we head back to the parking garage. It might be a long night."

Later, the team stopped at a Chick-fil-A for sandwiches and coffee which they consumed at the parking garage. It was a beautiful sunset for a dreaded time in the city. At twenty hundred hours, Ruth and Scott launched and positioned their drones in a hover over the suspect homes of the Antifa soldiers. The guards were still stationed outside.

"How long can you keep the drones up there," John asked. "They are fully charged so five hours max as long as we don't have to maneuver much," Ruth answered. "We both have ready drones in the chargers. It will take five minutes to swap them out if the time comes," Scott added. At twenty-one fifteen Scott announced, "I've got movement at the townhouse. A pick-up truck and an SUV just picked up passengers." John directed his binoculars. "That truck has a lot of boxes in the back." Ruth announced, "I've got people leaving the apartment building. Their walking down 2nd Ave to East 31st Street." "I see them, their faces are covered. Only the two guards are armed," Dutch noted.

Later. If you were a police officer guarding the Precinct entryways or posted on the formation line abutting the protesters, you would experience total chaos, but from a bird's eye view from the drones, you would see an organized attack. Protesters were filing out of the Lake Street station parking lot. Some protesters were leaving the parking garage the surveillance team was observing from.

The Antifa leaders were assigning people as they entered the CHOP Zone. Most were assigned as human road blockers to keep the officers at bay. When the police tried to advance, the blockers would raise their hands in surrender and stand fast. Meanwhile, behind the blockers, the Antifa soldiers and other rioters would throw the rocks or Molotov cocktails offloaded from the truck which later returned with another load during the night.

The attacks went on in spurts all night and into the morning. Disgusted, Scott asked, "Why won't the police do anything! They could kick ass and take names!" "Because their mayor is holding them back. This is a peaceful protest," John stated. "By what authority can the mayor do that?" Ruth asked. "The Chief of Police works for the mayor and the State Police work for the governor," John replied. "What you see before you, is an exercise of First Amendment Rights and if the police did anything forcefully, it would be televised as police brutality."

"None of the violence shows up on the news, look there," Dutch pointed, "that's a reporter and camera crew just waiting for something to happen," Dutch explained. "That's right," John said. "And while the police are loyally following the mayor's orders, the mayor is stabbing the police in the back by defunding their departments."

Before John finished his comment, the sound of M-80's or gunshots could be heard. Antifa was launching roman candles towards the police who deflected them with their shields. One of the businesses' inside the CHOP Zone plywood barriers caught fire. Moments later a man with an extinguisher was trying to put out the flames when he was knocked down from behind by one of the rioters. "Look! Why aren't the news reporters filming that!" Ruth yelled. "It doesn't fit their agenda," Scott said. "I fear what I would do right now if I had my sniper rifle," John said as the tears flowed.

As the new morning arose, the Antifa soldiers began leaving the zone. Protesters came and went. Things returned to normal. A couple of people came to the aide of the man who was knocked down from behind. Thankfully he was walking with the help of two others. Dutch ordered, "Pack up the drones and let's try to stomach some needed breakfast. When they returned to the base, Dutch asked John, "Join me in my room, we need to discuss a plan and call the Admiral ASAP."

Rescuing the 5th Precinct, September 16th

At zero eight hundred hours Wednesday morning, after the militia finished breakfast at the chow hall, they assembled in one of the older empty boot camp barracks, an open concept single floor. Rene worked his magic and requestioned a large map of the battle zone which hung on the wall. John and Dutch stood on both sides of the map and explained their plans. The plans were obviously approved by the militia with Oo-raahs and cheers.

Four leaders would guard businesses with 12 combat militia in each unit with Kevlar vests and helmets, four in each group would be armed with small suppressed Beretta 92 pistols and everybody would be armed with lead tipped batons. "Rules of Engagement: Return with force against Antifa rioters if they pose a threat to you or businesses only. Protect the Protesters until they take up arms against you, then become rioters.

Four snipers (including John) with spotters, would be armed with suppressed CSASS sniper rifles provided by Admiral Palton. One team on top of the New Horizon Academy, one on the Global Health Link, one in the Saint Frances Church's bell tower, and John's team on a high-rise apartment building. Each was an excellent observation nest and would have unobstructed crossfire views of the Chop Zone streets and be less than one-thousand yards from the zone. Combat militia call signs were Unit-one through four, snippers were Sky-one through four. Dutch would be Sky-zero and Ruth and Scott would be Drone-one and two.

Protesting Minneapolis

Kesha Holland, an anti-American ultra-leftist academic Antifa woman of color, long grunge hair tied back with a short-medium build, was striding back and forth with her loudspeaker stirring up the protesters, *"Every government is a minuscule fringe of the*

Left, just as its predecessors were. It's a major gift to the Right, including the militant Right, who are exuberant. We want liberation, not conservativism. We want the power to determine our own destiny. We want freedom from an oppressive government with a history of racism, they memorialize their injustice with statues of EVIL WHITE MEN like Thomas Jefferson, George Washington, and Abraham Lincoln. We want the immediate end of government sanctions controlling the masses and murder of our people by the police. And we are prepared to stop these government-sanctioned regulations, white privilege, white supremacy, and murders by any means necessary. We want the police completely disbanded NOW! We WILL destroy what we want! We will destroy their fascist regime, take away their wealth! Join me now! WHAT DO WE WANT? DEAD COPS! WHEN DO WE WANT IT? NOW! WHAT DO WE WANT? DEAD COPS! WHEN DO WE WANT IT? NOW!"

Kevin Murphy, a heavy built, young white man, brown wavy hair, a Junior at Macalester College in Minneapolis, stood listening to Kesha Holland pontificating about how messed up the society he lived in was. Realizing now, how much sense his studies were and becoming reality right before his eyes. Courses like 'The Empire Strikes Back:' *Resistance in the U.S. Empire, Internationalism or U.S. Identities and Difference*, or Barack Obama on the Global Stage.

I am FREE to rebel against this Judeo-Christian fascism and be part of the re-structuring of a Maxis Society. Looking around, he saw one of his brothers dumping a box of rocks and bats in street. He picked two, one he threw hard at the police line, "That cop would be in the hospital if it wasn't for that shield," he said to himself. Then he turned and threw a rock at a shoe storefront picture window. The store owner had hung a sign: *"This business supports BPM."* The store window shattered. *"They should have boarded up. That was too easy,"* Kevin thought laughing inside.

The rock flew past Mike Ackroff from three feet away as he was approaching the store. "I've got several rioters attacking a business!" Mike radioed. A group of rioters rushed towards the smashed window with the intent of looting the shoes. Before the looters could enter, they were met by four militia attempting to discourage them. "Walk away now or ride in an ambulance later," Mike shouted.

Keven just stood there starring at the militia when three rioters rushed past him with knives drawn. The rioters were able to make one swipe each with their knives before they were met with led tipped batons and hearing the crunch of their bones breaking before the pain registered in their brains. One of the rioters got up on his unbroken knee, drew a pistol and aimed it at Mike. Keven heard a Thwap! Before the rioter dropped his pistol as his hoodie sleeve began to turn red.

Kevin witnessed the militia take down the rioters with ease. Hearing a commotion to his right, ten more rioters were grabbing bats from the bed of a nearby Toyota truck to attack the militia with. They charged towards the outnumbered militia for revenge. Out of nowhere, four men bumped past Kevin almost knocking him down. In less than thirty seconds ten more rioters were left squirming on the ground. Kevin paused, like a child checking the coast is clear before raiding a cookie jar, picked up another rock. Then a woman dressed in Cammie pants, hoodie, and black mask stood there and said, "not cool." In a whirlwind blur, her fist met his jaw and everything went black.

Earlier, at the CHOP Zone border

The militia teams staged at the Blaisdell YMCA parking lot and waited until the CHOP zone was full and for Dutch to order them forward. Dutch, Ruth, and Scott watched as the scene played out the same as the night before. Antifa arrived at the townhouses with a truck filled with rocks and bats. Soldiers filed out of the Apartments and walked to the zone. Protesters entered the zone unabated by the blockade guards. They were dumping rocks in the street. Boarded up windows of local businesses were already being bombarded by looter-wannabes hoping for access through the windows. It was time. "All units approach your positions."

The two Antifa barricades were heavily guarded. The invading militia stopped just before turning the corner to the barricade. Ruth and Scott flew their drones over them. Ruth yelled her mic, "flash-bangs away." When the flash bang grenades dropped from the drones and exploded, it rendered the Antifa guards useless.

The militia units blew past the blockades, disarming the guards. In a single file, Richard's unit jogged through the disposed hypodermic needles and fesses up along the front of the stores in defiance of the rioters and was immediately attacked for it.

The attackers were addicts, appearing almost malnourished with psychotic wild eyes. They charged, clearly without any consideration of the physical discipline of their foes, expecting their numbers would have the advantage. The militia ducked, avoided, and countered with equal violence dropping Antifa into their own CHOP Zone's products on the ground.

The battle was less than one hundred feet from the police line. An officer in the formation line looked back to his Sargent, "What do we do?" "Stand fast! Do not engage! I say again, do not engage!" The Sargent yelled. Richard looked back to the Sargent and saw her nod and smile.

From his perch, John saw one of the rioters who was laying on the ground remove a pistol from his coat and fire at a militia soldier. John fired and took out the shoulder of his pistol arm. The weapon dropped. John heard "Man down!" in his radio and saw Dick Vinaldo helping the shot militia up and escort him behind the attack line. From John's scope, it looked like the militia took one to his chest's Kevlar vest. "That's going to hurt," John said in his mic.

Sky two yelled in his mic, "Unit three, you've got two Antifa with machetes at your rear." Unit three (Elijah Goffstien) turned and faced them. As both machete attackers rushed Elijah one lifted his arm telegraphing his move, Elijah simply dodged the blade and swept the attacker's leg and he went down with a thud.

At the same time the other machete blade, aiming for Elijah's neck, was blocked by Elijah's baton in his left and with his right thrust up the heel of his palm connecting with the attacker's nose. The crunch was so loud Elijah thought he had just killed a man by sending his nose into his brain. No time to check. He moved to the first attacker who was just getting up and before the attacker could position back into a fighting stance. Elijah threw a helicopter leg five feet in the air which connected with the right temple, knocking him unconscious.

John observed the scene with awe. "Lord" he prayed, "May our deeds not bring upon us Your wrath. Keep us safe from harm." The militia was plainly outnumbered, but their superiority was lopsided. The only reason John could think of why the rioters continued to attack was purely defensive of their precious CHOP Zone. The militia looked like lawnmowers leaving bodies lying on the ground as they passed through. If you threatened the militia, man, woman, white, black, Hispanic, you were left behind with a broken bone or a severely bad bruise. If you ran from the militia, you were left alone.

A militia named Rolley Winters from unit four was advancing ahead of his unit. An attacker launched a high swing with his fist, Rolley ducked and went low to the knee. Another advanced with a switchblade and slashed at Rolley's mid-section, he jumped back and swung his baton down on the attacker's collar bone. Another rushed to tackle him, the attacker got Rolley's knee to the stomach and a baton to the back of their neck while falling from their own momentum. Rolley's team leader yelled out, "Winters slow down!" Rolley walked back to rejoin his unit. All shots except for one were fired in defense and by the militia. The wounds were non-lethal (ordered by Dutch) and muffled with very little sound from the suppressors.

The news network cameraman was filming away. The reporter looked excited; her report would make headlines news on every station. The militia was masked, so they couldn't be identified and left no evidence behind. Dutch made a standing order before the invasion, No interviews! Finally, at twenty-four hundred hours, the order was given by Dutch, "All units, return to the staging area. Sky units, remain on station until all units are secure."

The destruction left in the militia's path September 17th

Before the night was over, Dutch invited John to have breakfast with him the next morning in his room at zero seven hundred. On the morning of the 17th, John left his room and met Dutch at the chow hall. Dutch was already seated and was working on a hardy breakfast. Scrambled eggs, hash browns, pancakes fruit, yogurt, and two urns of coffee. "How's our wounded man?" Dutch asked. "Sore as hell. He's been wrapped up by the surgeon. He's cracking jokes and pretty happy with our success to notice the pain." John answered. "Sit down John, we're about to be entertained." Dutch pointed to the 52" television screen hanging on the wall as several commercials and a few political campaign ads rolled through after which Fox 9 News introduced the top stories. Dutch and John didn't have to wait long.

"This is CNN 9 Morning News with this just in from WCCO-TV News" The television screen was split with the WCCO-TV's Anchor on one side and the CHOP Zone battle on the other. *"What started as a peaceful protest at Nicollet Avenue and East 31ˢᵗ Street in front of the 5ᵗʰ Precinct Police Department ended up in a symphony of brutality. Local hospitals were flooded this morning with eight gunshot wounds and seventy-two men AND WOMEN with broken bones and severe bruises. Many of those wounded in the hospital are from* **out of state***.*

An unknown terrorist militant group attacked the peaceful protest last night around 9 PM leaving behind a tangled mess of bodies. While the Police stood by guarding their own property saying they were merely following the orders of the mayor not to engage the protesters. So, rioters tried and failed to defend their CHOP Zone while the terrorist militants rolled through unhindered. The Police Chief has denied an interview. Nobody saw where the terrorist came from or where they went after the attack." Disgusted, Dutch changed the channel.

Fox and Friends: *"Democratic congresswoman Abdulla Omani didn't have anything nice to say about the President of the United States and is blaming David Travis for enraging NRA enthusiasts and his base with racist language. Republican Senator Majority Leader just said, and I quote, "Keep defunding the police? Keep tying their hands and you will see more of these vigilante groups popping up."*

The television switched to a Fox News reporter on the scene of the once CHOP Zone. *"I'm here at the scene of last night's battle and as you can see, citizens are cleaning up a very littered street."* Behind the reporter is a garbage truck with some citizens sweeping up and others picking up trash and throwing the trash into the garbage truck.

The television pans right to a man in his forties standing next to the reporter. *"I have with me Stanley Kirk, one of the business owners in this once CHOP Zone. What do you have to say about last night's battle?"* *"Fifty days ago, my business was destroyed by THESE peaceful protesters, so we boarded up and two days ago the THESE peaceful protesters lit our store on fire. My father who lives upstairs came down with an extinguisher to put the fire out and one of THESE peaceful protesters hit him in the head from behind. He's in the hospital with a severe concussion. Those SO-CALLED terrorists that cleaned out the CHOP*

Zone, in my opinion, were avenging angels." The man said. "That's my report from the CHOP Zone, back to you Lenard."

Black People Matter headquarters, September 17th

Rasha Tossa waited until her whole staff was seated, saying nothing. She just sat there waiting. Nobody was brave enough to speak except Mike Durham. There weren't many people he feared. "Is this about Minneapolis?" Mike asked. Rasha spouted off a string of profanity that would make a sailor embarrassed. "How about Portland Maine, Portsmouth New Hampshire and don't leave out Manhattan, New York! Can anybody tell me what's going on!? Is this one group or more? Are these groups some kind of special military that Travis is operating to try and sabotage BLM? With? I want answers and I want them yesterday! She waved her hands while yelling her last statement striking her gourmet Star-Bucks Cappuccino across the room. "DAMN IT!"

Sara Roseberg stood and spoke, "This can't be one group. Why travel almost one thousand miles from Maine to Minnesota? It's possible, but why? It's got to be military. I have a source that says they saw a very large Air Force Cargo plane at a Reserve Air Base around the time of the attacks." Mike Durham spoke next, "My sources say the group calling themselves the Maine Militia defeated the attacks at Portsmouth, captured one my operatives there and turned him over to the FBI. The FBI took out seven MS-13 in New York, I also doubt they had anything to do with Minneapolis."

Rasha interrupted, "By the way, did you have that bitch reporter fired? The one who did that interview in Portsmouth? And what about the media, they're supposed to be villainizing the militia? Tell the media to call these assholes White Supremacist!" Rasha demanded. Sara Roseberg spoke, "She was fired, and we put out a warning to the media, if they so much as report any positive clips of these militia groups, we will scream racism! But we can't do much about Fox News. It's time to cash in on our insurance to really give these militias a black eye!" Rasha demanded. "Great use the insurance. Mike, I want to know...Wait, I don't want to know. I want it to go away! Do your thing and TAKE OUT THESE militias!!!"

After the meeting, Mike Durham pulled out his phone and hit the speed dial. Chuck Mason picked up and waited as the pings and clicks of the encryption finished. "What's up Mike?" Chuck asked. "I have a very important mission for you. I want you to take out those sons-a-bitches Maine Militia. I wonder why you haven't done this without my asking after they humiliated you at the Shipyard!" "I already have a plan Mike. I'm real pissed about them taking out Carl Nelson, my chief lieutenant." Mason said.

"This is real important Chuck. What can I do to help you succeed?" I need more automatic weapons and people who know how to use them. I'm going to hit them hard right at their home!" "I'll send you a team and extra weapons from the New England Antifa Group. Where are you now?" "I'm in Boston."

"What are you doing in Boston? What's happening in Portland?" "I've been warned by one of my hackers that the cameras in Portland have been hacked and Carl got himself captured because of facial recognition," Chuck said. "Your Militia must have someone or something sophisticated working for them. Don't screw this up! I want you to take care of it personally!" Mike Durham ended the call.

CHAPTER EIGHT

Militia Command Center, September 17th, nineteen hundred-hour

The team returned early Thursday evening. John stopped by the command center to check in with whoever was standing duty at the communication desk. It was Paul Grant, one of the wounded veterans. Paul was not aware of the mission John was returning from, and John preferred it that way. The fewer who knew the better. The word was passed that the fifty-nine militia members were invited to help train the New Hampshire Militia and stayed over-night. John's ex-teammate from the Seals was starting his own branch. He was covering for John's fifty-nine people, claiming they were camping out at a training facility in Barrington New Hampshire. John spoke with Paul about everything he missed and read some of the reports filed by the patrols. Nothing big.

John's phone vibrated in his pocket. It was Admiral Palton. "Hello, Admiral," John answered. "John, I want to thank you for the outstanding results. As promised, I'm sending you the extra equipment on your list. Is there anything else you'd like?" The Admiral asked. "It's more than enough sir," John replied. "John, I'm a little worried that you're making some pretty unorthodox enemies. I've seen satellite images of your complex and you have a lot of weaknesses. Don't you think? You're not going to get careless in your old age, are you John?" "No sir! Dutch and were already planning on including our facility with perimeter patrols," John answered.

"Well, I'm going to send you sensors and cameras along with the monitors for your perimeter. Get Rene to set it up, he knows how." "Thanks Admiral, Dutch is going to love it." "John, are you getting any closer to capturing Chuck Mason? Don't forget my offer as my operative. What have you got so far on Nelson?" "He's gone to ground. He's not in the Portland area. Rene has hacked a lot of cameras and has gotten zero hits." "Well, keep trying, and get your perimeter secured, okay?" "Yes sir, Admiral." The call was ended.

Bi-Monthly Militia meeting, Kennebunk High School Auditorium, Saturday, September 19th Ten hundred hours.

The militia had out-grown the Command Center which could hold two hundred twenty people so, they moved their Bi-monthly meeting to the High School auditorium which could hold three hundred fifty. Dutch and John walked out on the stage and were applauded. John gave the opening prayer and when he finished, Dutch took the microphone waited until another applause quieted. "I stand in awe as I look out at the Maine Militia. We have grown from twenty-eight to three hundred twenty-four in just three months. We have ten snipers qualified at one thousand yards. Two hundred thirty qualified MK 416 marksmen, two hundred eighty expect pistol marksmen, one hundred qualified at tenth level Krav Maga. Our training camp is manned seven days a week. We have two outstanding UAV drone pilots, Ruth Nelson and Scott Hamlin. We are assisting the establishment of other militia groups. We're are now patrolling Wells, Kennebunk, and Kennebunkport from nineteen hundred to zero seven hundred seven days a week. The Kennebunkport police is gone, Kennebunk has decreased to sixty percent and the same with the Wells police. We are keeping things safe and quiet in our communities. Give yourselves a round of applause!!" The auditorium broke out in a roar.

"Recently, with the help of NSA's Rene Cyr, we captured the wanted criminal Carl Mason and turned custody over to the Manhattan Police collecting a $10,000 bounty. After taxes and expenses, that's $8,645. You should realize that we now have a common enemy with America, domestic terrorist, and Antifa." The crowd began booing. "As a safety precaution, all unit leaders agreed to use the amount of $3,060 to purchase concrete barriers along our property's parking lot to prevent anybody from driving a vehicle into our command center. John Colton's source in D.C. will be sending a free security system for our Center's perimeter using sensors, cameras, and monitors, along with materials to expand our armory size and equipment inventory to one hundred sets." The crowd roared.

I'd like to direct your attention to the incident in Minneapolis Minnesota. The Minnesota Militia successfully took down the CHOP Zone around the 5th Precinct. Did you see that on the News? The concept of the militia established on December 13, 1636, is rising again." The crowd roared. "Next is Portland Oregon, Seattle Washington until Antifa has been rooted out of our Democracy!" Standing ovation. "I'd like to appreciate some key people who have contributed to our success. John Colton for his sources and sniper instructions. Our techy, NSA's Rene Cyr. Michael Bird for his administration trailer. Elijah Goffstien our hand to hand combat instructor

Gunny Wilson, allowing us to use her property for our weapons training. The administrators, Helen Knowles our lawyer, Doctor Albert Cayer our surgeon. How about the seizure of One million two hundred fifty thousand dollars in street valued drugs by Richard Bloomer and Dean Tron or the burglary busted up by Mike Ackroff and Dick Vinaldo. As your Commander, I have one standing order for you. Get qualified in everything we offer. Make yourself the best militia you can be and be ready to defend your country." Standing ovation. We have several tables in the lobby with sign up sheets for the ranges, combat training schedules, and patrolling schedules, make sure you sign up. We'll need carpenters and a work detail on Monday at three PM to receive our expanded armory. Have a great weekend and see you at the center!"

The Maine Mall September 19th fifteen hundred thirteen hours

John, Dutch, and Richard and their wives had become the best of friends and enjoyed going to dinners and events together. When they could, they attended outdoor concerts held at a local outdoor gazebo in Wells Maine every Saturday from eighteen thirty until twenty-one hundred. Before meeting Dutch and his wife there later, John and Richard were taking their wives to the Maine Mall for a little shopping.

The men grudgingly agreed to go. They found a parking spot outside JC Penny's (The North side of the Mall) so they entered the Mall from there. The men faithfully followed their wives, stopping frequently inside the store as they coveted the latest fashion accessories, eventually entering the Mall's concourse and its highway of people. The women had their sights on Kay Jewelers and the men were liberated by the sight of a Starbucks.

Suddenly, gunfire. John and Richard were all too familiar with the sound of automatic AK47 gunfire which sounded like it was coming from the far south-side of the Mall. They both grabbed their wives and started pushing them back into JC Penny's. John told them to get out to the parking lot, into the car, and move to the farthest end of the lot. "Call 911 and tell them two friendlies are moving south from the north entrance!"

Both John and Richard always carried concealed SIG Sauer P226 pistols and drew them as they advanced automatically. Three shots were fire from inside JC Penny's "Oh God no! I'll take care of it!" He yelled at Richard as he ran back into the store. He followed the direction in reverse of how they came through the store. Trying to scan in all directions. There were so many places a terrorist could hide. He chanced to reveal his position. "Leah!" "Over here," He heard.

As he came around the women's coats, he found Leah standing over a moaning Terrorist holding the .22 revolver John gifted her which turned out to be a disastrous Christmas gift. That Christmas day she argued about how inappropriate a gun gift was for Christmas. And here she was, despite hating that gift, she still kept it in her purse as John pleaded. It had saved hers, Cheryl's, and who knows how many other lives.

John went over to a scarf rack and pulled a couple off the rack. "Leah, do you think you can tie him up? then will you and Cheryl please get out of here? I've got to get back to Richard," John said. "I can. Please be careful?" "I will." He kissed her and ran back towards the concourse.

People were rushing through JC Penny's to escape, John caught back up with Richard and ensured him his wife was safe and what

Leah had done. Then John and Richard pushed against the flow inside the concourse. Richard ducked into the storefront of GNC and John moved further down to US Cellular. They both watched as several people were slaughtered in front of the Starbuck's by a shooter who had entered from the Mall's main west entrance. They couldn't see him yet, but John had settled his sights at that intersection. When he appeared, he was lobbing a grenade down the east entrance. John shot him three times just as the grenade sailed away.

When the grenade exploded, John and Richard were around the corner and out of the way. John moved to the blindside wall with his pistol pointed and slowly moved toward the intersection. People were dead and dying everywhere. Nobody could help them until the threat was down. As John moved forward, Richard grabbed the AK 47 and three mags from the terrorist. Having an AK47 and three mags was an endlessly supplied weapon compared to a pistol. John was watching for the next threat and watching where he stepped. Blood is slick and stepping in a blood puddle was like walking on ice once your shoes were bloodied.

He walked along the wall of the concourse and Richard hugged the other side. If a second terrorist wanted to shoot John, he would have to expose himself to Richard who had moved to the US Cellular door and was waiting. A second terrorist jumped out from around the corner and was spraying bullets in John's direction, but John had dropped to his stomach and before the shooter could adjust aim, Richard walk several bullets up from the terrorist's chest to his head. John got up, grabbed the terrorist's gun and magazines, and continued his slow walk to the intersection and peeked around the corner to find it empty. He could still hear shots continuously being fired from the south side of the Mall.

People were running out of stores, rushing past their position. Richard ran ahead of John to check several people who had been gunned down. One of them was still alive, so Richard dragged her to a kiosk booth for phone sales and propped her up. She was hit in the leg. John grabbed a shopper before he could pass by and led him over to the young lady and told him to stay here, apply pressure, and wait for the police. John moved to one of the dead shooters and judging by appearance determined he was Middle Eastern.

They proceeded south down the concourse in staggered formation leapfrogging from one storefront to the next storefront. Another terrorist was leaving the Chico's store when he spotted Richard approaching. With a shocked look, brought his AK 47 up to his hip, but before he could get a shot off John took off his head with a spray of aimed bullets. Every store had people crowded inside and some screamed when John or Richard entered the storefront. They tried to quiet them, telling them "We're good guys" and it was almost over. They were approaching the next intersection when a chubby rent-a-cop with a pistol ran out of a store and up the concourse towards remaining terrorists. He either just woke up from a nap or there was an office upstairs. He didn't see John or Richard. John yelled to stop and only received a look back around the cop's shoulder.

The wannabe hero continued running until he entered the intersection, where he was cut down. At least ten bullets had torn him up and his pistol flew across the floor. He was still able to drag himself to a travel agent's stall where he laid, looking back towards John and as his life was draining away, managing to point up in the direction of the Sears store. There must be a shooter in the balcony above Sears. Before we could worry about that shooter, we had to worry about the east & west side intersection. Police sirens could be heard outside and AK47 shots were still be fired from what sounded like inside the Macy's store on the west and the Sears on the east.

John got on his cell phone and called 911. "What is your emergency?" Dispatch asked in her headset knowing this would probably be another call reporting a shooting in the Mall. "My name is John Colton. I am a retired Navy Seal. I am in the Maine Mall with one other man named Richard Bloomer and he is an ex-Army Ranger. We're both armed and have killed three terrorists and wounded one in JC Penny's and is tied up.

Tell your emergency responders the North concourse is clear, and the rest of the shooters are in Macy's, Sears, and also store above Sears." The dispatch was stunned, "You're in the Mall fighting the terrorists?" John didn't have time to say anything because one of the terrorists opened up on Richard from around the corner and Richard returned fire. Nobody got hit, and John was sure she heard it. John didn't wait and said, "Tell your SWAT Commander what I told you and don't shoot us. I am wearing a blue windbreaker and khaki pants and he is wearing a green sweatshirt and olive-green cargo pants." Then John hung up.

John looked at Richard who was signaling to move up to the intersection, then he pointed to his eyes with two fingers and pointed to where the terrorist should be, in the western direction towards Macy's. Then he pointed to himself and forward. Richard was going to set up the terrorist by presenting himself to the terrorist while John goes for the kill. John held up a fist signaling to wait and then leaned his AK47 against the wall and pulled out his SIG Sauer P226. If he used the AK 47 John would need to expose his back to the eastern concourse in front of Sears. John nodded to Richard. Richard stepped out and fired.

The terrorist fired back, and John leaned out. The terrorist had to step away from a kiosk giving John a perfect shot, which he took, and the terrorist went down. At the same time John leaned out, he also drew fire from the two remaining terrorists in the eastern concourse in front of and above Sears. Bullets struck the concrete wall above John's head sending pieces of concrete into John's face. John ducked back away from the line of fire and felt blood trickling down his face.

John didn't hear them or see them but sensed someone from behind. He swung around looking back and saw two lines of Swat approaching. There were eight on John's side and eight on Richard's side of the concourse. Every store they came to, one soldier broke off into the store to clear any possible terrorists and escort out any surviving shoppers. John called to Richard and held up his AK 47, Richard noticed the SWAT and did the same. The Swat Commander reached John's position and said, "I'm Captain Wilson, we found your wounded and dead terrorists, what's left for us?" "I'm John and that's Richard." Then the rattle of an AK47 sounded along with a different weapon, maybe an AR15 or HK416.

The Swat Commander then said, "the downstairs terrorist is tucked in with superior cover." We're going to use a flash-bang the disorient him." Cover your ears and close your eyes." John heard him say to his radio, "fire in the hole," then they heard the loud explosion.

A flashbang or stun grenade is designed to produce a blinding flash of light of around 7 mega-candles and an intensely loud "bang" of greater than 170 decibels. It may be a less-lethal explosive device used to temporarily disorient an enemy's senses but can render the good-guys blind and deaf too if not ready.

It did the trick because the AK47 opened up and bullets were whizzing by everywhere. The shooter yelled "Allah Akbar!" and just started blindly spraying and praying he would hit something. Next were a couple of shots from an AR15 and it was over. John immediately called his wife to tell her "we're okay, meet us outside of Macy's." Richard did the same. Once the wives knew the husbands were fine, John and Richard explained everything to Captain Wilson from start to finish. The SWAT Commander told John to have the cut on his face looked at, but it had stopped bleeding and neither Richard nor John wanted to hang around and talk to the Press.

Militia Command Center, September 21st fourteen hundred hours

John Colton and Rene Cyr had been at the command center since zero eight hundred hours along with several carpenters who were expanding the communication office in accordance with Rene's instructions in preparation for the soon to be added security monitoring equipment. The command center had become a daily bustle of people either training in Krav Maga or procedure training downstairs.

The administration trailer was always manned with administrators and militia members adding improvements and qualifications to their service files. The concrete barriers were delivered around noon by a flatbed with a crane that lifted each barrier to its place along the parking lot. The entrance to the parking lot was now narrowed plus one barrier was placed in the path to the parking area, so if you entered the lot, you had to maneuver your vehicle around that barrier.

Dutch caught up to John and Rene as they were going over a map of the area. Dutch looked at John and the band-aide on his face and said, "missed you at the Wells Harbor Concert Saturday night. I guess you and Richard had better things to do." "Yea, we helped eight Muslims get their seventy-two virgins in Paradise a little early Saturday, wish you were there." "Well, my wife doesn't like that kind of party. I understand your wife participated." "Yep, that's why I try not to piss her off."

Not knowing what happened, Rene said, "You two mind? Get focused please!" They all studied the property survey map together. The rear border of the property was 3000' of forest to a dirt road. To the left was 400' of forest to Old Cape Road. To the right was 800' of forest to Reynolds Lane, and School Street (Main street) ran along the center's parking lot. Rene plotted the locations of cameras and sensors and decided to walk the perimeter with John & Dutch for a visual.

"So how do you want to set up the locations of sensors and cameras?" Dutch asked. Rene answered, "I'll set the sensors 150' out from the command center, then the cameras will be attached on tree trunks facing the center from 125' feet out." "Why will they face the center?" John asked. "Because the only place to attach them is in the trees and would easily be detected if they're facing the intruders. So, say the intruder triggers a certain sensor. It alerts the monitor and when they proceed within the next twenty-five feet, the camera captures them. Works every time." When they returned to the command center, they found the expected cargo truck waiting for them and was already being offloaded by the work detail. John walked up to the waiting driver and signed for the equipment.

One female from the work-detail asked, "What's this crate stenciled radios, we've already unpacked the throat mics?" John answered, "Should be fifty hand-held radios with chargers. One for each Unit leader's home and for any key players we decide needs one. My source felt that we needed a quicker response method than our current phone chain. I also strongly suggest all unit leaders have equipment kits in their vehicles So, if an emergency call goes out, the unit leaders will be armed and ready. They should create their own phone chains within their units."

By twenty hundred thirty hours, the new armory and the new communications center was built. The sensors and cameras were set, and all gear was stowed away. Dutch called all unit leaders to come in to receive their unit radios and equipment kits as soon as they could.

On the trail of Chuck Wednesday, September 23rd

On a beautiful pre-fall morning, John arrived back at the command center and stopped in the administration building because he saw Gunny Wilson's car. "Hello Ann, how's the militia coming along?"

"Good morning sir seems the growth is actually slowing down. Three hundred forty-five members and we're still trying to catch up with the paperwork." "Ann, you know you don't have to call me sir, hell, you outrank me militarily." "Sorry John, just a habit. You might want to hustle up to the communications office, seems they've got some important developments." "Thanks Ann, on my way." The off-going Militia Patrol Dispatch, a wounded veteran marine by the name Troy Sked and Dutch Swanson were staring over Rene's shoulder as he typed away. "What's going on guys?" Dutch turned to John and said, "Seems Chucky's back in town." Rene starting filling in the details while typing not even slowing down. *How can people communicate both in words and typing and still be proficient in both?* John thought.

"I caught Chuck coming through the Maine Toll this morning around zero three hundred. He's driving a late model Ford Escort, Massachusetts license." "You were here at zero three hundred?" John asked. "No, my facial recognition program runs continuously without me being here. When I came in this morning, the computer already got pinged on him and I'm just now trying to track him.

He's made a couple of phone calls which I'm trying to triangulate thanks to the help of our old friend Marley Kilroy's phone. Also, the car he's driving belongs to one Phyllis Mulligan who just happens to be a missing person from two weeks ago. I did a background on Phillis and she's clean and not the type of person who would hang out with the likes of our Chucky. But that's just my opinion."

"Is he heading back to Portland," Dutch asked. "No, he's gone rural." What do you mean by rural?" John asked. "According to my GPS he's somewhere around Dayton, Hollis or Union Falls. I don't know what's out there, but I can tell you there's only one Cell Tower and not many roads. I won't be able to locate a specific house. All I will be able to do is give you a general area." "Can you find out who he's calling?" John asked. "Sure. I can give you who, but I can't give you what they're talking about because he's using an encrypted phone.

The good news is, he just stopped roaming. By my estimation." Rene looked at one of his other computers and pulled up a google map. "He's probably at some property along New Country Road, Gould Road, or Gordon Road in Dayton." "I'm somewhat familiar with New Country Road, my wife use to teach in the neighboring town of Waterboro. Some beautiful country out there, mostly farmland," John added.

Dutch leaned back in his chair and said, "We need to consider that Phyllis is either a hostage or complicit." "The property owners could also be hostages," Troy Sked added. "He's right," John agreed. "We need to send a fully kitted team with Ruth Nelson and Scott Hamlin with their drones and try and locate that farm."

"Should you inform the local police?" Rene asked. "There are no police up there only maybe a couple of Constables." "What about the FBI, Chuck is wanted by them?" Dutch asked. "I could get into trouble. I'm on extended leave from the NSA and not supposed to be using the NSA's resources, so that leaves no reliable evidence for the FBI." Rene informed.

"What if we have to kill somebody, that's really going to cause some havoc," Dutch pointed out. "If we're kitted in Kevlar, helmets, and masks, who's going to know? If there are hostages, we rescue them and have them call 911. Or there's another solution." John answered. "Let's plan on finding that farm today. Dutch, I'll need Ruth and Scott, one good sniper and five fully kitted militia with suppressors qualified in clearing houses, and I need them here in one hour. I need to make a call." John left the communication center and walked outside where he placed a call to D.C.

CHAPTER NINE

In farm country, Dayton Maine, Ten hundred hours, September 23rd

John's team conveyed in two SUVs east on New Country Road until they came to the intersection of Gordon Road where the northbound road turned to dirt. They turned left and drove by a barn and no houses. The barn appeared to be for equipment and tractor storage for near-by farming fields. They continued for another five hundred feet to the end of the road. The road ended on a nice rise which lent itself to a good view of New Country Road as far west as Gould Road, about one mile away.

They covered the SUVs with camouflage netting which also made shade for the team. Ruth and Scott got the drones in the air quickly and separated in two different directions to cover more area. From this rise, they could see a couple of houses beyond two thousand yards which John viewed from the scope of his compact semi-automatic Sniper System (CSASS). "I can't see anything suspicious about those two houses, don't bother sending the drones there.

It took the drone team almost two hours before Scott found something. "I have a large farmhouse, very isolated, two men on the porch with weapons." Referring to a map, Scott said, "it's the last house on Bittersweet Run, about three miles from here." "Ruth, fly to that location," John asked. The Team gathered around and while Scott observed the from a couple of hundred feet in the air, Ruth circled her drone around the farm about fifty feet up in the air and one hundred feet away. From that distance, the drone was practically invisible and quiet. The two guards would have to be alert and looking for them. They were not alert. One was sleeping and the other was reading. "Is that a frigging comic book? Ruth asked. "Very unprofessional," said one of the militia.

"Ruth, I need eyes in all the windows, see if you can find anybody inside," John asked. Ruth did a fly-around, "I see a man and woman tied to a chair front right window upstairs. All the other windows have shades," She said. John reviewed the map, "This is it. let's pack up and get to this dirt road, Deer Road. From there deploy to both sides and the rear of the farm. We can't drive up the driveway without being seen."

The team drove to the end of Deer Road and was divided into three units. They would have a good cover of trees all the up to a small back yard and even smaller side yards. John didn't have to assign call signs because on the ride up, using their radios, the team established their own call signs. They all knew John was called Cobalt while in the Navy Seals and all thought they would like their own.

Unit one's sniper was Hawk and Gambler. They carried Heckler & Koch (HK) 416 rifles. Unit two both Ruger and Grizzly carried HK416s. Unit three Cobalt was the sniper and Hobbit carried an HK416. Unit one would have the shortest distance to the farm, Unit two would circle to the rear and enter from the back, and Unit three would circle to the farm's right. Hawk and Cobalt would sniper the two guards on the front porch and enter through the front door. Ruth, Rogue-1's drone would hover above the farm to watch the guards, and Scott, Scout's drone would watch the roads for any visitors.

John gave his final orders before they deployed, "Get to your positions and hold until we're all set. On my command, snipers take out the guards and once they're down we will quietly enter using your computerized key picks (a gift from Admiral Palton). We will use house clearing procedures. Protect the hostages. If we can capture a bad guy, great, but don't get shot! Let's Go."

The six militia soldiers started through the woods until unit one got into position, then four of the militia proceeded until unit two was in position. When John's unit made it to his position he spoke into his mic, "No names around the hostages, make sure you pick up your brass, we don't want to leave any sign behind. Hawk, how's your target?" "Scope is full, awaiting your call." "On execute then. Three, two, one, execute." Both snipers fired simultaneously, and two guards silently died in their chairs.

All units rushed to the front and back doors which were unlocked. Ruger and Grizzly entered. Ruger went left into a coat room and Grizzly went right into a kitchen coming face to face with a perp. The perp went for his gun and Grizzly said don't, but the perp didn't stop, and Grizzly shot him in twice the chest. A well-silenced weapon, the HK 416 is so quiet, bullets striking the target, the cycling bolt or brass hitting the floor make more noise than bullets leaving the muzzle. Nobody else heard the sound except Grizzly and the perp.

John and Hobbit proceeded upstairs. John carefully stepped on the outside of each stair which has a less chance of creaking. His rifle at his shoulder aiming. Walking upstairs was considered a death cone because you presented an easy target to a shooter from the cover of a bedroom. Hawk and Gambler were clearing downstairs to the basement.

Walking downstairs was worst because your legs are exposed to a shooter long before you have a chance to see them. All the shooter has to do is take out your legs and after you fall down the stairs, finish you off. The basement was dark, and Ruger had the advantage of using NVGs. Ruger found an unfinished basement and both he and Gambler clear the basement without a problem.

John found a creaking step about half-way up and a voice spoke from behind the front bedroom door. "Is that you Tony? You got lunch?" John gambled and said, "Yea." One of the bedroom doors opened and out came an unexpecting perp. John was aiming his CSASS at his face and said, "Don't move." He froze. John didn't expect any problems given what the perp was seeing. Two masked militants, with military cargo pants, Kevlar vests, and helmets with attaching NVGs aiming a very scary military-style rifle in his face.

John approached him while Hobbit began clearing the other upstairs rooms. After clearing the downstairs, Ruger and Grizzly also came upstairs to assist clearing bedrooms. John told him, "lay down on the floor and don't budge." While he looked into the room where the bad guy came from. Inside, he found the Henley's (homeowners) tied up to kitchen chairs. John heard in his headset, "Ah shit Cobalt, this is Grizzley, you need to get in here!" John asked, "Hawk get up here." John checked inside the closet before he pulled out his K-Bar knife and cut the hostages retrains.

Ruger entered behind John and began attending to the hostages. John moved to the back bedroom and found Hobbit cutting the restraints of a naked woman tied spread eagle on the bed. John looked around and found a blanket in the closet and covered her. "Rogue1 get in here ASAP" When Ruth Taylor arrived, she began administering to the woman and after questioning her, confirmed she was the missing Phillis Mulligan. Ruth showed her a picture of Chuck Mason and Phillis immediately said, "Don't kill that bastard without torturing him first!" Hobbit call for John in the last bedroom. When John entered the room, he found Hobbit looking at maps laid out on a large table.

Hobbit looked at John and said, "That's our command center!" John pulled out his phone and made a call. He looked at the map. It had arrows pointing to the command center from all compass points. John heard Scott call, "we've got two black SUVs approaching fast!" John responded, "They're friendlies, let them pass." Ruth was helping Phillis out of the bedroom when suddenly she broke free from the blanket and Ruth's arms, ran, and sent a kick to the perp's side while he was tied up on the floor. With that kick, she could have made the starting line-up as an NFL punter.

She was about to stomp on his head when Ruth caught up to her and pulled her off. John grabbed him by the back of his shirt collar and threw him into the chair. "Your two guards and Tony are dead and you're about to join them. As much as I want to kill you right now, against my better judgment, I'm going to offer you another option. Answer a couple of questions and I'll let you live." "I don't want to die, I'll answer questions."

"Where's Chuck now and is he coming back?" "I don't know where he is, he moves around a lot. He knows you're looking for him. He's not coming back. We're supposed to keep the hostages until he calls and then we were supposed to kill them." "When's the attack?" John asked. "Saturday morning at shift change," he answered.

Scout radioed John, "The SUVs are here, six people, genders unknown because they were wearing medical garbs complete with head coverings, masks, aprons, booties, and gloves." They didn't speak to the militia and began cleaning up the blood and brains on the porch.

Two cleaned the kitchen and all three perps disappeared into body bags and were placed in the back of one of the SUVs. Two of them came upstairs and asked, "Are you Cobalt?" "Yes, that's me." John replied. "If you're done with the package, we'll take him." "Go ahead, take him. Make sure he never sees the light of day." Then they escorted the perp to the back seat of the SUV.

The cleaners finished within thirty minutes. The SUVs were driving away when Scott asked John, "dare I ask who they were?" "They're CIA Cleaners, somebody in D.C. owed me a favor." "You and Rogue-1 get your drones down and packed, I need to speak to the Henley's." John met the Henley's and ensured them that Chuck would not be back. They could call the police if they wanted, but the police will see it as a false alarm with no evidence to corroborate their story. John was sorry for their inconvenience and promise that Chuck and his gang would be severely prosecuted. The Henley's were content with that.

Phillis Mulligan was driven to a Kennebunk parking lot of a local grocery store where they met Captain Tee Parker of the KPD. They passed Phillis over to Officer Parker. Officer Parker would arrange for Phillis's return to Massachusetts and her loving family.

The team arrived back at the command center at fourteen hundred fifty hours where Dutch was waiting with a smorgasbord of pizza and soda. John grabbed Dutch and led him into the office. He gave Rene the phones he took off the bad guys which he also used to take their pictures. "We missed Mason, but we nabbed this." John said and showed Dutch the maps.

Preparing for the attack, Thursday, September 23rd

Dutch stared in shock. "They going to hit us at shift change so they can kill as many as they can. But now that we have this map, the trap is set and we're the bait. How do you want to handle it?" John responded, "we have two options: A. we can stop the attack by hitting them at their staging positions before they even get out of their cars or B: we can hit them after they're committed, which means we wipe them out." "What about the police?" Dutch asked. Rene answered, "It's a surprise attack. We didn't know about it." "We can call them after they begin the attack. John replied.

"How does this apply with your spiritual convictions John?" Dutch asked. "The world has changed for the worse. Evil is rampant and the justice system allows it to happen. Whoever gets arrested in this raid, will get off, just like Marley Kilroy did. When I saw what they did to Phillis Mulligan...."

"What happened to your prisoner John? I hear the CIA's got him?" Dutch asked. "If I know the CIA, he's on his way to a black site prison," John answered. "I'm sorry John, what's a black cite prison?" Rene asked. "After 9/11, the FBI were nabbing terrorist cells and the Justice System was taking a big hit because the terrorists would not reform and return to the fight, that's when President Bush's Administration created the Black site prisons. Captured foreign terrorists were sent to Gitmo Cuba and Domestic terrorists went to Black Cites." John answered.

"Where are these prisons?" Rene asked. "A farm in Nebraska, maybe Iowa or the Dakotas. They are gigantic underground facilities with top of the line technology. And sitting above them, farms, with acres of farming land, fully functional, working for America, with all amenities of prison life in seclusion," John explained. "And none the wiser," Rene concluded.

Looking back to the map Dutch began, "If I was attacking this facility, I would have all my troops staged before a frontal attack begins from Main Street. I would put my main force on the dirt road and attack from two compass points and then some elements on Reynold Lane to the right. Once in place, a line of cars, maybe twenty men start the fight in front of the command center, or start from the back, doesn't matter when the element of surprise is in your favor." "that would be logical if they're being logical. We can't underestimate Chucky," John said.

Dutch continued, "On Saturday, we place three units twenty feet behind the dirt road where their main force will attack from, another two units twenty feet beyond Reynold's Lane, and three units across Main Street. We'll add snipers on the roof, three on each side, and six on front and back. Three units will cover from fortified positions around the command center. We'll be hitting them from the rear and the front. They have access to RPG's, so we need to make sure we take them out first. Mortars won't be effective because of the trees." Let's arrange a work detail and build camouflage fortifications inside the command center's tree-line tomorrow, I want a safety zone in case any of the attackers make it that far. Now, how about we get some pizza and cold pop."

Fortifying the Command Center, Friday, September 25th

The activity around the command center was energetic. Ann Wilson (Gunny) and Richard were in charge. Mike Bird (The administrator who bought the Admin Trailer) ordered a dump truck of heavy loam out of his pocket and refused Dutch's offer to reimburse him. Crews were digging foxholes but could only go so deep because of large tree roots, so Mike Bird had the idea to build up the foxhole rims with loam. Another crew using wheel barrels, transferred the dumped loam around the foxholes. Another crew was using chain saws and clearing much of the forest area of chutes (young trees), opening up a more visual kill zone, then using the brush of the chutes to camouflage the loam piles so the fortifications didn't look too manufactured.

Dutch joined Gunny as she was taking a break and said, "I am so impressed with so many volunteers and the growth of the militia. When this thing is over, and Chuck Mason is either captured or dead, I won't know what to do with them all." "Don't worry about that Captain, after October you're going to lose about one hundred of them."

"Why? Why are they leaving? Where are they going?" "They're going back home to New Hampshire, Connecticut, Massachusetts, New York, Texas and so many other States for the winter." Dutch started laughing, "You mean we have a bunch of Tourists in the Maine Militia?" "And they LOVE IT!" Gunny replied. "Two of the requirements for joining the militia are: They must be patriots and they must be land-owners. Lots of Outer-Stater's have homes in Maine. They come here for the cooler weather, the views, the dining, the wives love the shops. After a while, it can get pretty boring for some of them. You'd be surprised how many renters we turned down."

Gunny and Dutch were having a laugh when John and Richard walked over. John asked, "laughing at a sobering time as this? Please fill me in, I could use a good laugh, because tomorrow, many will never laugh again." There was a moment nobody spoke. Then Dutch put his hand on John's shoulder. "Yes, and many will never kill, sell weapons, or deal drugs again.

These are domestic terrorists who rape and destroy innocent lives. I'm not as devoted to my faith as you are John. I admire you to the point of envy, I believe in God and His Son Jesus Christ. Tomorrow, we will be stopping evil, plain and simple." Then John remembered his conversation with Pastor Micah Dalton and the Scripture. *"For our struggle is not against flesh and blood, but against the rulers, against the authorities, against the powers of darkness of this world and the spiritual forces of evil." Ephesians 6:12*

"You're right Dutch, and God has laid things out totally in our favor from the beginning of the militia to tomorrow's attack. This coming fight would hardly be called a battle with such overwhelming odds in our favor."

Dutch suggested, "we need to take a walk around grounds for inspection and later John, you should meet with the snipers on the roof of the command center, Gunny, get a hold of the surgeon and see if he can set up a triage in the command center to treat any wounds occurring during the fight. Richard, let's call a meeting around sixteen hundred with the unit leaders and assign their attack positions and defending positions." Richard questioned, "NOW, if you will be so kind as to tell us what you were laughing about?"

The inspection was amazing. With the cleared cut forest, they could almost see out to the dirt road. Walking in from the dirt road, it was difficult to make out the foxhole bunkers, even knowing what the inspection team was searching for. Later, John met with seventeen qualified snipers and notice Paul Grant (the wounded veteran) standing in the group. He had a prosthetic leg which was unnoticeable until he walked. "so, you're a qualified sniper?" John asked. "I was a very good Marine sniper until the Humvee I was riding ran over an IED in Al Anbar, Iraq. It was easy qualifying."

An improvised explosive device (IED) is a bomb constructed of conventional military explosives, such as an artillery shell, attached to a detonating mechanism. The bombs are hidden behind signs and guardrails, under roadside debris, or inside animal carcasses, On 3

January 2020, President David Travis ordered a drone strike near Baghdad International Airport that targeted and killed Iranian major general Qasem Soleimani of Iran's Islamic Revolutionary Guard Corps (IRGC).

The General was the mastermind in the development of the undetectable IED and was responsible for many of the more than 2,000 deaths and numerous casualties suffered by U.S. and coalition forces since the invasion of Iraq. Despite the great victory and revenge of our troops, President Travis was vilified by the media and Democrats for Soleimani's death. John assigned each sniper their position.

Chuck Mason's hide, Friday night, September 25th

Over the fire mantle of the newly hi-jacked home in Arundel, Maine sat the goddess Santa Muerte (Holy Death in Spanish). A skull over a pile of bones dressed in a golden shroud and sitting before her bowl of sacrificed blood and a circle with a pentagram inside. Santa Muerte is a goddess of death in some Mexican religions. She acts similarly to the Grim Reaper of mythology, collecting the souls of the dead, and deciding when people die. Unlike the Grim Reaper, however, she is worshipped and loved by Mexican Cartels.

Chuck Mason sat before his fifty warriors. A glass bourbon in hand toasting with his men. "You have been blessed by the power of Santa Muerte, the same god worshiped by my very powerful friends of the Mexican Drug Cartel, the Los'Cartos family, and our leader, Mike Durham. They, my friends, are very powerful and have provided all the weapons we'll need to eliminate the militia. We will soon experience that power as we TAKE what we want and rape whenever we want. The house shook from the cheers of the men.

"Tomorrow I want Gus to take twenty-five men to the dirt road and invade their pitiful shack center (making a quoted sign with fingers). when you get my phone call you will begin your attack. I will assault them with twenty-five men from the parking lot. When their backs are turned to confront your forces, my fighters will strike from behind and wipe them out."

Someone asked, "What about attacking from Reynolds Lane?" "Two forces front and back should do fine," Chuck answered. Chuck raised his glass again and they all cheered. "Tomorrow, we will collect their blood and offer it to our faithful god, Santa Muerte! TAKE NO PRISONERS!! I want you sober and straight, wait until the victory celebration," he said with a smile. The group laughed. "When they're all dead, don't hang around for the cops. We'll torch the place and meet back here when we're done."

Command Center under attack, Saturday, September 26th

It was a warm Indian summer day, the sun in the eastern sky was just reaching the tops of the tree line. An ocean breeze brought a slight scent of seaweed. The Morning patrol was arriving early by Dutch's orders in preparation for the expecting attack. The scent of brewing coffee lingered inside the Command Center. Dozens of cars were parked in the parking lot, but the Command Center was practically empty. One hundred twenty-four militia troops car-pooled in and were in position outside since zero six-thirty. One hundred militia were armed with Heckler & Koch (HK) 416 rifles and eighteen were on the roof with compact semi-automatic Sniper System (CSASS) rifles.

Twenty feet inside the opposite tree line running along the dirt road behind the Command Center, Mike Ackroff moved up to the road and on a knee checked down the road where the Antifa attackers were expected to arrive from. The militia had been waiting and eager to engage. This was the third time Mike checked the road since setting up his team's position. In a crouch, while backing up, he heard Bob Simpson's transmission, jokingly, "are they here yet?" Bob Simpson (Drill Sargent) was another team leader further down the same tree line as Mike. "These guys can't even make it to their funeral on time."

Then Alan Carey, another team leader stationed behind the Reynolds Lane tree line transmitted, "We're clear here too. All quiet." Two minutes later, a two pick-up truck and the five-car convoy arrived and parked on the dirt road right in front of Mike Ackroff's team. They all got out and the man in charge lined up his team and waited. Richard Bloomer radioed, "I see a line of vehicles, convoy style, coming up Maine street." Richard and his teams were across the street in front of the Command Center. Mike Ackroff heard the man in charge receive a call. When he disconnected the call he said, "Okay boys, let's kill us some militia." His team got up and started forward into the forest.

Mike waited for John's signal. John didn't want any shooting until Chuck Mason and his team arrived out front, otherwise, he might retreat before getting out of his car. Alan Carey's and Dick Vinaldo's teams four and five on Reynolds Lane were expecting their attackers any minute, but they never arrived. Mike whispered into his mic, "teams one, two, and three move up. Listen guys, don't shoot anybody in the back, you'll hate yourself for it. But try to get them turned around to surrender or engage you, then they're all yours. Wait for my signal before you engage." When Mike got into position, he could see the attackers slowly moving forward through the trees. He radioed, "Larry, can you see them yet?" "All I'm getting are glimpses." Larry responded.

The convoy of two pick-up trucks, three vans, and one car arrived from Main Street and began maneuvering into the Command Center parking lot. They were bottle-necked because of the concrete barrier in front of the entrance. Three vans in front of the convoy were first to enter and park. The attackers piled out with RPGs and AK 47s while the rest of the convoy was still maneuvering around the concrete barrier. Four fighters with their RPGs waited for Chuck's signal to fire.

The attackers from the dirt road began firing at the Command Center. They weren't shooting at people because the windows of the center began to disintegrate. They were creating a diversion to bait the militia inside into the fight while the front fighters made their advance. Mike was puzzled at first, but it became clear. Inside the command center, Dutch hit 911 on speed dial to inform police they were under attack. Larry Wetzel, team six, could now identify the attackers approaching from the dirt road and ordered, "commence firing."

The Antifa team leader Gus watched as tracers zipped past, fired from the bushes by the command center, and yelled, "take cover!" Mike saw two attackers drop and one lifting an RPG up to his shoulder. If he gets that shot off, Larry's men will be dead. Mike quickly settled his receptacle onto the man's left center back and fired. "Commence firing!" yelled Mike. Gus watched in astonishment as his men started dropping even though they were concealed behind trees. *"How can they be picking off his men like this?"* he thought. His eyes widened, "They're BEHIND US!!" He screamed.

One of the men responded and swung his RPG around and fired blindly. The rocket flew right over one of the militia's head and hit one of the attacker's car and exploded. Three militia were tossed forward from the impact. Bob Simpson shot the RPG launcher in the chest.

Another attacker got a rocket off and it hit the side of the command center. Two militia was hit by wood shrapnel. As the attacker was reloading, two militias both shot him at the same time. One of the attackers found good cover with a large boulder in front and a tree behind. His weapon was an AK 47 but he saw a dead attacker with an armed RPG laying next to him. He reached the weapon and aimed it in the direction of Bob Simpson.

A bullet had found his right shoulder. The sudden jolt to his body caused the reflex of his finger and the RPG launched. But his aim shifted down and the rocket launched into a group of his men. He couldn't believe what he'd just done. The thought never occurred to him that he was surrounded when he picked up his AK 47. He knew the closest targets were behind him and swung the weapon from his hip and pulled the trigger. He fired in an arc-like style seen in a gangster movie, hoping his bullets would find a body. The last thing in his mind was a militia bullet. The forest had become quiet. The attack was over in under a minute. All the attackers were down.

Mike ran back to his downed men from the car explosion and from the bushes, Larry Wetzel ran to his men. "Two men down," He yelled. When Mike got to his men, they were just getting up and shaking their heads from ringing ears. He looked them over and found no blood.

Chuck Mason could hear the shooting and knew his plan was succeeding. He yelled, "RPG's FIRE!" Four men popped up with RGPs on their shoulders and four men dropped before firing their rockets. Paul Grant John Colton, Luke Logan, and his son Joshua Logan had every RPG shooter in their scopes before they had a chance to aim.

When Chuck realized where the shots came from, he yelled, "SNIPERS ON THE ROOF!" He aimed his AK 47 and began firing. The attackers were shooting wildly, trying to kill anybody they could see. One of the attackers next to Chuck lifted his RPG and his head blew off. Chuck thought, *"the blood splatter went in the wrong way, forward, not back."* He turned around and yelled, "THEY'RE BEHIND

US!" The attackers turned to fire on Richard's team, but Richard and his men had taken positions behind the concrete dividers. Chuck watched as his men were all dropping from the tracers behind, front, and now from the side.

Dick Vinaldo's team had a flanking position on the attackers from the trees of Reynolds Lane. One of his men, Dean Tron crept up to within eight feet of an attacker and said, "drop your weapon." The attacker turned to see Dean get hit in the chest. Smiling, the attacker was about to finish him off. Paul Grant saw Dean drop and set his scope on the attacker and shot him through the temple. From John Colton's scope, he could see the man who shot Dean and dropped him like a sack of dirt. Dick Vinaldo ran to Dean to see him squirming and holding his Kevlar vest. "Shit! It hurts!" Dean yelled. "You'll be fine," Dick gasped.

John swung his scope around the parking lot and could see all the attackers were down and not returning fire. He watched Chuck drop his weapon and raise his hands. John radioed, "All elements cease-fire." Chuck realized the fight was over, police sirens could be heard in the distance. He was the last man standing.

From inside the center, Dutch and Rene watched the battle unfold from the camera monitors. They could hear the windows shattering and felt the impact of the rocket hitting the center. Dutch ran downstairs to see three of his men being carried in the triage. The surgeon and his assistants were ready to begin treatment. He checked the injured militia and saw the wounds were all superficial. Splinters of wood embedded in the arms and legs.

Dutch wondered how bad the injuries would have been if they hadn't had Kevlar vests on. He turned and stared at the gaping hole in the center just forward of the armory. One of the militia stuck his head inside the door and asked. "We've got two attackers alive and badly hurt, what do you want to do with them?" "They can get in line," was all Dutch said. He could hear John running down the stairs from the roof before he saw him. John arrived downstairs and immediately checked the wounded too. Dutch thought to himself, "*A true leader is always concerned for the safety of his men.*"

Richard Bloomer stood over Chuck whose hands had already been zip-tied. "You ever hear of Black Cite Prisons?" The militia had no control over what was going to happen to Chuck. Rene had already called the FBI who'd been looking for Chuck for months. Richard placed the hot gun barrel of his HK 416 against Chuck's forehead and said, "you're not good enough to be prisoned by taxpayer's dollars. Answer me one question or you die right here, do you have any more hostages stashed around?" "466 Limerick Road," was all he said.

The police arrived. Three cruisers and two ambulances. Richard waited until Chief Cameron got out and asked, can you spare an officer and a cruiser. I have an address of where a possible hostage is being kept. The Chief would have sent a squad if it wasn't for the loss of personnel thanks to the governor's defund policies. "Captain Parker, take a cruiser and go get some hostages."

Limerick Road Hostages, Saturday, September 26th

Richard spoke into his mic, "John we've got a lead on some more hostages. I'm going to need a sniper and UAV pilot. John replied, "Ruth, grab a drone and meet me out front." When John met Richard, Captain Tee Parker was there with him. "Captain Parker, good to see you, sorry for the mess." She looked around and said, "You really know how to throw a party." Ruth ran up with a suitcase in hand and out of breath said," drones all charged, what's up?" John looked at Richard, "Yes Richard, what's up?"

"Chucky just informed me he left hostages on 466 Limerick Road. Officer Parker is joining us for the rescue." John looked around and saw Dick Vinaldo standing idle and called out to him, "Dick! Where are you parked?" He pointed at his SUV and John waved him over. "Richard, why don't you ride with Captain Parker, Ruth and I will ride with Dick." Harry Hodge ran over and asked if he could tag along.

When they arrived at the address, John got a call on his cell phone, "Go ahead," he answered. It was Rene. "John, Scott Paris just gave me Chucks phone and when I cracked his password, I found speed dial "5" titled bomb. I heard where you were going and thought you'd like to know." "Rene, find someone and ask that asshole what speed dial 5 is and get right back to me."

John turned to Richard and officer Parked and explained what the call was about and then called Ruth over. "Check the windows to see if we can identify anyone inside. You'll need to call your EOD Tee." "Our EOD is out of Portland; it's going to be a while." Someone tapped

John on the shoulder, it was Harry Hodge. "I did two tours in the Navy as EOD. I was assigned to the Navy Seals and did some disarming in Fallujah and Mosul."

"Okay, let's see what Ruth finds."

Before he got the words out, Ruth's drone was airborne. "Downstairs living room is a mess, look what they've got on the fireplace mantel! Gross! Okay, Coming around to the kitchen, what a frigging mess! Looks like....The dining room is clear, upstairs bedroom one empty, bedroom two....I can see people in chairs, one, two, three, four, all tied down. Bedroom three is clear. Can't help you with the basement."

John looked at Captain Parker, "what do you think?" "Tee looked at Harry and asked, "how extensive is your training?" In my experience, the calling cell phone needs a receiving cell phone to act as an electrical impulse to a detonation cord in contact with the explosive compound." Tee looked at John and said, doesn't hurt to look. Send your man in." "Okay Harry, don't get blown up."

Harry walked up to the window. "What's wrong with the door? Dick asked. "It could be wired from inside. No wires here," and with his 416 smashed the window, cleared the glass from the bottom sill, and jumped in. After a few minutes, the front door opened and Harry stood there with a smile and said, "I'm not going to get billed for the window, am I? John stationed Dick and Ruth outside as he, Richard, and Officer Tee Parker went in following Harry. They slowly proceeded as Harry scrutinized their pathway upstairs. When they arrived at the bedroom door, Harry's fist popped up, meaning everybody halt.

He knelt and examined a light fishing line strung across the bedroom doorway. From his knees, he looked left and turned and looked right. "Anybody have scissors?" John stuck his hand into his pocket and pulled out a boy-scout knife with all the accessories in one knife, unfolded the scissors, and handed it to Harry. Harry snipped the line.

When they walked in Harry pointed to a grenade taped to the wall with a fishing line tied to the pin. "Pretty primitive." The hostage's appeared to be a father, mother, and two adolescence. Their mouths were taped shut murmuring something. John told them, "you're alright now, we're going to get you out of here."

Harry did a quick walk-a-round the hostages and then laid down on his side to look under the hostage's chairs. "Here it is folks. Looks like a small block of C-4 with a detonation cord hooked to a cell phone." C-4 or Composition 4 is used by the United States Armed Forces and contains 91% RDX ("Research Department Explosive") combined with other compounds. When those specific compounds are mixed to form its end product, it results in a clay substance that can be thrown against a wall and not explode, but when you add an electrical impulse is when C-4 becomes a highly combustible explosive.

"How are you going to disarm it?" Richard asked. Harry reached under the chair and pulled the cord out of the C-4 and showed it to the group. "You can untie them now." Officer Parker was already on the phone with Chief Cameron letting him know the hostages were free and needed an ambulance. Also, they disarmed two bombs, and the house needed to be cordoned off for a crime scene investigation and should be cleared by EOD. John's cell phone vibrated in his pocket. He pulled out the phone and answered. "John, it's Rene, we've got Chuck's confession. Speed dial "5" will blow a bomb wired to the hostages." "Thanks Rene."

CHAPTER TEN

"RPG!" John screamed when he saw the tell-tale sign of a white smoke trail coming from the eighteen-wheeler, just before the black SUV in front of them was blown sky-high in an orange ball of flame. "Steve! Cap! back up!" Steve locked up the brakes and skidded to a halt, then he slammed the shift into reverse, and their Humvee started backward in a squeal of tires. Cap and Angie were leading the way backward. Almost immediately, there was a loud drumming noise on the outside of their armored vehicle as though they were being smashed by a severe hailstorm. But in this case, the hailstorm were bullets. They ricocheted off the windshield leaving behind scars from their impact. "We've got jammed traffic behind us! They got us locked in!" Cap yelled.

John noticed no guardrails on this section of Highway 91 and commanded, "Steve, exit right down the median field to that street! Come on Steve, move!" John snapped. They made it to the street and were making their way to a crop of apartment buildings and shops.

"Another RPG!" Richard shouted from the backseat. "On the right!" Steve Paris spun the wheel, the Humvee slid sideways on two wheels and landing back on all four wheels as the RPG rocket whizzed by barely missing them just above the hood, and blew up when it hit a building on the side of the road.

Back in Maine, Dutch yelled in John's ears, "John, report! What's your SITREP?!" "We're taking fire! I say again! We're taking fire!" he paused and said "Two FBI agents are dead. RPGs hit their SUV!" "There are tangos in the windows and the streets on both sides of the road! They have us in a crossfire! IT'S A TRAP!!" Shouted Ruth. "We need to find some way out of here!" "Damn!" John snapped, "Defend the package! Protect Chuck Mason!"

Two days earlier, Sunday afternoon, September 27th

It was two days of bureaucratic crap. John missed Church with his wife because forty-two tangos were dead, five wounded (not including two superficial wounded militia) and one very important captured Antifa leader, Chuck Mason. The good thing was Chief Cameron was on the militia's side. Although his investigators took hours on Saturday interviewing many of the militia players, inspecting all the bullet-ridden cars, the center's windows, and the huge hole on the back of the center's wall, the State Police didn't confiscate any of the militia's weapons.

Then, the militia had to do it all over again when the FBI arrived. Chuck Mason got locked up in a temporary cell in the Kennebunk's Police Station until the FBI could arrange a transfer to their headquarters at 26 Federal Plaza, New York, New York. John was feeling uneasy about how the justice system was going to handle the prosecution proceeding. John did not want Chuck to see the light of day again.

John found himself getting along with two of the FBI's agents, Tim Caplinger (Cap), who was an ex-recon marine. He was a large muscular man, early thirties with short hair a red mustache, and looked out of place in a suit. Angie Corwin was an ex-army, thirty-something, tall, athletic, long black hair, plain face, and very capable-looking. Both were patriots. Two other FBI agents were rather stiff. James Dupaul was a tall thin executive type who looked good in a suit and his partner Ben Carter was robust and out of shape, He appeared to be the leader and did most of the communication with the police and FBI headquarters. Neither of them spoke about any military service. John assumed both were life-long civilians.

By Sunday afternoon, the plans to get Chuck down to New York were finishing up. The FBI had the transfer documents and their man. John got a phone call from Admiral James Palton and had a long conversation about the whole affair. Admiral Palton was pleased John's mission was over with the capture of Chuck Mason, but he wasn't thrilled with who was transferring him.

Mason had critical information on the Antifa structure, Mike Durham's, weapons and drug smuggling operations. "What do you think about escorting Mason with the FBI?" the admiral asked. "Are the FBI expecting trouble?" John asked. "I don't trust the FBI," he said, "Mike Durham is wired into a lot of money and some of the FBI could be in Durham's pockets. Look how they treated the Travis Administration." "That's not very encouraging Admiral. Look, If I help escort Mason, I want some control of the escort team and the route." John demanded. "Just say yes and I will make a phone call," the Admiral replied.

Convoy to FBI Headquarters, Tuesday, September 29th

Red-faced, and with veins bulging in his neck, Agent Ben Carter stormed into the Militia Command Center. "Who do you think you are!" "Easy Agent Carter, we're not stealing your show, just a couple of us are coming for a ride," Dutch replied. "Why is the DOD hell-bent on you coming in the first place?" John answered, "I've been chasing Chuck Mason for five months now, and I what to ensure he arrives safely. I am now employed by the DOD as Operations Manager and although I currently out-rank you, I'm not going to flaunt it, and I won't take any credit for your successes. But, I do want to know your route and I want to know what you have for a plan and operational support."

Agent Carter had no operational support and no real plan. He was taking Interstate 95 to 495 to 84 through Hartford Connecticut then switching to Route 684, into Manhattan and FBI Headquarters. All he had were two black SUVs with bulletproof windows and four nice windbreakers with big bold yellow letters "FBI."

So, John recruited Officer Steve Paris and his Humvee. John would ride shotgun. Richard Bloomer in the back, Ruth Taylor, and her suitcase with a charged drone. Chuck Mason was strapped into the third-row seat. The militia escort were all armed with HK416 assault rifles, fully kitted in armor including NVGs.

Their biggest assets were the long-range radios (which John demanded all the FBI Agents wear) and Rene Cyr who was given access to satellites for overwatch. Agent Carter took one look and smiled. "Okay, this is a little over-kill, but I hope you're all comfortable for the ride." Because of Agent Carter's blundering attitude, John insisted that Feds at least take their assault weapons out of the trunk and put them in their back seats.

"Agents Carter and Dupaul you will take the lead in your SUV, the package vehicle will be next with my team and Agent Cap and Corwin's SUV will take the rear. This was a standard method of transferring prisoners. When John called "mount up" Mike Ackroff ran up to John. He was all kitted up. "Sorry Mike, no room." "I've got my team. We'll follow you and hang back a mile or so." "Who's we?"

Mike pointed to the command center as, Dick Vinaldo, Bob Simpson, and Dean Tron, all kitted up and were walking over. Practically the whole Carl Nelson transfer team, except for Dean Tron. "This is not necessary guys, we've got this," John reported. Mike smiled and said, "hey, we're just taking a short ride to New York. Don't concern yourself." John contemplated the idea and decided he really couldn't do anything about their decision to follow. "Okay, let's mount-up."

They stopped for gas outside of Hartford. Richard scared the crap out of some woman at the gas station when he stepped out of the vehicle looking like Robo-cop, wearing all the combat gear. He put his helmet on just to complete the ensemble. Everybody got their chuckles. Agent Carter flashed his FBI badge and apologized for the scare, then he gave John a long disgusting stare.

Once outside of Hartford, traffic became light and the convoy was making good time until they observed up ahead, an eighteen-wheeler had pulled over into the breakdown lane and then turned out across the highway completely blocking the road off. An RPG was launched from the cab which took out Agent Carter's SUV and automatic gunfire began pelting the Convoy from a row of buildings on both sides of the highway.

Edmund Road, Somewhere in Connecticut

It was Rene's voice, "John, I have eyes on you! Your coming to a dead end and a large field. It looks crossable to another street. Should get you out of the mess!" "Works for me! Anything is better than this!" They rounded a curve and had the dead end in sight. "SHIT! The dead end is blocked by three burning cars!" "Steve! Pull over onto the sidewalk and stop in front of that store. Cap, park your SUV behind us and we will corral a barrier in front of that alley ahead."

They pulled Chuck from his seat and pushed him deep in the alley and the team began firing back. The alley was bordered by two single story stores so at least they were not taking fire from above. "Ruth, check out the back of this alley, is that fence passably? Rich, cover right, Steve cover left, Angie guard Chuck, Cap shoot anybody in front!"

Richard brought his weapon up to fire at a figure leaning out of a second-floor window. The bullets stitched the antifa soldier across the chest, and he fell forward from the opening and landed with a thump. "Bet that hurt," he said. John fired his own weapon for a kill at another shooter higher up. Following him was Steve. He had his HK416 firing at an alley across the street. "Fence is passable, but it leads to a field with no cover!" Ruth Yelled. Ruth joined the fight.

Cap was using an HK416 with a scope. looking for a target, and saw a figure with an RPG. He shot the man just as the rockets left. "RPG!" Everybody ducked into their alley. The FBI's SUV Exploded in a ball of flames. The team was pelted with debris, but nobody was seriously injured. Cap got up and began checking the alley across the street and saw what looked like a small parking garage a couple of streets away.

John pulled out his phone to call his boss Admiral Palton. "Morning Admiral." "John, I can see you're in a fix again." "How'd you know?" John asked. "We have a video feed on your situation thanks to Rene." "Admiral, can you provide some overhead support and a ride?" John asked. "I've already got two Black Hawks inbound, but they're over an hour out. Can you find somewhere clear for an extract and fort up?" "I'll see what I can do. Looks like the FBI has a mole." John answered.

"The Black hawk call signs are Swordsmen one and two," the Admiral reported. Cap reported to John, "I see a parking garage a couple of streets away through that alley." "You hear that Admiral?" "Just let the Black Hawks know when you're there. And we'll find the mole." Admiral Palton ended the call.

"Steve! Richard! On me!" John commanded. When they both arrived, John pointed, "you two, fast-track across to that alley. We're going for the parking garage beyond where we can get extracted. I've got two birds inbound. Once you're across, cover us, and we'll follow." Steve and Richard strapped their rifles and ran across the street.

Bullets kicked up the asphalt around their feet. Fist-size chunks of road lifted up and both Richard and Steve did a dive for the alley. John knew the sound of an M2. He seen them used on top of some Humvees in Iraq. The M2 machine gun or Browning .50 caliber is a heavy machine gun that uses a much larger and much more powerful .50 BMG cartridges, which can blow right through bullet proofing armor.

Cap yelled, "Damn it! Where'd that come from!" "Its coming from our side of the road, Rich and Steve were damn lucky to have gotten across." John said. Suddenly Ruth ran to the Humvee and jumped in. "Ruth! Get out of there!" John screamed. She retrieved one of the suitcases and hauled it back and opened it. Inside were eight grenades. "You've been hanging around Harry Hodges too long!" John said.

John grabbed a grenade and inching forward while picking the window the M2 was shooting from, found the window, pulled the pin and threw. He jumped back in the alley and yelled, "fire in the hole!" The explosion rattled the alley they were in and sent wood, a body and the M2 flying across the street. "Everybody, grab the rest of those grenades!"

John yelled. "Ruth, you want to get your drone out of Steve's Humvee, or do I blow it with a grenade? Either way, the drone should stay out of their hands." John asked. "I'll take the drone," Ruth responded. "Okay Richard, Steve, we'll need covering fire, we're on our way." Richard and Steve began shooting at the tangos on John's side of the street. John sent Ruth and Cap first. When they were across, John, Angie and Chuck ran across.

Despite all the fire power against the tangos, they still managed to shoot more asphalt around the sprinting militia. When they made across the street, Chuck was cursing and cussing, "those bastards aren't here to rescue me, there here to kill me!"

"Real nice friends Chucky," Angie said. Two by two they crossed the next street.

It was quiet. The rebels stopped shooting. They were probably out of position and had to catch up. They crossed the next street and entered the parking garage where they walked up to the top of three levels. When at the top level, John started assigning positions. They had all points of the compass covered.

"Cap had his scope pointed down a street and reported, "I've got an SUV inbound and closing fast." John walked over and said, "That's Mike's SUV, they would have been better off staying home." John watched as they drove into the garage and traveled to the top level. "Calvary's a little late," Richard said to Mike. "We took out that eighteen wheeler's RPG and the SAW (M249 Squad Automatic Weapon) that shot your Humvee up. Where do you want us boss?"

"We've got two Black Hawks inbound for extract. Their still forty minutes out. I just need to call in our exfil position." You want to ride with us in the birds and leave your vehicle behind?" "I'd like to take all them antifa pukes out and drive back in Steve's Humvee," Mike joked. "Good luck," Steve said. "It died before I had a chance to kill the engine," and Steve tossed Mike the key. Mike tossed back the key and said, "I guess we'll have to ride with you, our SUV is badly shot up too."

The parking garage had a nice concrete wall around the top. Ruth was watching from the North wall and yelled back to John. "I hate to interrupt guys, but I have movement around the apartments next door." "Thanks Ruth, Mike and Dean, join Ruth, Dick join Cap over there, and Bob, your over there with Angie and Chuck."

While standing next to Mike's SUV, John radioed, "Swordsmen one, Swordsmen one, do you copy?" "Go ahead Cobalt, read you five by five." John then gave them their GPS coordinates and informed them that they would be picking up eleven passengers from the top level of a parking garage. "It'll be a little crowded. We're about thirty mics out, approaching from the west, do you read?" "Roger Swordsmen, Cobalt out."

Suddenly John heard a thump sound and look over and saw Cap slumped over. "Shit! Sniper! Dick, grab Cap, get him over to the North wall NOW!" Just as Dick got up, the concrete wall where he was crouching by, chipped from a bullet strike. The apartment next door was three stories higher than the parking garage. Antifa had reposition themselves on higher ground than the militia. John ran over to Cap while Ruth was checking for a bullet wound. Looks like he took one to his helmet. He's knocked out cold. "Will he be alright?" Dick asked. "He could have a concussion. He needs to get to a hospital."

"Where's Cap's gun?" John asked. "Actually, it's my gun," Angie said. "Why's Cap got your gun?" John asked. "Because you gave me Chucky to guard and Cap thought we needed a sniper in this fight." "You're a sniper? You any good?" John asked. "Only up to fifteen hundred yards." Angie answered. "Great, take the gun then and take position behind Mike's SUV. Find that sniper. They need to be dead before the Black Hawks try to pick us up. You've got about fifteen minutes."

Antifa started shooting. John yelled, "take it to them! Pick your targets!" Angie grabbed the gun and ducked behind the SUV. She checked the magazine, saw it was full and then slid the bolt back enough to see the brass bullet. She eased the rifle over the hood near the windshield and began her search.

She saw tangos shooting from the windows and she saw them getting shot. *"These militia are good,"* she thought. *"Okay, where are you my sniping tango. If I was sniping from that building, where would I be? On the roof!"* She saw the flash of the sniper's rifle before she saw him. He was shooting, but not at her. She settled her crosshairs on his scope. She held her breath and let it out slowly. Her finger tightened around the trigger until the rifle's recoil surprised her. The bullet went right through his scope and into the sniper's eye.

She continued scanning for her next target. Scoping through a window, she spotted another sniper laying on a table inside. He saw her rifle flash and was scoping her. *"Is he aiming at my scope?"* She thought. She didn't duck, she didn't flinch, and she didn't take her time. She fired and saw him fall but wasn't sure she killed him. She continued to watch the room and saw him stand. He was wounded and trying to get back on the table. She finished him off.

She radioed John, "Cobalt, two snipers are down. I can find anymore." "Good job Angie. Dean look down from his position and saw six antifa crossing the street below and moving towards the garage. He shot two of them and radioed John. "Cobalt, I've got six coming at us from the street below. I got two of 'em." Richard and

Mike, take two grenades, one of you take the stairs and one take the road. don't let them up here.

Ruth yelled, "RPG!" When she saw the white tail tracking their position. It flew over the wall and exploded behind them. Angie tracked her scope to the source inside an apartment room and saw a figure reloading. She sent a bullet through his head.

Rene radioed John, "Cobalt! You've got a pick-up truck coming up your street from the east!" Down on the street the pick-up arrived and parked at the corner of an apartment, In the bed of the truck was a mounted M2 fifty caliper. The gunner began firing. He was chewing up the Concrete wall the militia were covering behind. John crawled over to Ruth and shouted, "How fast can you get your drone up?" "One minute!" She yelled back. "Can you arm it with a grenade?" "Consider that bastard dead in two minutes!"

Ruth had the drone up in thirty seconds with a grenade in the pod's clutches. She guided the drone over the unsuspecting shooter and released the grenade. The explosion took out the threat and included a couple of antifa standing near the vehicle.

"All this for that low life Chuck?" Ruth asked. Chuck started laughing, "Not just me, all you fu**ers have a $5000 bounty on each of your heads." Suddenly, the team felt an explosion from underneath their feet and two minutes later Richard appeared and ran over. "Got two coming up the stairs!" Then they heard shots fired from inside the garage. John radioed, Mike, Mike what's your SITREP?" "Two tangos down, I'm on my way back."

Bullets began whizzing by and the team were once again taking fire from tangos on the roof. A voice in John's ear started, "Cobalt, Cobalt, this is Swordsmen one you copy?" "Copy, I read you five by five Swordsmen." "Cobalt, we are two mics out, how's your LZ?" (Landing Zone) "LZ is hot! I've got shooters on the roof at the apartment east from the garage, can you provide covering support?" "My pleasure Cobalt."

In the distance, they could hear the whoop, whoop, whoop of the two UH-60 Black Hawk Helicopters. Within two minutes they were circling the apartment laying down heavy fire from two M240 machine gunners. Antifa figures were down and wiggling violently as multiple rounds hit them. An RPG was launched from a window which couldn't have been aimed because it flew past fifty yards below one of the Black Hawks. Before the first Black Hawk landed, John ordered, Bob Simpson and Dean to carry Cap into the gunner's bay. Angie and Ruth, carrying her suitcase followed. The next Black Hawk took the rest of the militia.

CHAPTER ELEVEN

American Cut Steakhouse, Manhattan NY, Tuesday, September 29th

The FBI arranged that the Roxy Hotel open to allow the militia team a place to stay. The hotel was a few blocks from the FBI Headquarters. The FBI also arranged that the team was treated to a steak dinner at a five-star steakhouse which also had to be opened for their dinner.

"So, what's going to happen next, are we getting a ride home or will we be walking," Richard asked. "I've been told we will fly out in a G700 Gulfstream to Sanford and Dutch will meet us there," John replied. "I guess Mike and I are out two vehicles?" Steve asked. "Maybe they'll replace your rides, but I don't know with what," John answered.

"I heard you say you are now employed by the DOD as Operations Manager. When are you leaving us?" Ruth asked. "I have no idea. My new boss hasn't spoken to me since he arranged our ride in the Black Hawks." "Do you think your new boss will continue to use you to work with our militia?" Bob Simpson asked. "It will be my request," John answered. "We have a lot of talent in our militia. I won't like leaving that talent and so many friends behind."

"Do you suppose Antifa still has a bounty on us?" Ruth asked. "The FBI Supervisor told me the Antifa didn't drag off their dead and wounded. The body count was twenty-one dead and fifteen wounded. Hopefully, that will deter any headhunters, but I'm not betting on it." "You know what I think?" Dean said, "We need to declare war on Portland Oregon, Seattle Washington, Chicago, and rid those cities of Antifa and violence." John smiled, "I'm all for stopping the violence. Oregon and Seattle, I'm okay with, but Chicago would look too much like white people attacking Afro-Americans. Chicago needs its own militia. That's the only way it would work."

"I've got a question," Dick Vinaldo asked. "Where were all the civilians of that ghost-town we fought in yesterday?" "When the FBI did the clean-up of the town, they didn't find a single civilian." "I asked the Feds the same question. There were a couple of factories nearby that the governor closed due to the pandemic. The governor calls the factories 'super-spreaders'. All the civilians abandoned the town, packed up, and just left. The governor's lock-down caused the factories to claim bankruptcy." Businesses are filing lawsuits against those governors" *"Democrat Governors, in a disturbing and gross abuse of their power, have seized the COVID19 pandemic to expand their authority by unprecedented lengths, without any proper Constitutional, statutory, or common law basis therefor,"* the lawsuit states. (USA Today).

"How's Cap doing?" Ruth asked. "He was taken to a hospital. He is awake and alert. If we have time, I'll be stopping by for a visit. Anybody want to join me?" "Everybody said "I do" in unison.

Going home, Wednesday, September 30th

The FBI drove the team in two vans to JFK International and escorted them past customs because each carried a duffel bag issued by the FBI which held their arsenal. They left the terminal and walked one hundred yards to a hanger. When they entered the hanger, they got their first look at their ride home. When Mike saw the G700 Gulfstream, he asked, "are we flying with the Rolling Stones? Damn! That's for us?"

When the flight attendants started taking their duffel bags for storage, John ordered, "Richard and Mike, take your duffel bags onboard. Ruth, take your drone. I'm just being paranoid." "No problem with that thinking boss," Richard said. When the team was all settled in and the aircraft was finally in the air, the flight attendants served the team drinks and snacks.

One of the attendants told John he had a call and escorted him to a special video phone in the back out of earshot from the team. When John sat down in the executive's chair, the video phone came to life and Admiral James Palton's smiling face was before him. "You did a great job yesterday. You actually had me worried." "I have to admit, it got pretty nasty!" John replied. "Now that Chucky's captured, I suppose I'll be packing for Pax River, Maryland."

"Not so fast John, I've been reconsidering that move for now. Would you mind staying in Maine for a while?" "Really? I'd love to but for what purpose?" John asked. "The main reason is you and your militia impressed my boss, President David Travis. But there's a catch." The Admiral continued. "President Travis and I want to send your militia a more resourceful leader, and we're not suggesting that Dutch has been anything less than an outstanding leader!"

"I don't get it then, why send a new leader?" John asked. "Two words, Regulated Militia, read the second amendment. We want an active-duty soldier making decisions with you and Dutch. This person will also get priority with any requisitions you may require for a mission, and we have a couple of big missions for your militia's future." "Admiral, our SOP (Standard Operating Procedures) is not for saving the world, it was for saving Maine. You want to turn the militia into a team of mercs (mercenaries)?"

"Come on John, you're exaggerating a bit, aren't you? I saw your man's interview on Fox TV after the Portsmouth event. You were far from being mercs there, you were patriots! I want patriots, not mercs!" The Admiral demanded. "I'll need to talk with Dutch, and he'll want to bring it before the unit leaders." "I'm sending you a video file. Look her over and call me IMMEDIATELY with the militia's answer." "HER?!"

Back in Maine, Wednesday, September 30th Ten hundred hours

When the plane landed, the first thing he noticed was Leah standing in a crowd of people. When his eyes scanned the crowd, he recognized many of the wives and girlfriends. Dutch stepped out of the crowd and yelled, "Steve and Mike, ON ME!" They followed their orders and John proceeded over to see what was going on. When they all got there, Dutch threw a set of keys to Steve and Mike and said, "you'll find two Humvees in the parking lot. You're the olive green one Steve and you're the black one, Mike." John laughed and said, "Are they bulletproof?" "Yep and they come with a package of bells and whistles. It's going to take you weeks to figure them all out."

Leah grabbed John and they kissed. He started to leave with his arm around her when Dutch got his attention. "I'll need a debrief from you, John." How about lunch with the wives at Duffy's later today?" John Suggested. "I don't know Bro, last time we ate there you dropped that trip to Minnesota on me." "You're right. We don't need lightning striking twice at the same place." Dutch smiled and then his face scrunched, "What do you mean by that?" "What do you say we meet at the Maine Diner at twelve forty-five."

Dutch and John along with their wives were seated at twelve thirty in a tent outside the restaurant thanks to COVID-19. The waitress brought their drinks while they all caught up with their lives. The wives asked for NO business for the first thirty minutes, but time flew and after lunch, the wives asked for ice cream at Big Daddy's down the street. That's when John delivered the news.

"The Admiral WANTS TO SEND US A GENERAL?!?" Dutch exclaimed. John explained all the details and reasoning. Dutch's first reaction was, "we need to bring this before the unit leaders." "That's what I told Admiral" John replied. "Is this what you meant about lightning striking twice?" Dutch asked. "I believe we're going to see a lot of lightning if we agree to this," John answered. I'll radio all unit leaders before the day is over and we'll meet tomorrow morning. We're down to twenty unit leaders because seven of them were out-of-state property owners and I don't know how many soldiers." Dutch reported. "We're still an effective bunch now aren't we," John answered.

Militia Unit meeting, Command Center, October 1st

Dutch, John and Rene sat with twenty-unit leaders. These men and women have gone far. When not at work and making a living, they were training. They've been called to missions which could have ended badly, but they continued to serve their State. Now Dutch presented a new protocol, one which serves America.

John let the cat out of the bag, revealing his source for the first time with the unit leaders. "He's the Deputy Chief of the Department of Defense, Admiral James Palton." He's been the source of the militia's arsenal and now the Admiral is asking for the militia's help. To make it official, the Admiral is asking us to take on a new Boss. Dutch will work hand in hand with a Regular Army General. The General has an impressive record as a tactician, no doubt she would be an asset to our militia." Almost in unison, they repeated, "SHE?"

Dutch took over, "Our unit leaders still have a card in the game when strategizing the missions, but the General will have the final say. We aren't military, so you can walk away anytime if you don't like what you see, but the Admiral vouches for her, and I have read her file and She's legit." Dutch reported.

"Can I say something?" One of the unit leaders Ronald Brown (a black man) asked. "please," replied Dutch. "As a patriot, it makes me sick to see great cities falling to criminals while they burn and burglarize businesses and then villainize the police because of one idiot. That's prejudice. Count me in." Richard and Mike said "I'm in," in agreement.

Dutch asked, "Just speak up if you oppose, you will not be viewed adversely." Nobody opposed. Many commented about taking on bigger missions, all were positive about the General. John whipped out his phone and call the Admiral. "Yes sir, good to go, yes sir, excuse me sir? She's here? Yes sir. Thank you, sir." John hung up and walked over to the door and waited. He opened the door and in walked General Gail Lipton. When John viewed her file on the plane's video phone, she looked younger. Now, maybe in her early forties, with dark hair up in a severe-looking bun. She was athletically built, and her not-so-attractive face bore no signs of aging. Her uniform had a shoulder patch, one John recognized, a ranger patch. Since 2015, women had been allowed to go to ranger school, one of the toughest courses in the US Armed Forces. Not many passed. Apparently, this one did. Which attests to her grit.

"Ladies and Gentlemen, this is General Gail Lipton, she is your new commanding officer." A murmur rippled through the room as the members of the militia glanced at each other in confusion.

"Captain Swanson, Chief Petty Officer Colton, Militia unit leaders, you now work for me. I hope you will continue to work as well as your reputation precedes you. On the other hand, you know nothing about me, and I hope to change that soon. Dutch and I will be the top of your chain of command. But it will be my ass hanging out in the wind when it comes to paying the Admiral. John or whoever is designated as the mission leader out in the field will be in charge. Missions can change in a blink out there and I won't override their call.

If you want a Hellfire R9X Ninja missile launched by the MQ-9 Reaper drone, you'll get it. Unit leaders, rest assured, If your unit is involved, you will be included in all mission briefs and you will be responsible for briefing your people. It's going to be a while before I can remember all your names, but to get on my fast-track memory, either do something exceptional or something stupid! Any questions?"

Leslie Cunningham raised her hand. The General pointed at her. "What can we expect as our next mission." I'd like to explore a deployment into Seattle and squash the protest violence." Why not go after the Kenosha, Wisconsin rioters? Their closer, "Terry Wells asked. "Kenosha is under a Republican Governor and he is calling the National Guard to restore order."

"Will you do anything different in Seattle than what we did in Minnesota?" Dick Vinaldo asked. "Nobody figured out the Maine Militia spoiled Antifa's attack on the Naval Shipyard in Portsmouth. The Base did a great job keeping your identities secrete, but in Minnesota, just because you're on a military base, your secret isn't safe. Some of the best spies eat in the chow hall on military bases.

Believe me, I'm not saying your plans were nothing less than extraordinary with the resources you had available. If I attack the protests in Seattle, you will be complete ghosts. Any more questions? No? Okay, Rene, put the map of Seattle on the big screen.

The problem with Seattle is the protest will move when all the stores have been looted. If we were to fly in today based on a particular occupied street, we may have to re-strategize because they move, wasting our time and causing us to leave a bigger footprint. When they move, they usually stay a few days to cause optimum damage.

What I propose right now, is to collect video using a Predator Drone and analyze their next move. What do you think Dutch?" "You're making this easy with a Predator. Your strategy is sound General, but what's your plan to make us ghosts?" "Rene, zoom in over here please." Gail circled her laser on the screen. "This is a school bus parking slash maintenance warehouse under construction. It's almost finished but the governor's shut down the construction company until the pandemic is under control.

We will fly into Naval Air Station Whidbey Island on a C-17 Globemaster III. We will be picked up by school buses and stage at the school bus warehouse. No red flags there" Two shell company SUVs will be waiting at the base for John's snipers and spotters. *A shell corporation is a company or corporation that exists only on paper and has no office and no employees, but may have a bank account or may hold passive investments or be the registered owner of assets, such as intellectual property, or ships.* They will deploy to their overwatch positions and recon ASAP." "Where will we stay if this is an overnighter?" Mike Ackroff asked. "Oh, it WILL be an overnighter, and we will stay at the warehouse. You will receive one box lunch at the base and the rest of your meals will be MREs (Meals Ready to Eat). As far as the base is concerned. This is a typical training exercise."

"The Admiral will provide the construction company with a special PPP (Paycheck Protection Program), not to raise any red flags until we leave. From now until boots on the ground, President Travis will be calling for curfews to be enforced. In the past, when the governor or police called a curfew, increased protesters and rioters. "What's a normal crowd compared to an increase?" Larry Wetzel asked. "We have seen increases doubled from one hundred fifty to three hundred people. The more the merrier."

John made a request, "I'd like Ruth Taylor and her drone for my spotter." "I don't have a problem with your request except we will have a Predator drone overhead recording a one-mile area, you won't need Ruth's drone. Her drone will be important for other missions, just not this one." "Are you aware we only have equipment for one hundred?" Dutch asked. "Yes, Admiral filled me in. We will only need one hundred people for this mission." That drew murmuring from the militia. "One hundred against possibly three hundred? I don't like those odds!" Doris Waite moaned.

"No worries, there will be two hundred of us. Very good odds for our trained soldiers. Another asset of my position is, I can coordinate with other militias." "There are others?" Richard interrupted. "Oh yea, they're popping up in most states. We will join forces with Washington's version of you. They're called *"The Sixth Branch"* You were their inspiration to form a civilian force and they can't wait to link up with you."

"This just keeps getting better and better," Mike said. "I want you to brief your people and then I'd like you to pick the eight-unit leaders and twelve militia per unit who will go on this mission. John, I want four snipers and spotters from you. Everybody takes some time off, you deserve it and we will meet back on Monday, the fifth of October, zero eight hundred hours. Anything else Dutch?" "Yes, Check the patrol schedules and training schedules before you leave. Have a great weekend."

CHAPTER TWELVE

Fox News: President Travis sounds like a broken record. Every news brief he attends, you can expect the same message about curfews in the violent cities. Quote: "If your city is under curfew, it begins at 8:00 PM. If you're out after that time, you are participating in the insurrection. If you not causing violence or looting, you are abetting, and you will be dealt with. Get off the streets before 8 PM!"

Plans to move on Seattle, Monday, October 5th

At zero eight hundred hours, the militia unit leaders were assembled, and Dutch took the podium. "Before we begin General Lipton handed down some interesting updates concerning our mission. We will not be alone in this mission. The President has called for the National Guard to overtake the Kenosha, Wisconsin riots. According to the General, Oregon has a Militia and they will overtake the Portland riots. We and the Sixth Branch will overtake Seattle's riots and we will all accomplish these missions on the same evening of October seven." This caused discussions within the group.

"Do we know what kind of ROE the others will use on the rioters?" Luke Morgan, an ex-marine who was other than honorably discharged asked. "The leaders of all these groups have been briefed to avoid causing death, and use force to protect businesses and yourselves from harm." Dutch replied. John spoke, "When we hit Minnesota, we rushed in and were met with major resistance. We maimed, or I should say broke a few legs. The snipers had to wound a few of the armed rioters to keep them from shooting our people. The whole mission was a success because the protesting stopped as a result, out of fear of reprisal, and hasn't started back up.

Bruce Gorham commented, "So we're going to storm in and start crippling these people?" Mike Ackroff jumped in, "Have you watched the news? Haven't you seen these riots in action? People are burning the American flag yelling 'Death to America.' Maybe you never served in-country when ISIS fighters were screaming 'Death to America.' over and over in Iraq? The protesters burn businesses without discrimination, blacks, whites, Hispanics. Then they beat the owners for trying to douse the flames. And Oh man! You might be the best, kindest cop in America, but you put that uniform on and you're a racist murderer!

Did you know that Black People Matter is a Marxist group? It's on their frigging website! You're looking at a major domestic terrorist group in American right there on the evening news! And the best part of being an American Marxist is? When you get arrested, you get out jail the next day to get back into the fight!" Thanks to the Democratic President's running mate! Mike rose to his feet and pointed at Bruce, "If you're not ready for this fight, please let another unit leader take your place!" Bruce raised his hands in surrender, "Jeeze Mike, just asking man, I wasn't at the first gig. I'm all in here!"

The General walked in and stood next to Dutch, "Settle down people, let's not fight amongst ourselves! The fight is out there! But I will emphasize that Mike is correct about these people EXCEPT, and let me make this clear, the Marxist part of BPM is in Antifa and the top echelon. Most protesters don't even know what Marxism is! Which also means, innocent protesters are under our protection,"

Elijah Goffstien stood, "I was in Minnesota and let me warn you, If you let what you think is an innocent past you while in this attack, you better have eyes in the back of your head. I was attacked twice that way." The General chimed in, "Very good point! We will not be there to make friends. Any more comments? Great. Rene bring up the first aerial photo please. A bird's eye photo appeared.

"This is from the reconnaissance predator drone taken at last night's protest. These rioters are leaving behind eighteen burning buildings, multiple burning vehicles, one dead cop, and several injured. We have determined their next attack will be the Seattle City Hall, the Municipal Court, and the police station on the next block on James Street. All the Streets and Avenues boarding City Hall have hundreds of stores and businesses, a looter's dream."

Dutch spoke next, we will place two snipers and spotters here, and here," as he pointed to the photo. John interrupted, "Why are our snipers doubling up and only covering from the East and South?" "Because the Sixth Branch will cover the West and North." Dutch replied. "How do we know they're reliable?" Richard asked.

The General answered, "The leading sniper is well known for hitting a moving target moving at fifty miles an hour from two-thousands yards." "Are we talking about Reggie Austin, AKA the Reaper?" John asked. "Yes, the Reaper got out of the Shipyard security business to form his own militia thanks to your militia. He's actually from Seattle."

Dutch laid out the plan, "our militia troops will move north on 6th Avenue to James Street. Two units will continue up to 6th, six units will proceed west on James. Three units will break off and proceed north on 5th." The General continued, "The Sixth Branch will confront the rioters on Cherry Street behind City Hall and 4th Avenue. They will have snipers here and here," she pointed with the laser pointer at the aerial photo.

Skyscraper, Seattle, Wednesday, October 7th, twenty-one hundred

One half-hour after curfew, Reggie Austin (The Reaper), was watching through the prototype computerize Argos BTR optic scope as the crowd grew. Paying particular attention to a tall black man with a bald head. He was armed with what looked like an AR-15 strapped to his back. Other armed men were congregating around him joking and laughing. Next to that group, men with baseball bats were gathering like they were waiting for the tall black man who was now pointing up and down the street.

"Hey Cobalt, are you seeing the tall black stud on James?" "Yea, Reaper, looks like he's in charge. You notice almost all his minions are white?" The racial composition of the Democratic city of Seattle in 2019 was 65.7% white, 14.1% Asian, 7.0% Black, 0.4% Native American. This baffled the prominent white community when Seattle was hit so hard by the Black People Matter movement.

"I see that Cobalt and they have more armed soldiers than we expected too." "I'm thinking he's prior military." They both watched as the armed men broke off and began walking in different directions, then the tall black man began speaking to the baseball batters, who later moved towards their assigned areas. Cobalt radioed, "all snipers, armed tangos are dispersing to the ends of each corner of the two blocks, you should be able to see them in your scopes now." Cobalt listened as each sniper confirmed that they had eyes on the armed men.

A Sixth Branch sniper radioed, "I've got two pick-up trucks turning down 4th Avenue. One truck has bricks and the other, boxes. Could be fireworks." The truckers were stopped by the tall black man. He waved some idle protesters over and they began unloading the truck. "Looks like our party might be starting early," Reaper radioed. "Yea and our forces aren't even staged yet," the sniper Hawk said. "School busses are one mic out." The General radioed, "militia and Sixth Branch forces will be ready to deploy on Cobalt's call."

Earlier that day, General notified the police chief something would go down tonight and asked the police to continue guarding their buildings. So, the police had all their officers in riot gear and lined up in front of City Hall, the Municipal Court, and the Police Department. While the protesters were forming up in front of the police lines, the rock throwers were setting up behind the protesters. The batters were lingering around the storefronts. The armed soldiers stayed on station at the entrances of the two city blocks.

You didn't need a lot of intelligence to figure out how the violence was going to unfold. Cobalt radioed, "Okay General, let them loose, shit's about to hit the fan here." When the militia began their jog up 6th Avenue, John and his buddy sniper Gambler were observing the guards posted on 6th and James. "Those guards were going to see the militia coming," John warned. Sure enough, they both brought their weapons up in threat. John and Gambler fired simultaneously at their tangos, wounding them both in the shoulder. They fell as if they had died, and when the militia arrived, they pulled the weapons from them. Two militias sent kicks to their groans. John shifted his aim to the armed guard aiming an AR-15 on James and 5th Avenue and shot him in the shoulder.

From a different sniper's nest, Hawk and Hobbit took down two more threats at 6th and Cherry and on 5th and Cherry. All militia assigned guards were no longer a threat. Cobalt, Gambler, Hawk, and Hobbit were now scanning the streets along with their spotters for any armed rebel they might have missed. None of the rock throwers or batters were yet aware their guards were down or that they were under attack. They heard no reports of the suppressed sniper rifle, and the screams from the wounded guards were masked by the fireworks and the chanting noises the protesters were making.

John scoped one rock thrower from far behind who had an impressive arm. He was nailing the police shields. John took aim and timed his shot to throw off the brick's launch, John purposely nicked his arm and the brick fell short and landed on one of the protester's head. Three protesters turned to confront the poorly aimed thrower and saw militia troops engaged with crowds behind their lines. They started pointing and yelling. Half the protesters ran off screaming and the other half charged the militia.

Richard Bloomer's unit was part of the 6th Avenue assault, Richard saw the armed guards laying on the ground squirming from shoulder wounds. Luke Morgan grabbed an AR-15 off one of the guards and tossed it into a nearby trash dumpster. Clashing with the rebels, the two units found themselves outnumbered two to one and each of the militia was struggling to take down the resistance.

Luke swung his baton at two attackers in a proficient Krav Maga style. Suddenly he was hit from behind. As he felt from the initial impact, he felt confusion, how'd they get behind me and everything went black.

Back at the warehouse, the General and Rene watched while the predator drone filmed the battle. They had the whole picture of both militia and the Sixth Branch. The batters were the biggest threat after the guards were down and several of them were shot by General's troops. None of the wounds looked serious. Some of the batters wounded some militia troopers. Some militia re-engaged; some were escorted out of the fight. By twenty-one fifteen the troops were checking on the wounded while the ambulance sirens could be heard in the distance. The fight was over in forty-five minutes. John radioed, "All elements muster your troops and move back to the buses."

One missing man in Seattle

John (Cobalt) was breaking down his gear at the top of a financial Investment building when he heard Richard call on the radio, "Anybody see Luke Morgan? He was operating on 6th Avenue tonight." John stopped loading his compact semi-automatic Sniper System (CSASS) into its case. He removed the scope and told his spotter to scan the streets for Luke Morgan. While scanning, he radioed, "any snipers on street level?" Hawk answered, "Hobbit and I just got here and are checking bodies." John could see them now. "He's not here, but he could have been put on an ambulance." A few minutes later, the General radioed, "All elements return to your bus and get back to base ASAP. That includes you too John."

When John entered the school bus warehouse, he rushed over to the General and Dutch leaning over Rene's shoulder. Rene was on his computer. "What's going on? Why did you call off the search?" The General answered, "the UAV Drone found him. He was beaten over the head and captured. Three tangos dragged him down an alley and into a building. When the coast was clear, they moved him into a truck and drove off on East Madison Street. The tangos were a tall black man, a masked white male, and the other a twenty-something unmasked white male. We're running face recognition and we're trying to pick up their vehicle with the drone."

"Was the tall black male bald?" John asked. "Yea, we heard you and Reaper talking about the suspect." "I got the unmasked white male!" Rene announced. "His name is Whitney Cohen, one arrest for possession, lives at 5 Glamour Heights Seattle, an expensive gated community. A Junior at South Seattle College. He's a frigging rich kid." Dutch ordered, "dig into the parents, I want a phone number. Call him, see if he's home." "What about the black guy," John asked. I have a friend helping at the NSA, he's working on him," Rene answered. "What about the drone, are we re-tasking to find the route of the truck?" "The drone pilot is on it."

Cohen Lodge, Washington Park, October 7th twenty-three hundred

Luke was waking up from what felt like a black dream. He remembered being in the fight on 6th Avenue but couldn't remember what happened. He opened his eyes and couldn't see. *I was hit in the head; I can feel the pain, did it affect my sight?* He thought. As his head began to clear, he realized there was a hood over his head and felt relief, he wasn't blind, then the relief moved to the dread that he'd been captured! He tried to move and felt he was tied to a chair.

These are ropes around my wrists, they obviously don't have my utility belt rig, they would have found the zip ties. Somebody is standing close in front of me, I can hear them breathing. The hood began to rise off his head and bent over and inches from him was a bald black man. Fear rushed over Luke when he remembered the conversation Reaper and Cobalt were having about a tall bald black man. Was this him?

"How's that bump on your head?" He asked. "Oh, I'm sorry, you don't have a bump because you were wearing a combat helmet. In fact, you had all kinds of cool military gear on. We had to remove all that shit just to carry you to the truck."

"Where am I, what do you want with me?" Luke asked. "That's a very stupid question. You invade our peaceful protest, shoot people, break their legs, and YOU want to know what I want from you?" Then the black man punched Luke twice in the face and twice to the stomach and was about to hit him again when someone shouted, "Lenny, stop." While catching his breath, Luke was able to look around and saw a half dozen people standing around in the room. The room looked like an elegant den with a picture window looking out at a small pond and trees. The room had plush furnishings, oak paneling, and a polished oak table.

"We don't need him knocked out, and the rest of you, to your posts!" Luke now focused on the man who just saved him from another punch. He was white with spikey hair with too much gel. He was much shorter than the black man and wore a hoodie and ripped jeans. Now it was just him and Lenny left in the room. "I want to know who you are, who all your friends are, and who you all work for. Let's just start with who you are." *I can't tell them who I am, they can't find out the Maine Militia is here,* Luke thought.

Although Luke only served two years in the military. He was never trained in what to do when captured. Maybe he would bring it up at the next militia meeting. *What should I say? Should I give them a fake name? bullshit them about everything? What about my militia team? Are they looking for me? I'm sure they know I'm missing.* "WHO ARE YOU!!" Luke was trying to figure out what to say when Lenny pulled out a military K-bar knife. "I won't knock you out, but I will stab you in the leg if you don't answer."

"My name is Lex Morris." The initials were true but that's all, hopefully, they'll never know. "Okay Lex, that wasn't so bad. Now, who are your friends?" "We're just local citizens who don't like the violence in our city!" "Bullshit," Lenny said, "Let me stab the mutha!" "You want me to believe you and all your friends got all that military gear and WHAT ABOUT THE SNIPERS!!! Do you think we're stupid? STAB HIS LEG LENNY"

Lenny couldn't wait to inflict pain and jabbed the knife into Luke's right thigh. Luke tried to take it like a man, like in the movies, but he cried out. He looked at the knife sticking into his leg a watched the blood begin to stain his cargo pants.

School bus warehouse, Seattle

"Hello, this is John, is Whitney home?" "Hi John, this is his mom, he's not here." "When will Whitney be home?" "He's staying up at our camp at the moment. How do you know Whitney?" "I met him at South Seattle, I'm just a friend." "Well if you're a friend, he would have told you about the camp. Are you one of those Black People Matter friends?" John thought about what a mom wanted to hear from a stranger friend of her sons. He wouldn't want to turn her off about Whitney's affiliations. "No, ma'am, I'm not into them." Then she got short and sounded upset. "You dealing drugs?" "No, ma'am, If I sell him anything, it would be the Lord Jesus."

There was a long pause. John figured he would hear the phone hanging up. Then the mom said. "He's up at the camp and probably with a bunch of Black People Matter people. I wouldn't go there if I were you. We pray for Whitney all the time. I hope you can get through to him." "Me too, ma'am, what's the address of the camp?"

It's not an address, you just take East Madison Street to

Washington Park. When you see the Welcome to Washington Park sign, count 1.7 miles to a dirt road on the right. It's a mile to the camp. I would not go there though, they might hurt you!" "Thank you, ma'am, I'll bring him back safe and sound. May the Lord bless you and your family." "Please be careful and don't tell him I told you how to find the camp," she pleaded. They hung up.

Rene's phone rang, he answered it and put it on speaker. "What do you have Lester," Rene asked. "His name is Lenny Hoffman, no home address, dishonorably discharged from the Army in 2002 for assault of an officer. Lenny doesn't like to be told what to do. He has a few domestic assault charges. It appears he finds a girlfriend and beats them up within a week. Incarcerated once for a two-month stint." "I owe you one Lester, thanks a million!" "Your welcome, take this asshole out Rene, bye."

Then Rene called the drone pilot and re-tasked the drone to Washington Park. Before the General had a chance to speak, John was organizing his team, "Richard, Mike Ackroff, Dick Vinaldo, Ruth Taylor, Larry Wetzel, Steve Paris. John needed another good sniper, so he picked Reggie Austin AKA Reaper.

Cohen Lodge, Washington Park, twenty-three fifty.

The white male had Lenny wrap Luke's leg and placed a garbage bag under his chair. Someone would catch hell for bloodstains on the hardwood floors. "You want Lenny to stab you again?" "We're a militia group out of Billings Montana called to assist a smaller group in Seattle." Luke knew that town in Montana because he had a cousin who lived out there.

"See, now that wasn't so hard, was it? Who do you know in the Seattle group Lex?" "I don't know anyone, I'm just a private in our group." Luke figured he'd done well in his lies because the white male and Lenny left the room to talk. Luke could hear yelling outside his door, but the words were muffled. Then he heard thumping like a struggle, and all became quiet.

Luke was in pain and pulled on his wrist binds to try and loosen the ropes. When that didn't work, he looked around the room for something he could use to cut the ropes. He spotted a side stand in the corner of the room with a picture of a nice family. He recognized the young man as one of those in the room earlier. Luke's legs were tied, but his feet were planted on the floor. His legs were not tied to the legs of the chair, an amateur mistake of his abductors. So, if he could balance on his feet, baby step to the side stand, break the glass, and cut the ropes, he'd be free. *Hell, who am I kidding, this plan has too many moving parts,* he thought.

Cohen Lodge road, zero two-thirty

About fifty yards down from the Cohen Lodge's entry road, Steve Paris pulled over at a widened part of the Park road. They parked there and walked in on the dirt road. They were fully kitted complete with night vision goggles. All of the militia were armed with HK416 rifles except John and Reaper who carried CSASS sniper rifles. The dirt road was curvy, Mike Ackroff was the point man and walked fifty yards ahead and Larry Wetzel was rearguard and watching their six. While Mike on point moved silently on the edge of the road, somewhere a night-bird made a sound that was accentuated by the stillness of the darkness.

John readjusted his grip on the CSASS and stopped when he heard Mike's voice over the net, "hold! danger close!" and there was silence. The radio was quiet a minute before Mike came back on and said, "tango down." "Copy" John replied. They moved forward and found Mike waiting beside a black Antifa fighter. Mike had used his Strider SMF marine corps folding knife to neutralize the threat. "Well, I guess we better step it up a bit, we can't be far away from the camp and somebody's going to miss this guy."

Suddenly, a phone rang. "Who's got a frigging phone here!" Reggie asked. Mike bent over and retrieved the Antifa's phone and pressed the answer icon. "What are you doing!" John whispered. "Why haven't you checked in yet?" the phone said. Then mike covered the phone's mic with the cup of his hand and started making static sounds.

"Try charging your damn phone!! Finish your rounds and get in here!" and the caller hung up. "That will buy us a little time," Mike said. John turned to Reaper, "Reaper, we're heading up a hill, see if you can find some high ground for overwatch." John ordered and Reaper was gone. John called Dutch on his radio, "Boss, is the UAV overhead?" "Roger Cobalt, and we're seeing two roving patrols around the main cabin, at your ten o'clock and two o'clock" "Any idea where they might have Luke stashed?" John asked. "We see a garage and the main cabin; my guess would be the cabin." Reaper eased through the foliage and swept the perimeter with his CSASS suppressed sniper rifle. He found a large boulder on a hill and set up. He picked up the two roving patrols and in a low voice said, "eyes on." John ordered Dick and Larry around the front (pond side) and told them to check it out. He then told Ruth to put her drone up with an attached flash-bang grenade.

A few minutes later John heard, "Cobalt, this is Larry. We've got one sleeper on the front deck." "Copy Larry, hold and watch him." John turned to ruth and said, "Hold here, and wait for my call." Then John whispered to Richard, Mike, and Steve, "We'll make our way up until we can see the rovers. Reaper and I will put them down and then we'll breach the camp." When we get to the door, Richard, you take right and Mike take left, I'll go straight and Steve, check out that garage. Ready?" They all nodded.

They quietly moved up and John could now see the two o'clock rover. "You still have eyes on the ten o'clock rover Reaper?" "Ready when you are Cobalt." "On my call, all three go down, three, two, one, execute!" The count was slow and deliberate, and when he finished, his finger squeezed the trigger at the same time as Reaper and Larry did.

When fired, silencers don't make weapons completely silent. Unlike their portrayal in the movies. They suppress. There is still some noise. It worried John as his team fast-walked to the camp door with their weapons up, they were out in the open. Richard was scanning right, and Mike left as they crossed the yard to the back door, John tried the knob and found the door unlocked.

As Steve silently approached the garage, he saw a side door open and two tangos stepped out. At the cabin, just before John opened the door, he heard two shots from the garage, and a few seconds later heard, "two tangos down." Steve reported. John opened the door and Richard quietly went to the right, Mike scanned left and John scanned straight. A stairway was in front with hallways on right and left. At the top of the stairs was a "U" shaped railed hall/loft with four rooms. Richard and Mike began clearing rooms and John moved upstairs.

After John's first step up, one of the doors opened and the tall black man looking surprised to see the intruders brought his gun up to shoot, but John already had his CSASS up and put one bullet into his bald head. John radioed, "Steve, need you in the camp. Help me with the upstairs. Larry and Dick breach through the front door."

When John reached the top of the stairs, he turned left to check two doors. Steve was coming up the stairs. John felt the tango before he saw a white male coming out of one of the rooms from the right of the stairs. John turned to see the shooter aiming his rifle. He heard a suppressed shot and the white male crumbled over the railing and thumped below. Steve nailed him.

Mike radioed, "we found Luke, he's good, he'll need help to walk." "I've got another white male hostage," Richard radioed. John and Steve finished clearing the upstairs and came down to see the hostages. Looking at the white male when the tape was removed from his mouth, "Who are you?" John asked. The hostage said, "I'm Whitney Cohen." A surprised John walked outside and call General Gail Lipton, "We have two packages, Luke Morgan and Whitney was a hostage victim. We're going to need a clean-up, eight tangos down. What do we do with Mr. Cohen?"

School bus warehouse, October 8th zero three-twenty-five

When the team returned with Luke, the warehouse roared with cheers. Luke, limping around received multiple hugs and the rescue team got a lot of handshakes. John kept Whitney close by and he was able to observe the camaraderie of the militia and Sixth Branch. Questions were answered except where the militia groups were from. General introduced herself to Whitney and he shared what happened and why he was tied up.

When the Black People Matter militant group discovered Whitney's upscale status, they tricked him into giving Lenny the location of the camp. The camp was then seized as their headquarters. At the protest, Whitney saw BPM captured Luke and was forced in helping load him into the truck. Whitney was against torturing Luke. When Lenny and Tim Page (the masked white male) decided to kill Luke, Whitney fought the decision and they turned on him, so they tied him up and decided that Whitney would also have to be murdered.

The Militia were packing up and would soon have to leave for the Naval Air Station, so John volunteered to take Whitney home in the rental SUV and he would link up with the militia before wheels up. "So, you're a Navy Seal?" Whitney asked. "I'm a retired Seal, yes." "Your friend Lex took quite a beating, I'm impressed." "He did, but I've got a friend who took a much bigger beating than that." John answered. "Was he captured by Iraqis or something?" "No, he was captured by Romans." "Romans?" "Yes, and His name was Jesus Christ." "You're beginning to sound like my parents now."

Then John asked, "Your parents didn't teach you about Jesus?" "Sure, they did, but I'm in college now and I believe in science, not fiction." Jokingly, John asked, "Oh, the 'Big Bang Theory'?" "Yes, what's so funny?" "You mean to tell me you believe that something came from nothing?" "It sounds a little weird when you phrase it that way, but yea, I do."

"So, you believe the earth and sun formed from nothing, then mysteriously the earth began orbiting around the sun, rotating for 24 hours in a day.

The Earth just happened to be the perfect distance from the sun, then gravity formed keeping the earth from spinning out of orbit at 63,000 mph.

Then the Earth's atmosphere formed itself, water happens to appear, the Earth's moon appeared and happened to be exactly the right distance for optimized gravitational pull controlling our tides.

Inanimate matter appeared, the first simple cell produced itself and became complex and ONE complex cell formed millions of all plants, animals, and eventually formed human life?" Whitney paused and was shocked at how stupid the 'Big Bang Theory' sounded.

you to deny history?" "No why do you ask?" "Because true history shows the generations of the world, and Jesus was a very big part of that history," John replied.

"If you/re talking about the Bible, that book was re-written so many times by man, it got all distorted and full of superstitions."

"Yea? If one-quarter of the Bible is true, then you must conclude the people of the Bible experienced God. If God is marginally as powerful as He is depicted, He is indeed awesome. God has done in the Bible something no other holy book has ever dared to do. He based its credibility upon His ability to tell the future with one hundred percent accuracy. More than one-fourth of the Bible was prophetic when it was written. No other holy book comes close in this regard.

In fact, most of these other secular books contain no prophecies at all! The Bible sets the standard very high. You can not afford to deny it when your life after death is in the balance. And you came very close to death tonight." Whitney stopped talking and John knew he was pondering what he heard. They were about ten minutes from home when Whitney turned to John. "I need to repent!" "You're making the right choice Whitney." "I need to repent right now! Pull over."

When they arrived at the Cohen residence, Whitney's dad was getting ready for work. He saw his son get out of the stranger's SUV and met Whitney at the door. He was about to reprimand Whitney when his son attacked him with an intense passionate hug. Whitney cried into his father's chest and mumbled, "I want you to meet John, he saved me twice tonight." While still holding dad with one arm, he waved John over with the second.

John was considering driving off but decided it was best if he debriefed the Dad and asked for secrecy of what happened at their camp. Mrs. Cohen came downstairs when she heard her husband speaking to somebody. When Whitney saw her, he met her with the same passionate hug dad got.

"Puzzled, all she could say was, "can I get you a cup of coffee?" John knew their coffee would be better than what he's had all night and said, "Black and one sugar." She handed John the cup while he was debriefing Mr. Cohen about the night's event. "That was you? We saw it on the news last night. We were amazed and pleased that justice was finally served."

Then Mrs. Cohen interrupted and said, "you're him. The voice on the phone, you're him." Mr. Cohen turned to his son and asked, "you said John save you twice, what did you mean." When Whitney explained he had rededicated his life to Jesus, Mrs. Cohen broke down and fell on her son's lap. It was the most beautiful thing John had ever seen.

Later, John explained the clean-up of the Cohen camp would leave no traces what-so-ever. John asked for some paper and wrote down some information, then handed Mr. Cohen the sheet and explained everything about what was going to happen soon and asked for their secrecy. They whole-heartedly agreed! John slept soundly on the trip home in a very noisy C-17 Globemaster III.

CHAPTER FOURTEEN

Fox News: *Sara Roseberg, the Accountant and fundraiser for Black People Matter, and Vice-chair of Thousand Currents of California, a charity that handles fundraising for Black People Matter, was arrested last night after the FBI received a tip which led to the discovery of a damning video recorded by a security camera at the defense weapons storage facility at Tobyhanna Army Depot outside of Philadelphia. An anonymous source says she was clearly identified working with two rouge FBI Agents stealing a case of C4 explosives. Rosenburg has had a history of terrorism.*

In 1984 she an active participant of the Communist movement that carried out bombings in Washington D.C. Rosenberg landed on the FBI's most-wanted list and was arrested with stolen explosives. The terrorist drew 58 years but served only 16 because in 2001 President Bill Clinton commuted Rosenberg's sentence. Also discovered in her vehicle were five logbooks sources say are BPM financial records from the past five years of illegal practices of treason, extortion, and bribery which may be damning to some congressional representatives, senators, and the Black People Matter organization. We will keep you informed as the story unfolds.

Also breaking; Michael Durham, the Operations Manager of BPM, and Juan Los'Cartos, the famous drug lord of the Los'Cartos Cartel were arrested by Arizona State Police and Border Patrol yesterday while attempting to unload Drugs, weapons and...can you guess?... C4 explosives into a Mexican Cartel's warehouse in the United States. The warehouse was also the entrance to an ingenious tunnel system that led to Mexico.

Not far from where the two were arrested was evidence of a battle between Americans and Mexicans. Ninety-eight dead bodies were recovered along with several burned-out pick-up trucks called technicals. Both Michael and Juan claim the dead were killed by US militia. As for the two FBI Agents that assisted with the thief, they are still at large.

Militia Command, Kennebunkport Maine, October 21st

General Lipton, Dutch, John, and Rene were in the communication center. "I don't get it. How could the Admire corroborate all the elements to make the offenses stick?" Dutch asked. "I mean, a video linking the C4 to the FBI Agents Brian Jones and Keith Johnson?" "Rene, why don't you show the damning video the FBI found," General Lipton suggested. Rene turned to his computer and said, "Watch screen one." The fifty-four-inch screen came to lift. The Army Depot security camera's view was from high in the room, probably from the corner of the room.

Three people were filmed entering the defense weapons storage facility at Tobyhanna Army Depot outside of Philadelphia. Agent Jones was filmed opening a caged room while Agent Johnson and Sara Rosenburg stepped in and picked up a case of C4. When they turned to leave the room, the picture clearly displayed who they were.

The timestamp was October 18th at zero two forty-two. "That's them all right, but how?" John asked. "Sara claimed her alimony was with Durham in his office the night of the alleged theft," Rene answered. "Her alibi just got himself busted in Nogales Arizona, not good," General Lipton added. "Meanwhile, the FBI Agents, Johnson and Jones were secretly on a mission to find Lenny Hoffman who is from Philadelphia. They were in Philly the same night this robbery went down and with no alibi but each other.

In the damning video, what you're really looking at are three of Admiral's operatives, with similar physical builds, stealing the C4, and some real good manipulation of the video. I just scanned the target (bad guys) video's faces to isolate phonemes of the subject. Then I matched the phonemes with corresponding visemes, which are the facial expressions that accompany each model's face replacing the target (good guys) video faces.

There aren't many software programs out there that can manipulate a video with such quality and not be available to the public. The Defense's experts will not be able to deny it as admissible evidence, in a court of law," Rene explained. "Also, when I turned Sara's security cameras back on after your break-in, I looped the video and re-established the time clock, so the evidence will show no anomalies." "You are a world-class hacked!" Dutch said.

"So, they are innocent," John stated.

"INNOCENT?" General spouted. "THEY ARE GUILTY AS HELL! and have been for at least five years! You heard Fox News; they have committed treason! Extortion! Bribery! The list goes on! Sara and our two agents belong behind bars along with Rasha Tossa! BPM hires thugs to destroy businesses by looting and fire, assault the police and shoot each other in the process, and when they get arrested for these crimes, BPM lawyers come to the rescue, they pay-off or intimidate the Courts and the criminals get off and are free to re-commit crimes. We're doing the lesser of two evils." "Why is it every time I hear the lesser of two evils thing, I feel like I need a shower?" John replied. "Okay, so what's next on the list of our good deeds?" Rene asked. "The Admiral wants us to take a break," the general replied.

"The election is in two weeks and he believes even if Travis is re-elected in a landslide, the country will suffer major problems because the Democrats are pushing universal mail-in voting., which is not the same as absentee voting. Statistics say mail-in voting will be used by mostly Democrats. It will take weeks to count all the votes. So, say if Travis wins, even though Joe Black is ahead in the polls, mail delays, election board incompetence, and massive disqualification of mostly Joe Black ballots will be the recipe for corruption.

Hell, Democrats rioted at the 2017 Inauguration even though Travis won fair and square. You CAN expect rioting, looting, arson, and violence that will dwarf what has happened so far post-George Floyd killing. A court suit by the Democrats will likely happen, delaying our country of a president. Unless one candidate wins by a margin outside of delayed and disqualified ballots, there are going to be problems. Big league. Go home, take a break, I will need you all refreshed for the next mission," the general ordered.

A necessary stop, October 21st

Later that day, John was on his way home when he decided to make a call. "Pastor Dalton, do you have a minute?" John asked. "John, I've been praying for you, my brother. Do you have time to stop by and have a cup of coffee with me?" Pastor Dalton proposed. "I can be there in five minutes," John accepted.

After catching up with the goings-on of the church, Pastor Dalton asked, "is there something wrong? Something bothering you?" "If I tell you, are you obligated to keep it secret? John asked. "What is said here, is between you and God. Who am I to intercede with that?" Pastor replied. So, John filled him in on the battle in Arizona and setting up evidence against Sara Rosenburg. He told his pastor how he felt about the lies making him feel dirty.

"Did you get a chance to look in the logbooks you stole?" Pastor asked. "I did." "What did you see?" "I saw incoming contributions in the millions of dollars. Twitter, Facebook, Apple, Amazon, Google, big tech companies from Silicon Valley. I saw big payouts to Democratic Congressmen and Senators, MS-13 Antifa gangs, The two FBI agents, Circuit Court Judges, and Mayors. I saw how deep it went," John wept. "John, did you see the movie Star Wars, the first one?" Pastor asked. "Of course!" John choked. "Remember the 'power of the force,' the good side?" "Yes, Luke Skywalker had to learn about the force," John answered. That whole concept of the force is not far from the truth.

In this world, there are two forces: One: the Spirit of Christ, and Two: the spirit of the anti-Christ. The spirit of the anti-Christ is subtle in our day. Many messengers of liberalism disembowel the message of the gospel. They deny the Bible as the Word of God. They deny the deity of Christ. If you do not accept the Spirit of Christ, you auto-default to the Spirit of the anti-Christ. To receive the Spirit of Christ, you MUST be 'Born Again,'" Pastor Dalton retorted. "I know all that Pastor, and I try to help people understand, but what's that got to do with what the militia did to Rosenburg?" John asked.

There are many levels of the anti-Christ spirit. You can be a great person, deep in charity, a Nobel Peace Prize Nominee, a Sunday school teacher in your church, you do good things because you think you're earning points with your image of God. But if do not accept the Spirit of Jesus Christ, you are on the opposing side of Christ.

The deepest level of the anti-Christ is where you might find the Sara Rosenburg's of the world. They are gods in their own eyes, looking out for only themselves, or their personal god of power and wealth. Nothing can stand in their way. "Just like the levels of the anti-Christ, there are levels of the Spirit of Christ. The highest level is how well you mirror Jesus Christ.

To get to that level, you MUST read His word to know all about him, you MUST talk to him in prayer and know His voice, and you MUST go and do what He asks you and when He asks you to. The lowest level of being a Christian is sincerely accepting Jesus Christ as Savior and then just walking away and doing nothing,"

"What about me? Where do you think I am on the level?" John asked. "I can't answer that John because I don't know what's in your heart. I can see the fruit of your heart, like your sincerity in wanting to do the right thing. I know you're reading the word and I see you pray. I can see you have a gift. God set your path as a Navy Seal, a sniper, a good strategist, and God called you to be a Christian. What you did to Rosenburg just may be the beginning of her freedom in prison. Remove the power of the anti-Christ on her life and she might be susceptible to Jesus."

"What about taking a life as a Christian?" John asked. "All through the Old Testament, you can read about life-taking warriors who fought for God, King David, Sampson, and the Maccabees to name a few. The heroes of the New Testament were the Apostles and they fought with the words and teachings of Jesus Christ. But also, in those days of old, they had wars over the stakes of good and evil. I believe most American wars were just that. In the world's societies, Police try to enforce justice, courts weigh the evidence, and the judge's hand out sentences, no different than the days of the Apostles. Whether those sentences are just or not depends on the truth of the judges.

I truly believe that God inspired Thomas Jefferson and the fifty-six men to write the Declaration of Independence. Without a doubt one of the most important documents ever to be written in world history. If God inspired it, then who's going to enforce it? As for me, I sleep better at night knowing you and the militia are at work in America. I will sleep better knowing the Sara Rosenburg's and Juan Los'Cartos are behind bars. But what you need to do is be totally sincere, on your knees, talking to God and reading His word for the answers," Pastor Dalton replied. "Thank you, pastor, it can get pretty confusing." John replied. "The Apostle Paul wrote to the Corinthians that 'Satan is the author of confusion.' Talk to Jesus my brother and clear up the confusion." Pastor suggested.

Post-election results, November 5th Command Center

Fox News:

Two days after the election, there is still no winner. The count is 264 for Joe Black over 213 for President Travis. Travis has challenged the integrity of the vote to an unprecedented and breathtaking degree. Quote, "This is an embarrassment to our country. Socialists are all about tearing down institutions in the United States, and because the battleground States saturation their cities with unsolicited mail-in ballots has introduced the potential for fraud in the presidential election.

When every election can be called into question and thrown into the courts, a power-hungry party doesn't have to develop a sound strategy or run a viable candidate to win. There was a time when an attempt was made to count all of the votes right away. The mail-in scam gave officials an excuse to punt that responsibility. So, Election Day becomes election week and probably election month. The longer the process goes on, the easier it is to introduce fraud into it. You will be told otherwise by "experts," but this is true." President Travis told supporters that he won the election. It's comforting that he's going to fight any ensuing mail-in ballot shenanigans.

General Lipton, Dutch, John, and Rene were in the communication center enjoying their morning coffee, but not enjoying the news. They were expecting President Travis would win in a landslide. "Why do I get the feeling we'll be traveling to D.C. soon?" John asked. "If D.C. becomes a mission, I would think Travis will use the National Guard and keep us in reserve." General Lipton remarked.

"Hey guys, I just received an email from a source in the FBI. They will be storming Rasha Tossa's BPM office with warrants for hers, Sara's, and Mike Durham's computers. They are also collecting warrants for five judges in the Democratic States." "What kind of charges would the FBI arrest her on?" John asked. "My source says the RICO Act, whatever that is" Rene replied. "Let's get Helen Knowles in here and see if she knows what the RICO is," Dutch suggested.

Helen was downstairs when General Lipton called for her. She entered the office and Rene told what was happening. "That's interesting, the RICO Act (Racketeer Influenced and Corrupt Organizations), is a United States federal law that provides for extended criminal penalties and a civil cause of action for acts performed as part of an ongoing criminal organization.

The RICO Act focuses specifically on racketeering and allows the leaders of a syndicate to be tried for the crimes they ordered others to do or assisted them in doing, closing a perceived loophole that allowed a person who instructed someone else to, for example, murder, to be exempt from the trial because they did not actually commit the crime personally. Do you remember John Gotti, the syndicate boss of New York? Rudy Giuliani used the RICO Act to take him down" Helen explained. "Looks like BPM is going to have to start a new chapter," John said, pleasantly sighing with relief.

Suddenly, General Lipton's encrypted phone started ringing. Before she answered it, John said, "Here come our marching orders to D.C." The General was listening, her conversation consisted of only "Sir" and "Yes Sir" then she turned to Rene and asked him to pull up a map of Mexico on the big screen. She walked in closer to the map and listened some more. "Yes sir, I understand, I will brief them right now, Yes sir, goodbye sir." And she hung up.

She sat back down, took a long pull on her coffee, and seemed to be clearing her head. "We have a new mission," she said. "We are going into Mexico to blow up a fentanyl storage warehouse. Apparently, Juan Los'Cartos made a deal with the FBI, in exchange for the warehouse, General Lipton said. "What's in it for him," Dutch asked. "He will get extradited to Mexico for the charges of multi-murders and drug trafficking.

Mexico's been trying to apprehend him for a while." "Why do that? American prisons are like the Hilton compared to Mexico," John asked. "Maybe he has a better chance of getting broken out in Mexico. His brother is now running the Cartel and they are very close," The General replied. "How do we know the factory isn't a trap?" Rene asked. "Because he'll remain in isolation until we blow the factory," The General answered.

"Where in Mexico is the warehouse?" Dutch asked. The General stood and walked up to the fifty-two-inch screen and pointed. "Maijoma Mexico." They all got up to find the tiny town fifty miles south of Texas. "Admiral says the National Guard will handle the protesters for now. The President will be using the Insurrection Act and is now calling the protesters domestic terrorists. Meanwhile, Juan has given us a big gift that will severely hurt the fentanyl market. The President cannot send US forces to do it without Mexico's permission and Mexico will not allow it, so we're perfect for the job," the General explained

"The Admiral says, Cobalt, our Navy Seal, has done something like this mission while operating from Kabul FOB. A Seal Team drove a shitty vehicle forty miles to Ramak to blow up a weapon storage bunker," General Lipton stated. "The Admiral will arrange a Mexican asset to meet you after you cross the Rio Grande near Alamo Chapo. The asset will provide the vehicles to get you close to the warehouse. You will sneak in, kill the guards, blow the warehouse, come home but with no predator support on Mexican soil," The General explained.

"By-the-way, what the Admiral didn't express was what a SNAFU (Situation Normal All F**ked Up) it was. The bunker was two miles away from where the GPS said it was. We had to fight fifty insurgents on our way there, we blew up the weapons, but then got chased back to the FOB by an arsenal of technicals!" John explained. "We better get a team picked for this mission," Dutch suggested.

Los'Cartos Warehouse, Maijoma Mexico, November 5th

Orlando Los'Cartos, the younger brother of Juan, was a small man with a large ego, medium build with thick black wavy hair and mustache, sat in his office with Qassem Soleimani, leader of an Iranian terrorist group. Qassem was a tall lean dark-skinned man with dead shark eyes and a greying beard. "When your men arrive, I will provide supplies and an arsenal for your men, I will loan you my best coyotes to guide you to the best and safest crossing point to America, then my men will guide to Albuquerque New Mexico," Orlando said. "What is a coyote?" Qassem asked. "A name we call our smugglers," Orlando explained.

"My men should be landing at the port, Guaymas tonight. They will immediately travel the two hundred kilometers to Maijoma and will require rest before we leave for America. Then you will give me these coyotes to take us to America," Qassem demanded. "Yes, yes, but I will require two million payment for the weapons and of one million when your feet touch American soil," Orlando demanded. "I agree with this," Qassem replied.

Qassem hated doing business with the Mexican infidels but dealing with the Mexicans was a means to an end. America was on the brink of a revolution and this was the time to attack when America is so weak. *"Someday in the future, these Mexicans will also die by the edge of Allah's Muslim sword,"* he thought.

Orlando showed Qassem around the storage area, proudly displaying the assortment of weapons, pallets of fentanyl, and cocaine. "You sell these drugs in America and yet you assist me with bringing your American customers to their knees, Why?" Qassem asked. "It's our business, it's how we provide for our families, the money is very good.

Our American customers will always need my products and I don't believe your attack will decrease our sales, but my support of helping you isn't about sales, it's about my revenge for the capture of my brother," Orlando swore in Spanish. "You underestimate the terror we will inflict on your customers, my friend. The current revolution in America will magnify the damage I will inflict for Allah's glory," Qassem announced.

Fort Davis Texas, November 6th

Two SUVs arrived at a Fort Davis Texas Walmart where John, Richard (call sign Fog Hat), Ruth (Ebony), and Mike (wolfman) got out of one SUV and Reaper, Steve Cocci (Bam-Bam), a Marine, Explosive expert, Joe Little (Raindancer) a Seal guerrilla combatant got out of the other. "Hey Colton, long time huh? Looks like we declared war on the Los'Cartos family, my brother," Reaper said with a hug. "I sure hope we have a chance to inform Orlando his brother signed his death warrant.

Most of the fighters there already knew each other from the Arizona battle last month and they were all catching up. "So, where's our rides," Reaper asked. "It's two-thirty, they should be here soon.

Not too late I hope, we have an asset waiting for us," John replied. They all stopped talking and watched two beat-up vans drive into the Walmart parking lot and stopped in front of the group. One was a blue dented Ford 1980 something Econoline and the other was a maroon 1990 something Ford Aerostar.

The two agents who drove the junkers there got out and showed their IDs. One said, "They may look like shit, but the engines are in mint condition." They showed the militia how to access secret compartments. There were hidden latches under the floor carpets. When released, the middle and rear seats flipped back revealing largely hidden wells. The eight militia warriors took turns placing their equipment into the wells. "Who rides with who?" Reaper asked. Nobody wanted to ride in the Aerostar because that's where Steve Cocci stored his C4 explosives and Ruth's grenades. Richard drove the Econoline with Reaper riding shotgun and Mike drove the Aerostar with John riding shotgun.

The objective was to cross the border at Presidio City Texas to Ojinaga Mexico then travel south to El Mirador and link up with a Mexican asset in the rural area of Alamo Chapo. The assets would be dropped off by their people and would be waiting for the militia team.

When they arrived at the agreed destination, they approached a dusty beige Ford Expedition. Two people dismounted and started walking towards the vans. One was a young woman; she was tall and thin with black hair cut like a boy. She was pretty but had angry eyes. The other was a teenaged boy. He was a scarecrow in baggy clothes, with a smudgy face and unkept short hair. They boldly walked up to John, who got out of his van and the girl stuck out her hand.

"My name is Michelle Rodriguez, I am Poderoso Uno, but you may call me Micky, and this is Hernandez Gotto, my cousin." "We need to leave now. The police are very curious when people park in the middle of nowhere," she said. The Ford Expeditions drove away towards the dessert and Micky got in John's van and Hernandez got in Reaper's van.

Suspiciously, John commented, "Looks like you're well-funded to have that SUV." When he made eye contact with Mickey, she was smiling and said, "It belonged to Los'Cartos, we stole two from them after we slaughtered the asesinos who drove them." "What are asesinos?" John asked. "Murderers," was all she said. "Turn here." They turned off the dirt road and began driving south through the desert.

Alamo Chapo, Mexico, zero five thirty

"I have a good place to drop off you and your men. It will be less than two kilometers to the warehouse. It will be south of your destination and you will have good concealment when you arrive," Micky explained. "What about our vans," John asked. Me and Hernandez will take them to a safe place. If you can survive your attack of the warehouse, you call me, and we will pick you up at the front gate." The plan made John nervous. Relying on two unknowns with their vans and trusting they will arrive on time when the militia needed them.

"How do you know about our drop-off area?" John asked. "Me and my bandidos raided the warehouse three months ago. We killed everyone and destroyed as much of the warehouse as we could. The Los'Cartos' was back in less than a week and I am told they are at full capacity." "Sounds like you don't like the Los'Cartos' very much," Ruth commented.

"They tortured and murdered my brother and several men raped me, all in front of my parents before they murdered them. Now, these same men are dying one by one by my hand. This is how I got the name, Poderoso Uno," she proudly said. "What does it mean?" Mike asked. "Mighty one," she proudly replied.

They traveled ten kilometers south of Alamo Chapo. They picked up a dirt road and although it was full of potholes, it was smoother than the dessert. The journey was slow and dusty. At zero six forty, the sun was already baking the desert, causing the far away mountains to sway as the heat reflected from the desert's floor. They skirted the Parque Canon de Santa Elena Reserve. They could almost see the green oasis' with cactus and mangroves.

The dirt road turned east and after a couple of kilometers, Micky pointed, "Turn here, south off the road and into this field." "The vegetation is flourishing here," John commented. "Before Juan Los'Cartos came here, this was all farmland, our people are farmers, now they are slaves to the Los'Cartos animals," Mickey replied. After ten more kilometers she told Mike to stop. She got out and informed John, "Your people can get out here. Show me your map." Reaper's van pulled up and he got out. John laid out the map on a hot hood of the van and Micky pointed to where they were.

John checked his GPS and found her to be very accurate. Then she pointed southwest and said, "That is Maijoma." John looked through the scope of his rifle and could make out a village in the distance. You see those hills further south of Maijoma? You will find a good place to camp during the day." Then she pointed south from our position, towards some outcrops and crags and said, "You will find narrows that will take you behind the Maijoma hills and the warehouse will be on the other side.

John opened his backpack and took out a wad of US bills, ten-thousands dollars. She wouldn't take it until John said, "As a leader, my first priority is my people, that's what leaders are supposed to do." She thought about it and took the money.

She handed John a torn-off piece of paper from a cigarette package with her cell number on it. "Call me when you want me to pick you up. I'll be fifteen minutes away. If you capture Orlando, if possible, don't kill him. Tie him up and I will give him what he deserves." John gave her a confused smile. "We'll see you later." Reaper broke up the awkward moment and said, "That kid you brought with you looks like he could use a meal." Micky laughed, "He can eat three chickens and not gain a kilogram." After the militia offloaded all the hidden equipment, Micky got in the Aerostar and Hernandez got in the Econoline, and they drove away.

The desserts of Maijoma Mexico zero seven hundred

They watched the vans disappear into a dust cloud as they drove away to the east. "John folded up the map and said, "Mike, take point and head for the outcrops. Don't move in, we'll send the drone in to check them out. If I wanted to set up an ambush, that's where I'd do it."

When they caught up to Mike, he was on a knee outside the mouth of the outcrops. "Set up a defensive perimeter, Ruth, break out the drone and fly it in for a look," John ordered. Ruth had the drone up and flying in no time. "What's your max distance and battery power? Reaper asked. "The General has been very resourceful; we have the best remote and batteries on this portable drone. How will ten miles and ten hours suit you? Plus, I carry two extra batteries" Ruth answered.

John and Reaper leaned over Ruth's should watching her controller's screen. She flew up the west side of the outcrops and the return flight on the east side in a matter of ten minutes. "All clear," Ruth announced. "Mike, take the point, let's move people, two columns," John ordered.

They started through the outcrop narrows. Steve Cocci, the Marine explosive expert commented to John, "I heard about that mission you were on in Ramak. That was a real gutsy move to continue the mission after fighting through the fifty or more of the insurgents." "Well, It cost us dearly, nobody died but two good men were severely wounded and had to be medically discharged." "You spend any time in the sandbox?" John asked. "I was stationed at the Outpost," Steve replied. John stopped to face Steve, causing his column to also stop.

"You were at the Outpost?" John asked. There were many outposts in Afghanistan, but John knew what Steve was referring to "The Outpost" also known as Camp Keating, a poorly, indefensible base situated in the Kamdesh valley surrounded by Afghan mountains. While business as usual was being shot at by the Taliban from high up in the mountains, the Marine's mission was to try to gain respect from local village elders and convince them to instill peace in the territory.

One day, four-hundred Taliban rallied for a surprise attack. The fight raged on for hours and many Marines died while running out of ammo. The base was overrun and when air support finally arrived, the Marines called the air support to drop their bombs on the base. As Joe Little continued walking past the two, he said, "Your two resumes are making me feel sorry for the hurt we're about to bring on these Mexicans."

They walked on under the heat of the Mexican sun for two miles until John looking down at his GPS on his phone raised a hand and halted the group. In his mic he whispered, "on me." The group gathered around and took a knee. He pointed up to the hill and said, "the warehouse should be on the other side of the hill." The hill was rock, sand, and shrubs. Not much of a vertical climb and not tall. Judging from the rocks and footholds it might take five minutes to climb. There was a small crop of low trees not far from where they were so John ordered the group to get some rest in the shade. "Richard, set up security while Reaper and I climb up for a look."

On the hill, Maijoma Mexico, November 5th

Just as John thought, it was an easy climb, although they had to be careful not to jimmy loose any rocks causing them to tumble down which could create a lot of noise. At the top, they both squeezed in between two large boulders, keeping their silhouette to a minimum. It was enough room shoulder to shoulder. They eased their heads up for their first look.

Down below was a well secure warehouse. It had a six-foot perimeter fence with a double-wide gate for truck access. Between the fence line was thirty yards to the warehouse, plenty of easily defendable open ground for the Cartel. To the left of their position, about a quarter-mile away was the village of Maijoma. The warehouse had a concrete ramp up to a landing for a personnel access door. The loading dock was high enough off the ground for truck loading and a roll-up door. The only problem with having this location for a drug factory was the hill John and Reaper were spying from. Now John understood how Micky must have planned her attack.

There was one guard on the road at the access gate with a small roof for shade. Two guards roamed the perimeter fence moving in opposite directions and they all carried AK-47's. John wondered whether it was Juan's or Orlando's ego considering how inadequate three guards could protect their prize, or even if this was an upgrade since Micky's attack.

Attacking the property of a powerful Cartel family is serious business. John leaned in close to Reaper and whispered lowly, "It's getting close to noon, let's see how they change the guards." Suddenly, they both smelled it at the same time. Cigarette smoke. Reaper slowly moved his head over the crest of the hill and looked down below their position and slightly to the right was a machine gunner's nest outside the perimeters fence on the hill. He lowered himself back and whispered to John, "one man, looks like a twenty cal." So maybe that's their added protection.

Then an SUV drove up and stopped at the front gate, two men got out one took the guard's place, the other walked towards the hill and the off-duty gate guard got in. Then the SUV drove into the compound and two men got out and traded places with the fence guards.

Shortly after, they heard him before they saw the man walking along what must be a path of crushed rocks at the bottom of the hill. He came from the direction of the gate. After a short pass-down with the off-duty gunner he left the nest and met the departing SUV at the gate. John and Reaper had seen enough and made their way back off the hill. After explaining what they saw from the hill, John ordered, "Joe, take over on the hill, radio anything unusual."

Raindancer was a small man but lean and solid. He was a full-blooded Sioux Indian. His last name used to be Littledeer, but he got harassed about it in boot camp, so he eventually had it legally changed to Little. "Everybody else, on me." John and Reaper drew out the target in the desert sand indicating the positions of the four tangos.

"The perimeter guards and the gate guard will be easy, but the machine gunner will be a problem," John explained. "Let Joe take out the gunner. He can sneak up on anything," Reaper suggested. "Put Joe in bare feet and he'll sneak up to a spooked fox," Reaper added.

"Okay, we'll put Joe on the Gunner, but I want scopes on the guards and fingers on the triggers when that happens. If the gunner is alerted before Joe gets to him, it's going to get messy. Execute on my call," John directed. "Ruth, I need your drone ready to fly." John added. "Already waiting," Ruth answered.

Suddenly everyone's radios came to life, "Cobalt, we have visitors. Two troop trucks just arrived," Joe whispered. "Ruth, get your drone up and check it out!" The drone was away in seconds and soon hovering sixty feet above the troop trucks. They all huddled around Ruth's controller screen.

"Hey some of them are in Taliban Pashtun dress!" Mike noted. "What the hell are they doing here?" Richard asked. The Islamic men were disembarking from the troop carriers and going inside the warehouse. "If the Taliban are here, they're on their way to America," Steve commented.

John switched his radio to VOX which is a feature commonly found in higher-end radios. "Striker base striker one," John called the General at Racoon's facility. "Striker one, striker base, reading you five-by-five," radioed the General. "Striker base, our mission just went pear-shaped. Estimate twenty to thirty Taliban just arrived in two troop carriers, please advise," John asked. "Striker one, how is the warehouse?" "Striker base, the warehouse is easy." After a pause. "Striker one, keep your eyes on the Taliban. I want to know where they are going. The warehouse is secondary, take it if you can, but keep eyes on the tangos," the General ordered. "Striker base, tangos priority, house secondary, striker one out."

"John, we're outnumbered and outgunned if Orlando has a cash of RPGs in there," Reaper said. "The Ragheads can't be staying here, they're going to the US, and when they leave, we will need to follow them. We might have to split up and take the warehouse separately," John replied.

"They've come a long way to get here, maybe from the south or they landed on the west coast, either way, they'll need to rest before continuing north. Richard and Ruth, you'll follow the Taliban, the rest of us will take the warehouse and catch up to you. I'll contact Micky and ask her for a safe place to meet you in Maijoma. We all brought tourist clothes on this trip in case things went pear-shaped, I suggest you two break them out now."

Los'Cartos Warehouse, Maijoma Mexico, November 6th

Askary Mabeen got out of the troop carrier and embraced Qassem Soleimani "As-Salam-u-Alaikum wa-rahmatullahi wa-barakatuh" ("*Peace be unto you and so may the mercy of Allah and his blessings*"). Wa alaikum assalaam ("*And upon you be peace!*) "How was your journey my friend?" Qassem asked. "We are grateful for the Chinese hospitality to make us as comfortable as possible on their supertanker," Askary replied.

"How is the situation in America? Is President Travis still in charge?" Askary asked. "Yes, they are still counting votes, but he will lose. The people are still protesting and Travis has directed the National Guard to suppress them," Qassem responded. "I have contacts in a group called Antifa and they will be coordinating a diversion for Border Patrol so we can enter America and safely travel to New Mexico. Come now and meet Orlando Los'Cartos and see what weapons he has for us."

They were met by Orlando as he commenced his tour. They move inside the warehouse and weave their way through pallets of barrels fill with fentanyl and cocaine. They moved in deeper to the villager's section as the slaves packaged the drugs into small plastic wrappers for individual use. They entered through a door and stopped to gaze at the arsenal of weapons and ammunition, AK47s, RPGs, mortars, grenades, C4, and the most impressive, a stack of fifteen crates marked with *9К38 Игла́*.

"What are these Qassem?" Askary asked. "These are 9K38s, Russian/Soviet version of the US Stinger missile, a man-portable infrared homing surface-to-air missile (SAM)" Qassem replied. "I have purchased five for us. Five groups of five men will travel to five National Airports. Their mission will be to shoot down an airliner. If only two groups succeed and shoot down just two airliners in America, they will shut down all flights until their FBI investigations are satisfied. It will take months and cripple the country," Qassem explained. "Allah Akbar!" Askary triumphantly expressed. "Gentlemen we have offices, rooms, and food for your men upstairs. When will you continue your trip north?" Orlando asked. "At dusk," Qassem answered.

On the hill, Maijoma Mexico, November 6th

At sixteen hundred hours, Reaper had Ruth fly the drone because a work detail began loading equipment into the troop carriers. "Looks like RPGs and creates of ammo," Ruth said. "What are those long crates?" Ruth asked. "Zoom in for a better look," John suggested. "Those are Russian markings, 9k38, I've seen that number in security briefings back when I was in.....SHIT! They're stinger missiles! Russian version! They're SAMs!" John announced. "You think they're taking them across the border?" Mike asked. "Why not, what better time when our country is in a revolution," Reaper answered.

John made a phone call and when he hung up he said, "Ruth, pack your drone and bring it with you and Richard. Richard, she's now your girlfriend, make your way to Lana's café on Eldorado street and act like tourists. Carry hidden pistols only, have a meal if you like," John ordered. "Just don't drink the water, Steve joked.

"Micky says you'll have a good view of the warehouse gate from the café. One of her people will be parked right around the corner in one of our vans. These terrorists won't be staying long. When they leave, follow them, and keep a mile behind. Use the drone to track them. Here's a wad of pesos, (three thousand one hundred fifty pesos)." The exchange rate was Twenty-one pesos per dollar. The General gave John four wads of Pesos for their mission.

When John finished his instructions, Joe radioed from the hill, "Cobalt, a school bus just entered the compound." "Great, now what?" John relented. After the bus pulled in, the personnel door to the warehouse opened and about thirty villagers left the building. "Cobalt, the villagers are getting off work. The laborers are leaving. NO replacements," Joe radioed. "Finally, we get a break! No innocents to get in the way," John said.

"After the troop carriers leave, I'll send Joe for the machine gunner. When the gunner is down, on execute, Reaper you take the gate guard, Mike take the left guard and I'll take the right. When they're down I'll bring the wire snips and make a hole in the fence. We'll all fall in on the door and breach. Suppressor fire only, everybody is a target. Steve, you do your thing with the explosives, say, thirty-minute fuses. I want the warehouse evaporated. Micky will meet us out front for exfil. Got it?" John got nods all around.
They were all in positions at nineteen hundred hours when the terrorists started to pile into their carriers, Orlando said his goodbyes and watched Qassem get into the front with a driver and Askary got in front of his carrier with his driver. Soon, they were on their way and Orlando re-entered the warehouse. John whispered into his mic, "Rain Dancer, go ahead." John watched as Joe surveyed the perimeter guards, waiting when both of their backs were turned.

In bare feet, he slowly and quietly stepped down from one boulder to another until he was six feet above the gunner. "All elements, scopes on guards, Rain Dancer, whenever you're ready." Joe gently pulled his k-bar knife and dropped into the gunner's nest completely taking him by surprise. "Execute," John commanded. All three guards dropped as their brains splattered across the ground. John jumped out of his hide and climbed down the hill to the perimeter fence and pulled out his snippers while the others climbed down and set defensive positions. Mike was carrying Joe's ruck and Steve carried Richard's.

Los'Cartos Warehouse, Maijoma Mexico

Twenty seconds later, John moved through the hole in the fence, took a knee on the other side, and immediately set up a defense. Reaper came through next, took a knee, and with his gun up, he was ready. Once they were all through, they had to cross the one hundred feet of open ground to the personnel door. They all fast-walked, crouching, guns up, and covering all directions until they were all at the personnel door. John tried the doorknob and found it unlocked. He slowly opened the door for his first look inside.

The warehouse seemed to be empty except for the pallets of barrels throughout the floor. Single file they moved inside. With hand signals, John directed each to their defensive positions behind pallets. John could hear voices coming from above in the mezzanine. It could have been Orlando talking on a phone. It was in Spanish. He whispered into his mic, "Okey Steve."

Steve moved to the first pallet and opened his assault pack full of C4 explosives and initiating systems hanging from his shoulder. Moving quickly, he planted half of a block, then he pulled out the igniters on the time fuse and primed the charge for thirty minutes. He moved a few pallets away and set another charge and continued to the villager's tables filled with baggies filled with drugs.

John was thinking about how this operation was going too well. No operation went this well. Murphy's law always had a say in operations. No longer crouching he was able to look around the warehouse floor at the millions of dollars' worth of drugs. The rest of the team were also in relax mode and were no longer crouching but guns at their shoulders and watching their defensive assignment.

When Steve got to the weapons storage, he planted the C4 on a crate of RPG rockets. Now he was sure the whole warehouse would be completely destroyed. Still in bare feet, Steve returned to John and gave a hand signal that he was done.

Suddenly one of the mezzanine doors flew opened and four Mexicans filed out. *"Shift change?"* John thought. Everybody froze but were ready to engage. The Mexicans didn't notice the intruders and were casually moving for the stairs when John spoke into his mic, "Take them." The Mexicans were in a tight group and all fell as the suppressed rifle reports, sounding like large hard covered books hitting the concrete floor.

Much to the team's surprise, John shot up the stairs, leaping over the dead bodies, taking the steps two at a time. When he got to the catwalk, with his back to the wall at the unopened door, tried the doorknob. He pushed the door open as a blast of a shotgun splintered the door. John grabbed a flashbang from his vest and held it up for his team to see. They all knew what it was and shut their eyes and covered their ears.

John tossed it in and covered. The less-lethal explosive device used to temporarily disorient an enemy's senses, produced a blinding flash of light filling the warehouse with an intensely loud bang. Immediately after the explosion and with his ears ringing, John stormed into the room to find Orlando squirming on the floor. He zip-tied his hands behind his back and grabbed the back of his shirt collar and started dragging. Keeping watch outside the exit door, Mike heard his team approaching, he radioed "All clear," and they all filed out of the warehouse. John got Orlando on his feet and passed him off to Mike who perp-walked him to the front gate.

Heading for the border, November 7th

One of Micky's rebels arrived in the Aerostar. Micky followed in the other van and behind her was Hernandez driving the SUV. The vehicles pulled up to the guard shack and waited for the team to stow the equipment and pile in. Micky waited at the van's wheel while John pushed Orlando into the back of the SUV. Orlando started screaming, "NO, NO, NO, WHY IS SHE HERE?!?!! Please! I can give you five million US Dollars! Don't leave me with her," and started crying.

John turned to Micky, "you want five million?" "He's worth much more dead to me and our village," she said. "Hey Orlando, you know how many of my Americans you kill each year?" Mike asked. Orlando stopped crying and became silent. "Eighteen thousand DEAD from fentanyl alone!"

Reaper followed Orlando into the SUV, while John rode shotgun in the van. Micky pulled away from the guard shack, she made a phone call speaking in Spanish. John radioed Richard, "Fog Hat this is Cobalt, you have eyes on the package?" "Cobalt, Fog Hat, we are northbound on 18 heading for Potrero Del Llano, the drone is above the package, how did you do?" came his reply. "We're done here, stay on it," John replied.

About ten miles later, they were coming up over a rise in the road when John spotted headlights of a vehicle. Micky said. "They will take Orlando." John tightened his grip on his rifle as Micky got out and walked over to Hernandez's SUV and started manhandling Orlando out. She passed him off to two rebels from the newly arrived SUV carrying AK47s. When the exchange was complete, Micky yelled something in Spanish as the two rebels drove off. "What did you say?" Mike asked. "Save some for me."

A little while later, John was checking his watch, counting down the seconds when the road rumbled under them. Steve was sitting behind John. "Bam Bam, you didn't blow up Maijoma did you?" "Negative Cobalt, it was a controlled blast, that was the RPG ammo cooking off." At the beginning of the mission, John's team had a chuckle back at the Rio Grande when Steve gave his call-sign Bam-Bam. It made perfect sense with explosives being his expertise.

"Okey Micky, let's catch up to the target!" John commanded. John switched his radio to VOX, Striker base, Striker one, do you copy?" "Roger Striker, read you five-by-five." "Striker base, the warehouse is eliminated, the terrorists are moving north on 18. Will keep you advised on the border crossing, out" "Striker one, we'll bring the Calvary to your border destination, Striker base out."

John pulled out his map. Using a red lensed mini light, found Route 18 and radioed Reggie in the SUV behind. "Reaper, Cobalt, they can't try to cross at a border gate, they must have a tunnel under the Travis wall. Maybe they will leave this road between Alamo Chapo and Ojinaga before crossing the border." "Affirmative Cobalt, they can't fly out," Reaper replied.

It was twenty-three hundred hours when Richard radioed John. "Cobalt, Fog Hat, we just left Potrero Del Llano and still north on 18. The next possible town is Alamo Chapo. Maybe they'll fly across the border?" "I really doubt that Fog Hat, they'd never get past out defense radar, guess we'll see soon," John replied.

At zero hundred hours (midnight) Richard called, "Cobalt, Fog Hat, turning off 18 and onto southeast 200, moving south of Alamo Chapo." John reviewed his map again, and switched his radio to VOX so the General could listen in. John called back, "they still have options, but it looks like maybe El Carino and north to Barranco Azul to New Mexico or through the Mexican National Park to Rancho Blanco and cross the Rio Grande into the Big Bend Ranch State Park in Texas. I'm figuring option one." "Rog-o Cobalt will keep you advised."

"No need Fog Hat, I think we're approaching your six if you can see headlights behind you." "I hope that's you and not some Federal Mexican Police." "Fog Hat, we're flashing our headlights." "Welcome to our convoy Amigo. Hey, don't tell Cheryl about my new girlfriend!" "Your secret is safe." John replied. "He's not my type! I prefer dark meat!" Ruth called.

At zero thirty hours, Ruth called, "Cobalt, Ebony, package has turned north towards El Carino." "Striker base, striker one, Package is northbound to El Carino." Was all John had to say. The terrorists still had options to the border, but he knew Dutch and the General could read a map. John's team follow behind through several small farming towns and a couple of wrong guesses as where the terrorist would cross. But now the guesses were all but over. With no question, the terrorist was crossing at Monte Marqueno.

Border Patrol Base Presidio Texas, One hour earlier

General Lipton and Dutch Swanson were met by Captain Manuel of the US Border Patrol. "Now, what's this about? Middle Easterners smuggling weapons across the Rio Grande into the US? According to your phone call, you don't know where they're crossing, but it could be between here and Redford Texas? When do you figure they'll cross? How do you suppose they get over the wall?" "As I said on the phone, I have eyewitness HUMIT (Human Intelligence) in Mexico who have positively identified SAM missiles, RPGs, and thirty armed Middle Eastern terrorists who left the Los'Cartos warehouse in Maijoma driving two troop carriers.

The HUMITs have been following the troop carriers and are expected to cross anytime within the hour. I have no idea how they will get past the wall. My team in Mexico will radio the GPS where they will be crossing. I just need a dozen Border Patrol Officers ready to deploy when I get confirmation where they will cross." The General asked. If they're terrorists, why not call the National Guard?" Captain Manuel asked. "Have you been watching the news? The National Guard is busy busting up riots in Tucson, Portland, Los

Angeles, and Seattle, I couldn't get the National Guard Marching Band if I wanted!" The General said.

"You also said something about troops to support the Border Patrol. What troops are you talking about?" Captain Manuel asked. "I am an active duty General of Regulated Militia. We are armed and can render your Border Patrol support." The General said with resignation in her voice. "Okey, here's what I'll do..." Suddenly a Border Patrol officer ran up to the Captain. "Captain Manuel, "shots fired at the Presidio Border Gate!" the officer said. "What? Are the Mexicans charging the gate?" The Captain asked. "No sir, the shots are being fired from our side. They're shooting at our officers! I think they're rioters!?"

Captain Manuel just stood there trying to wrap his brain around what his officer just said. "Get everybody together and break out combat weapons!" Captain Manuel shouted. After he said it, he realized he needed to be at the barracks to organize the patrol units so they wouldn't bunch up tactical units with patrol units. He started to turn when the General asked about the terrorist threat.

"I will send some units to your crossing. Just let them know where you are and then you can coordinate with them. Use channel two on your radio!" He turned and ran off. The General and Dutch watched him leave. "It's got to be a distraction. We better get back to the troops. We'll find a spot somewhere in the middle of the crossing possibilities." The General said. "You really think Antifa would go as far as to help the Taliban?" Dutch asked. "Without a President right now, nothing is off the table." General Lipton said. As they were walking back to their SUV, they heard John call. "Striker Base, Striker One, Tangos have left the road and are staging to cross at coordinates 29° 28' 0" North, 104°."

The General and Dutch immediately took a knee. Dutch already had his map out and red lens mini flashlight searching for the coordinates. Pointing at the map, he said, "there! They'll need vehicles to receive the weapons and troops. I would post a watch on the Patrol road if I were them, so we can't just drive up on them," Dutch stated. "We'll approach slowly and without headlights, then we'll disembark into the trees. Their trucks will have to travel over two thousand feet through trees off the road to get close to the river at those coordinates." General Lipton stated.

"There must be a hidden road to the river that's not shown on the map," Dutch added "Striker One, Striker Base, your coordinates are confirmed. Close in but don't engage until my call," The General radioed. The General switch the channel "Border patrol, Border patrol this is the militia, do you copy?" Nothing. They assembled with the forty militia soldiers, got in their vehicles, and started down the road. "Border patrol, Border patrol this is the militia, do you copy?" "Go ahead militia." "Terrorist will be crossing at coordinates 29° 28' 0" North, 104°, within the hour." "Copy militia, we'll catch up momentarily."

The Border at Monte Marqueno Mexico and the Rio Grande

They stopped one quarter mile west on the patrol road before the coordinate location, they disembarked, moved into the trees on the opposite side of the road from the river, and began walking. The patrol road runs along the Rio Grande which borders Mexico from El Paso to the Gulf of Mexico in Bagdad. Dutch assigned Leslie Cunningham on point.

Technically, they were in the Big Bend National Park. There was plenty of cover, low trees, and shrubs along the Rio Grande. Dutch could see Leslie ahead of them by using the function of the thermals of his NVGs, so when he saw Leslie's fist rise, he halted. Everybody behind also halted. Dutch couldn't see other thermal images, so he moved up next to Leslie. "There's a northbound dirt road thirty feet ahead," she said. "Move up and check for security watching the road, radio your findings," Dutch ordered.

It took Leslie five minutes to travel the short thirty feet because she was thorough. "No security. There is good cover on the other side of this road. Recommend crossing and setting a superiority defense."

Once the militia had crossed the road and got set up, they saw fresh-cut stumps of trees and the ruts made by coyote's trucks towards the river. General heard, "Militia, border patrol, we're on our way to coordinates." She heard the radio call because she was monitoring channel two and Dutch was monitoring Striker One.

"Border patrol, militia, leave your vehicles next to ours and quietly walk in. The crossing is one thousand feet from our SUVs, Out." She whispered in Dutch's ear, "get a SITREP from Cobalt."

"Striker One, Striker Base, what is your situation?" Dutch called. "Three boats on their way over, SAMs and RPGs onboard with fifteen Tangos. The other twenty are standing by to cross," John answered.

The Rio Grande was about three hundred fifty feet wide at the crossing and didn't take more than fifteen minutes to cross. The real work was carrying the SAMs and RPGs up the wadi and into the awaiting trucks. Once that was done and the boats started across again, Qassem ordered Askary to take five men up to the patrol road and set up security.

The General, Dutch, and two snipers, Larry Wetzel and Scott Major found some high ground, a small knoll some fifty feet behind where the militia was set up behind trees and rocks. Scott and Larry spotted the Taliban's security approaching the patrol road.

Earlier at the Border Patrol Base Presidio Texas, Friday morning

Captain Manuel jogged up to the barracks staging area and was barking out orders organizing the retaliation teams when he received the call of the illegal crossing coordinates. "Terrorist will be crossing at coordinates 29° 28' 0" North, 104°, within the hour," the militia leader called. "Copy militia, we'll catch up momentarily, over. Damn it! Lieutenant Cooper, get over here!" Lieutenant Cooper was lean muscular with a shaved head and crisp uniform. He was a son of a Democrat Congressman and was quickly promoted even though his performance was substandard. Lieutenant Cooper was egotistic and trigger happy and the Captain did not want him anywhere near a shooting with civilians around.

"Yes sir!" Lieutenant Cooper yelled as he approached the pandemonium. "Take Staff Sargent Kramer and four men, two SUVs west on the patrol road to coordinates 29° 28' 0" North, 104° Now! Hook up with a militia General and deal with an illegal crossing, Channel two on radios, GO!" Sargent Kramer heard the Captain's orders and had four agents already picked and standing by two vehicles.

"Great! I have to work with Kramer" Cooper thought. Sargent Kramer was actually a former Marine and who spent time in Afghanistan. Cooper didn't like him for that reason and for sometimes ignoring Standard Operating Procedures and following his instincts. "Kramer, show me a map with coordinates 28° 29' "'0"

North, 104°. Kramer heard the Captain call out the coordinates and Cooper flip-flopped the numbers. Although he did show the Lieutenant the map and pointed to the correct coordinates.

"Carthy, McDonald with me, Brandon and Douglas with Kramer. Mount up!" Lieutenant Cooper ordered. They were all armed with AR-15 rifles and were driving west. Cooper radioed "Militia, border patrol, we're on our way to coordinates." Kramer heard the militia call back, "Border patrol, militia, leave your vehicles and quietly walk in through the trees. The crossing is one thousand feet from our SUVs, Out." When Sargent Kramer saw the SUVs ahead, he called Cooper, "There are the SUVs, why aren't you pulling over?" "We've got six men, enough to handle an illegal crossing, I'm not walking three football fields because some militia thug says to. Turn strobes on." Both vehicles turned on their blue and white light bars.

The Taliban's security saw the headlights before the roof lights came on. One of them had an RPG.

Militia defense at the border crossing

"Border Patrol, militia, you are DANGER CLOSE! Back off! I say again back off!" Kramer stopped his vehicle when he heard the General, but Cooper kept going and hit the siren. Askary had no other option and ordered his man with the RPG to take out the patrol vehicles. Lieutenant Cooper's eyes bulged when he saw the tail of smoke of the approaching rocket. It was the last thing he'd ever see again.

His vehicle exploded in a fireball. "Idiot!" Dutch yelled with disgust. Kramer already had his vehicle in reverse and was spinning up a dust cloud of dirt when the General called, "Militia engage!" The man with the RPG already had another rocket loaded and was pointing at Kramer's patrol truck when the Taliban's head exploded, and he crumbled down next to the RPG. Askary looked across the road to see multiple rifle flashes as bullets riddled his body. The five Taliban security were dead.

The boats were just landing on the Mexico side of the Rio Grande to pick up the rest of the terrorists when the shooting began. John heard the General's order to engage but wasn't sure the order was also meant for his team. In his head, he analyzed the situation and decided not to let the ten Taliban cross the river to join the fight, so he ordered his team to engage. The Taliban on the Mexican side of the river were taken completely by surprise. The half-second it took to switch off their safety's and point their rifles they were all either dead or dying.

One of the two coyotes who were operating the boats jumped out and ran, the other pulled a pistol and got off two shots into the trees before he dropped dead. Richard pursued the running coyote and ran into an opening to find the coyote had stopped and turned, he had Richard in his sights. Richard could see him smiling as the coyote's finger tightened around his pistol's trigger.

When Richard heard the shot, he flinched knowing it would be the last thing he heard. Instead, he looked and saw someone approaching through the trees. He automatically raised his rifle in defense to discover the skinny smudged face kid, smiling at Richard. "Hernandez!?" The kid who drove the team's second SUV into Maijoma. Hernandez stood over the dead coyote smuggler and said something in anger over the body. "Thank you, Hernandez, I've got to get back into the fight." Richard turned and started jogging back when he heard, "Be careful!" Behind him.

Kramer got out with Brandon and Douglas in tow and moved into the trees on the riverside of the road and called over the radio "Friendlies approaching the terrorist flank from the east beside the river," he called. "You've got two trucks and at least ten terrorists ahead of you." Dutch radioed. The General ordered the militia to advance across the border patrol road. The Taliban had good cover of the trucks and a couple of large boulders.

John's team took cover behind what trees they could find and began to engage the Taliban from across the river. From his position, he could see a large section had been taken out of the border wall and two trucks parked on the other side. "Ruth! Can you send a drone with a grenade?" He yelled. "Working on it boss!" She yelled back. It took time to hook up a grenade into the drone's release mechanism so when the grenade dropped, it would leave behind the grenade's pin attached to the drone. Harry Hodge (the former Navy EOD) was a genius coming up with an idea like this. By this time, some of Qassem's Taliban were returning fire at John and his team.

John could hear the bullets buzzing past his head. An RPG rocket flew past their position and exploded somewhere behind them. Splinters flew in his face when a couple of bullets hit the skinny tree he was standing behind. *"All the Taliban needed was to get lucky with one of those RPG rockets and take out his team's position, and it would kill more than one of us,"* he thought. "Striker Base, Striker One, they have us pinned down, we're going to need a little help."

Then, John heard Ruth's drone take off. John yelled, "Ruth, drop it on one of the cargo trucks!" *"maybe we'll get lucky and cook off a SAM missile,"* he thought. then he radioed, "ALL MILITIA, FIRE IN THE HOLE!!"

One hundred feet away, Sargent Kramer could now see the rifle flashes of the Taliban's AK47s. He ordered his two patrol officers, "take cover, set selectors to single shot, pick your targets, aim small, hit small," he instructed. A few seconds later, three shots were fired from Qassem's flank and three of his men fell. In Arabic, he yelled, "they're on our flank!" Now what was left of his men were shooting in three directions. When the General heard John's call, fire in the hole, she switched back to channel two, "border patrol, militia! Get your heads down, fire in the hole!"

Inside the right cargo truck, one of the terrorists saw that they were surrounded and began opening a crate of grenades. Unknowingly, the drone hovered above the truck and released its grenade. It dropped on top of the canvas that covered the troop area of the truck and exploded. The chain reaction started when shrapnel peppered the open grenade crate causing the grenades in the crate to explode. Twenty-five exploding grenades blasted the two SAM crates blowing up the warheads of the missiles.

Leslie Cunningham was one hundred feet from the cargo truck when she saw the explosion. The blast looked like the sun had just risen. The brilliant flash was followed by a hammering boom as the shockwave wave sucked the air out of her lungs and swept by overhead, making the trees sway and creak. The heat might have singed her hair on her head if it wasn't for the Kevlar helmet she wore. When it became quiet again, she realized she was still alive.

Kramer pushed off the brush that covered him from the explosion and looked up. Ten feet away was a skeleton of the second truck and three missile crates skewed around his position. He immediately checked Brandon and Douglas who were pushing off a small tree that toppled on them. "Holy shit, that was fierce!" Private Simon Douglas exclaimed. As Sargent Kramer was standing, he yelled, "Friendlies!" When he heard, "Come forward!"

Kramer and his officers began to trudge through the debris. When Kramer approached the explosion site, he saw the crater and the cab of the truck which was twenty feet away. He looked at the wall and saw a double-sized doorway hole in the wall. The Mexicans must have used torch welding units to cut the hole. People were standing around observing the destruction. Kramer called out to everyone there, "Don't touch anything. This is now a crime scene."

He saw a woman walking towards him. She had a presence of authority. "You heard him, don't touch anything," she said. She stuck out her hand, "General Gail Lipton." He shook her hand, "Sargent Donald Kramer ma'am." "Why the hell did your officer continue to drive up on a hazardous situation?" The General asked. "I repeated your warning to Lieutenant Cooper and warned him myself. He was an egotistic, power-hungry asshole who got two good men killed!" Kramer said in disdain.

"What did you hit the truck with a Hellfire missile from a predator?" Kramer jokingly asked. "We used a grenade attached to a portable drone. It must have ignited something very volatile inside." Dutch said as he approached the two.

On the other side of the Rio Grande, John and his team were saying their goodbyes to Micky and Hernandez. John rummaged in his backpack and pulled out the rest of the money and handed it to Micky. Again, she refused to take it. "Micky, Maijoma needs this money, it's not for you. You said Maijoma use to be farmlands. Buy seeds, cows, and chickens. I'm sure with the warehouse gone, wages are gone too," John explained.

She snarled, "what wages! My people were slaves." She practically tackled John with a hug and said, "Come back and visit us, you and your people will be treated well!" John returned the hug before he turned and got in a boat. He looked back and saw Richard still embracing Hernandez. "Com'on Rich, we got to get back." Soon, they were on their way across the river, going home.

Fox News:

Border Patrol met heavy resistance from terrorist when they tried to illegally cross the border. Lieutenant Dwayne Cooper who is the Son of the Democratic Congressman George Cooper came upon the terrorists as they landed on the US side of the Rio Grande in Redford Texas. The terrorists were smuggling weapons into the United States.

Lieutenant Cooper was killed after displaying a heroic attempt in challenging the intruders. Much of the evidence exploded when Border Patrol engaged in a gun battle and inadvertently hit hidden explosives. Fifteen bodies were identified by the FBI as Iranian Fundamentalist, two of which were on their watch list. Two other Border Patrol Officers were also killed. Their names are being withheld until their families are notified.

Not far from that battle, was another development in Presidio Texas, as Border Patrol were fired upon from the American side of the border. Three Border Patrol Officers were wounded, and five Americans involved were captured. An anonymous source says that the Americans were identified as Antifa members and were conspiring with the Iranian terrorists crossing in Redford.

In more news, the Grand Jury has acquitted two of the three police officers involved in the no-knock shooting incident of Brenda Taylor in Louisville Kentucky yesterday. The three officers serving a warrant on the boyfriend of Brenda Taylor were fired upon, wounding one officer. Taylor subsequently died when police returned fire. Shortly after the announcement of the acquittal, the protest went from peaceful to burning buildings, violence, and looting.

As expected, the 2020 presidential campaign season has evolved into a post-election battle consisting of legal challenges in crucial battleground States after the discovery of vote watchers blocking, dead voters, and sworn affidavits of tampering. The game isn't over, the Republicans are taking it to the courts.

CHAPTER FIFTEEN

Militia Breakfast Celebration, Saturday, November 14th

General Lipton's team had returned from their successful mission in Redford Texas, and all the Militia members and spouses were celebrating by throwing a Militia Breakfast. Although the militia was never mentioned in the news about defeating the terrorists in Texas, the local public was aware it was General Lipton's Militia who blew up the Los'Cartos drug and weapon's warehouse in Maijoma, Mexico, then defeated the terrorists from crossing over to Texas. The breakfast was a festive event with congratulatory conversations and laughter.

Richard and his wife Cheryl approached John and Leah with plates of breakfast foods, finding a table they could all share, they all sat down. When they finished eating, Richard asked John if he could have a word in private. "What's up brother," John asked when they were alone. "You know I had a close encounter with death at the Rio Grande. That kid Hernandez saved my life when that coyote had me dead to rights." "Yes, I heard. I see a trip to Maijoma in your future," John replied. "Absolutely John, but that's not what this is about.

You know, I never made the decision about accepting Jesus Christ in my life. That's what went through my mind in those few seconds starring down the barrel of the gun that was going to kill me. I was about to die in my sins. I need to make that decision and Cheryl does too. What do we need to do to receive salvation?" Richard asked.

"I can promise you this Richard. THAT decision is THE most important decision in life. If we're lucky enough to live eighty-five years in this life, it's but a fleeting moment in time compared to life in eternity, and there are only two places to go into eternity, heaven or hell," John expressed.

"Can I ask why God would send anybody to an eternity in hell?" Richard asked. "Richard, God does not want to send ANYBODY to hell. People reject God, not the other way around. God has made it abundantly clear He exists. Everybody can feel His promptings. But people either harden their hearts or create a god in their own minds. God sent Jesus Christ into our world to die in our place, but instead of worshiping Jesus, we use His name as a cuss word. Look how simple it is," John explained.

There's a scripture in the Book of Romans Chapter 10 verses 9 & 10 that says: *'If you declare with your mouth, "Jesus is LORD," and believe in your heart that God raised him from the dead, you will be saved. For it is with your heart that you believe and are justified, and it is with your mouth that you profess your faith and are saved.'* All you and Cheryl need to do is talk to God. For example, just say:

God, I confess that I have sinned, and I know that sin will keep me out of heaven. I realize there is not one single thing I can do to earn my way into Your kingdom. Right now, I am placing my trust in Jesus' death on the cross, His burial, and resurrection from the grave as payment for my sin. I now receive Jesus as my Lord and Savior, and I commit my life to you. Thank you for forgiving me and giving me Your Holy Spirit. I submit this prayer in Jesus' name. Amen," John explained.

"Can it be that simple? We don't need to get clean before approaching God to ask for such a great favor?" Richard asked. John giggled, "How can you possibly get clean if only God can cleanse you?" John explained. "Can I pray that prayer right now and be saved?" Richard asked. "Absolutely brother! And I'll help you if you want!" John said. So, in his own words, Richard spoke with the God of the universe and asked to be saved.

After the prayer, Richard looked at John and had a tear in his eye. "MY GOODNESS John! I feel so different!" Richard expressed. "That's the quickening of the Holy Spirit entering into your new life," John explained. Just like the hug Richard gave Hernandez a few days earlier, he gave to John and said, "Let's go get Cheryl!"

Militia Communication Center, Monday, November 16th

The twenty unit leaders were assembled in the general function area outside the communication center, awaiting General Lipton's presentation for the next possible mission. John Colton was assisting Rene with his workstation which would display a map of the next mission theater. "So, Rene, where are we going this time?" John asked. "We've been working all these years together, have you ever known me to break a secret?" "Hmm, I guess I'll have to wait," John replied as he was just taking his seat among the unit leaders when General Lipton walked out of the communication center.

"We've been asked by the Kentucky militia to assist them in breaking up the riots in Louisville. As you may have seen if you've been watching the news, Black People Matter has been protesting the fatal shooting of Brenda Taylor, and two days ago, the Grand Jury released its verdict acquitting two of the police officers. The third will be brought up on the reckless discharging of his firearm into the neighboring apartment. The protests have increased in the violence, destruction, and looting since the verdict was announced. "I have a question," Mike Ackroff said raising his hand. "How does a militia in Kentucky know how to contact us in Maine?"

"Gunny Ann Wilson has developed a website encouraging States and Townships to develop Militias. We're not identified on the website but have a one-eight-hundred number to call for more information on how to get started. If you haven't noticed, Bob Simpson, Elijah Goffstien, and Helen Knowles have been missing lately. They have been traveling around helping some of these militias to get off the ground with weapons handling, Combat fighting, and the legal use of force."

Dean Tron raised his hand and asked, "I get the cops were doing their job serving the warrant, but do we know on what grounds the warrant to search the apartment was approved?" "When did you become a legal beagle, Dean?" Dick Vinaldo asked with a chuckle

"There is a Detective named Josh James who was investigating a drug traffic ring in Louisville. He submitted an affidavit describing substantial evidence that Brenda Taylor's house was being used for drug trafficking by her boyfriend Jake Walker and two others. He noted pending drug charges against the two men and during his investigation witnessed fifteen to twenty vehicles going to and from the house within a week. He set up a surveillance camera which caught one of the men dropping and concealing a large, blue cylinder-shaped object the night of the warrant which led to the shooting and a house empty of any drug evidence."

Dutch Swanson spoke next, "The reason we're being asked to help is that the protests may be on one street, but the violence and looting can happen anywhere within a ten-block location and neither the Kentucky militia nor the police have enough personnel to cover the area." "So, we'll fly down with ten five-man ground units and ten sniper teams, link up with their militia and develop a plan with them," The General explained.

"Okey Rene, get the map up," The General asked. "We'll fly an Air Force DC9 into Louisville International, by-pass customs and picked up by the Kentucky militia using school buses. They will take us to their facilities at Jeffersontown. After a meet and greet luncheon, they'll debrief us, and we will establish a coordinated plan to protect business with force if necessary. Dutch will choose the unit leaders who will choose five people for their teams and John will choose his sniper teams."

Louisville Kentucky militia, 2nd AM Center, November 17th

When the General's team got dropped off in Louisville, they were standing in front of a two-floor warehouse-size building with the neon sign "2nd AM Center." Two men dressed in desert camouflage escorted the team inside. The first floor was a paintball entertainment center with a jungle of fake trees, hills, small cottages. Elevators were available to the 2nd floor but would take too long carrying the 62 militia upstairs only one floor. When they arrived there, they were looking at an open space gym type area much like their own.

The General, Dutch, and John were met by a woman named Viola

Waite. She was a beautiful woman with shoulder-length brown wavy styled hair, glamorous make-up, a beauty mark on her left cheek, and a figure of a model. She reminded John of a young actress of the 1950s, a brunette version of Hedie Lamar.

"I am Captain Viola Waite and I'd like to welcome you to our militia center. Next to her was a big black musclebound solid six-foot bruiser with a bald head dressed in a custom made suit. "This is Master Sargent Leon Russel, Leon owns this business," Viola said. "What are you a Captain of?" John asked. Leon put his hand on John's shoulder giving him a tight squeeze and said, "Captain Waite served in the 15th Marine Expeditionary Unit and fought courageously in Operation Moshtarak, the Battle of Marja; and Operation Mountain Reach II, Battle of Daridam.

"I was in Daridam after that battle. My Seal Team's mission was to clear the town of snipers. I would have noticed you there unless you were in that unit that got cut off in Tor Shezada?" John replied. "That was us," The Master Sargent said. "We were surrounded but managed to fight through a fortified bunch of pussies who went crying to our government complaining we didn't fight fair." "Come on gentlemen, let's quit comparing dicks and get something to eat," Viola said with a smile. John and Dutch just looked at each other and then followed behind her towards the food.

The two militias seemed to be getting along just fine. The food was prepared in the facility's kitchen was good and there was energy in the room with friendly conversation and laughter. Captain Waite finished her meal and walked to the front of the room where she pulled down a sheet covering a ten-foot-long and six-foot-wide map of Louisville's Route 264 beltway nailed to the wall. On the map were red pins and black pins. She explained that the red pins were businesses violated and the black pins were the unmolested businesses. "As you can see, there doesn't seem to be a pattern of destruction. The rioters have evolved in their tactics. They have learned from other big city riots not to be in the same place as the protesters. This is why we asked for your assistance. Our numbers can't be in every place the rioters go to burn and loot.

By this map, you will also notice the destruction remains inside the Route 65 and 60 corridors. I understand you have brought ten snipers who can aim well over three hundred meters and I have three. I believe if we can strategically place those snipers in positions where they can call in where the groups of rioters are attacking, our ground troops will be able to travel to those locations and discourage the cowards. General Lipton stood up from her table and approached the map for a closer look. "I assume you already have overwatch positions and a plan determined?" "I do General, with twenty units of five militia, we can cover the city.

I plan to assign my drivers for all of your teams. The city will be divided into grids and each unit will be assigned a grid. The driver will know their grid, we've had time to study them. The snipers will also have grids and will call in disturbances in their grids," Captain Waite explained. "Excellent plan, you've done your homework. When do you want to set-up?" The General asked. "Tomorrow night, the action doesn't usually start until after curfew."

Unit Four, West Oak Street, Louisville Kentucky, November 18th

Dean Tron was in a rented Ford SUV. They were parked in the Filson Historical Society parking lot which was currently boarded up due to the riots. "Man! This city has a lot of streets! I always thought Kentucky was mountains, coal mines, and forests," Dean commented. "Brother, we have the most spectacular mountains and forests in the country but dah! We have cities too," the driver Jason said. As they were laughing, sniper Larry Wetzel radioed, Unit four, Unit four, I'm looking at a half dozen insurgents with battering weapons gathering outside the "Stop and Go" on West Oak Street, I can not identify any arms."

"Copy Sniper four," Dean radioed. Jason started the car and was spinning his wheels in seconds and fishtailing onto Hill Street. They quickly traveled five blocks down West Oak, arriving at the "Stop and Go" within two minutes. When they arrived, the rioters were already breaking the glass to the grocery store. The Rioters had two vehicles, a van, and a pick-up truck. Jason and Dean's unit piled out of their vehicle. Armed with concealed pistols and batons Kevlar vests and helmets, approached the insurgents. "Halt what you're doing and step away from the window!" Dean commanded.

The Insurgents all stopped and turned in surprise that somebody was confronting them. One of the insurgents ran away when he saw how Dean's team was well equipped. A short white man wearing a hoodie had a concealed pistol in the pouch of his hoodie, quickly drew it out, and pointed it at Dean. Smack! Dean jumped when he heard the sound. The insurgent dropped his pistol as his bicep began bleeding, stumbling, he fell.

Of the remaining four, three held bats, and the fourth pulled out a switchblade. "I strongly suggest you drop your weapons and let us cuff you, we'll call the police and you can make bail within the hour!" Dean said.

Each insurgent waited until one of them dared to attack. When they finally did, Dean and his team avoided the initial attacks and answered with batons aimed at arms and legs. Within forty seconds, the four insurgents were laying down, groaning on the sidewalk while Dean's team zip-tied their wrists and ankles and applied a tourniquet to the bleeding arm.

The storefront door opened up and a man in his sixties came out with a shotgun. "I saw everything, thank you so much! Can I offer you all a six-pack of beer, your choice?" "We appreciate your offer sir, it's not Miller Time yet. Can you call 911 and explain what you saw to the police?" Dean asked. He looked down at the groaning rioters and said, "These won't be returning to the streets anytime, soon right? "I suppose not," Dean replied. So, the store manager kicked one of them in the gut and pulled out his cell phone. Dean smiling, returned to his SUV, and radioed Larry, "Nice shot sniper four, I never heard the report of your rifle." Larry radioed back, "aren't suppressors great?"

Unit One, West Breckinridge Street, Louisville Kentucky

John and his spotter were in the bell tower of St. Stevens Church when the spotter noticed two vans pull into the Heaven Hill Bernheim Distillery. "Hey John, check out that plant on West Breckinridge Street. Two vans just barreled through the front gate," his spotter Alice Gray said. "Unit one, Unit one, I have a breaking and entering at the.." "It's a distillery," Alice interrupted after referring to her map. "I have a B&E at the West Breckinridge Street Distillery. Two vans, eight insurgents, three with long rifles, identify weapons as AR-15s. Alice, call 911 and tell the police friendlies have robbers cornered inside the distillery." John ordered.

Mike Ackroff's unit was parked at BJK Industries three blocks away. John watched as their lone Humvee ran a red light from South 15th Street onto West Breckinridge Street and turn off their lights as they entered through the distillery's front gate. When Unit one arrived, the door, according to the sign, "Employee Entrance" was already opened. Unit one piled out on the opposite side of their Humvee from the robbers just as shots were fired from inside.

Mike could hear the sound of bullets pelting the vehicle and buzzing by overhead. Mike's team was pinned down. From his perch, John watched as one robber would step out of the doorway every time he shot. So, John set his receptacle on the spot the shooter would emerge from. When the shooter exposed himself, John fired his Heckler & Koch M110A1 CSASS from two hundred fifty meters. The shooter went down but John wasn't sure where he hit him.

The other shooter opposite from the shot burglar continued to fire. All John could see was his rifle sticking out the door. His team-mates were pinned down and John had to do something. He aimed, controlled his breathing, and let his finger break the trigger, and fired. John's bullet hit the stock of the shooters AR-15 and fouled the slide. By this time police sirens could be heard in the distance. Mike radioed John "Sniper one, can we enter the building and go after the robbers?" "Negative unit one, debrief the police and let them handle it. Maintain support," John answered.

As they were finishing their communication two cruisers sped into the parking lot and pulled up behind Mike's team. The police aimed their weapons at Mike's team yelling "HANDS!!" When John saw what was happening, he called the General. After reporting in, John watched on as the police were cuffing his team. One officer in charge sent two officers around the back of the building to watch the back exits. *At least that officer in charge knows what he's doing,* John thought. Five minutes after John reported in, the officer in charge obviously received a radio call and ordered his men to uncuff the militia unit.

"I don't know who you are, but my Station Chief just told me to let you go. Now would you please leave the area?" The Sargent suggested. "Before we go, can I offer a suggestion?" Mike asked. "Make it quick, I'm busy here," the Sargent said. "Take out your blow horn and tell the shooters that SWAT will soon arrive and enter the building and will shoot to kill. We neutralized at least one of the robbers who were firing on us, so they know you'll be serious. Maybe they'll surrender," Mike explained shrugging his shoulders up. The Sargent took the advice and as Mike expected the robbers came out and surrendered.

That night, back at the Police Station when the seven robbers were questioned (One robber was killed) the police discovered one of the robbers was an employee of the distillery who disabled the security camera and stole a key to the door. They intended to steal a few barrels of bourbon and sell them to any unspecified bar across the border in Indiana.

Eastern Parkway Protest, Louisville, Kentucky

Richie Foley, a leader of Antifa, was in the dining room of some college kid's home on Dixie Street with a dozen others. Three college students shared the house and unable to attend their college due to the pandemic. Foley was a black man of medium build with dreadlock hair. Four of the twelve people there were actually from the Antifa organization, the others were college friends of the house just there for the rush. They were making plans with Foley for the revolutionary attack on the fascist establishments by creating violence while under the protection of Eastern Parkway Protesters.

The Antifa revolutionaries traveled from Philadelphia, all expenses paid by some secret support organization. On the table were dozens of M-80 firecrackers, roman candles, Bic lighters assorted aero spray containers with alcohol in the ingredients, American Flags for burning, and a box of Molotov cocktails. Also, on the table was an ounce of marijuana laced with angel dust (PCP). Two joints were being passed around while discussing their strategy.

"Look for anything burnable like dumpsters, burn the plywood boarding up storefronts or houses, burn your flags inside the groups of protesters, and rally them up. Harass the pigs. We'll have frozen water bottles there. Throw them at the pigs!" Foley ordered. "We are 100% Antifa! We will be a pain in this administration's ass," Foley yelled. "We will harass those frigging Republicans for voting for Travis!" another Antifa leader yelled. "LET'S GO!" Foley yelled. "LET'S GO!" the others yell in unison, and they piled out of the house.

Steve Paris (Sniper six) was watching the protesters in front of the Louisville Metro Police Station from a high rise on Reasor Avenue. His spotter, Scott Hamlin, was flying a portable UAV Drone above the protesters looking for insurgents. Steve spotted a large group of people approaching the protester from Lydia Street. "Unit six, this is sniper six, I'm tracking ten to twelve people approaching the protesters. I can't see any weapons but they're carrying boxes. Looks like trouble to me," Steve radioed. "Roger sniper six, we'll dismount and join the protest from East Burnett Avenue," Maggie Lester replied.

Maggie was a light-colored black woman, small in stature, but solidly built. An ex-Army Lieutenant of the 1st Cavalry Division ("First Team"), one of the most decorated combat divisions of the United States Army during Operation Iraqi Freedom. "Scott, fly your drone over that group and see if you can identify what's in the boxes they're carrying," Steve asked. "On it Steve," Scott replied.

Maggie's driver found a parking spot on East Burnett Avenue and the unit dismounted from their Ford Aerostar van. They began the short walk north to the intersection of the Eastern Parkway and turned right towards the protesters. They passed a lot of private homes and soon could see a large park-like area where the protesters were making their stand.

Using the UAV's zoom camera, Scott reported, "I can see what looks like Molotov cocktails, bottled water, and American flags?" "Unit six, the Antifa group will be approaching the protesters from your opposite direction and are carrying Molotov cocktails and possible frozen bottled water. Be aware, police have all entrances to the building guarded," Steve reported. Maggie's unit arrived at the same time as Antifa. Unit six began intermingling with the protesters while Antifa was doing the same.

Foley was carrying the M-80's and roman candles and began passing them out and lighting them off right in front of one of the militia.

"Where you from? The militia driver named Josh Buscemi asked. I'm from Philadelphia, here to help you people," the Antifa answered as he threw another M-80 near the police line. "This is a peaceful protest and we don't need an out-of-stater here to help us with anything!" Josh said as he got in the Antifa's face. When the Antifa pushed Josh, Josh unleashed a quick aimed shot of his baton into

Foley's groin. He went down and couldn't squeeze out a sound. Another militia named Alice walked up to another Antifa who just set down the case of Molotov cocktails and struck him in the knee at the same time another militia struck the Antifa carrying the frozen bottled water.

The violence happened so quickly, and the sounds were suppressed by the chanting for the protesters, nobody noticed except for the college students who came with them and a few others. The college students who were stoned on the PCP and pot combination looked on as one thousand thoughts ran through their minds. PCP has a vast spectrum of effects on people based on their characteristics. While some experience a sense of strength and invulnerability, violent hostility, and psychoses indistinguishable from schizophrenia, others receive Auditory hallucinations, image distortion, severe mood disorders, acute anxiety, and a feeling of impending doom.

Everybody's heard the stories of the crazed psychopath, who continued to attack after being shot several times. The college students just stood there watching their Antifa leaders go down in slow motion, confused with whether it was a hallucination. The adrenaline rush was gone, now paralyzed in the state of impending doom. They were either speechless or pleading with the feared militia. "Go home or face pain," Josh told them.   In a matter of minutes, the Antifa group was neutralized and the students were leaving. The militia picked up and carried off the boxes as the protesters turned on them and began criticizing the militia's tactics, turning away from the police they began yelling and chanting. The militia just walked away unmolested.

Mayor's Office, 527 W. Jefferson Street, Louisville Kentucky

It was turning out to be a long day for Democratic Mayor Greg Foster who was still on a conference call with the City Council, the governing body of the City. The City Charter lays out the rules and regulations under which the City operates. The Mayor is elected at-large and two council members are elected from each of the City's three wards, each to a four-year term.

The protests being the number one issue and the Mayor was still resisting that the Black People Matter platform disbanding the police be implemented and the Mayor should appeal to a higher court and put pressure on the Attorney General Daniel Cammer to find all three officers involved in the shooting of Taylor be found guilty. "Has anybody told that asshole Cammer that he's fu**ing black and betraying his race?" One of the councilors said. "Look, it's unfortunate that Cammer has a different political philosophy, but because of his role as the attorney general and special prosecutor in the Taylor investigation, he believes he is leading with all the facts and truth. As for his color? Who's being the racist here?" Mayor Foster replied. "I May be a Democratic, but I'm not drinking that Kool-aid," the mayor added. "You need you to get on-board or face the consequences. If you won't agree with this council, we will have to report this to the media," another councilor threatened. "I am a Democratic, true blue! I AM NOT a Marxist!" The Mayor yelled and cut off the conference call.

Holiday Inn Express & Suites, Louisville

Antifa leader Don Lemmon was on a Zoom call with the co-founder of the Black People Matter movement, Patrisse Colon, a black woman with short afro hair and a mole in the middle of her forehead, who is a protégé of Eric Manning, former agitator of the Weather Underground domestic terror organization for over a decade, spending years training in political organizing and absorbing the radical Marxist-Leninist ideology which shaped her worldview.

The politics of BPM had fallen on her after the arrest of Rasha Tossa.

"I want you to invade the Mayor's office and threaten him or his family, whatever type of violence works in changing his mind. He needs to submit to the Marxist movement, adopt the BPM ideology and fire that Uncle Tom Crammer!" Colon ordered. Don Lemmon was a medium build, a handsome black man with close-cut afro hair from Philadelphia.

"I visited the building today. His office will be easy to attack. My hacker is disarming the security as we speak," Lemmon replied. "Do you have enough Antifa to secure the Mayor?" Patrisse asked. "My team is all I need to secure Mayor Foster. I'll call you from his office when I have him," Lemmon said and hung up.

Don Lemmon left his room and rode the elevator down to the lobby to find his Lieutenant Dave Scully waiting for him. "We all set?"

Don asked. "Van is warmed up and ready to go," Dave answered. They walked out to cool air to find the running van, Dave got in the driver's seat and Don got in the passenger side. Behind him, Lloyd Davis was tapping on his laptop and a large man named Fred Lawrence (the muscle) was drinking a large coffee.

Kentucky International Convention Center, Louisville

Arty Nelson was one of the three snipers on Viola's team. Although in his late sixties, he was in very good shape and had 20/10 vision. He and his spotter, Connie Sked were on the western edge of the Kentucky International Convention Center's rooftop. "Hey Art, it's just a gut feeling, but check out that black van that just pulled up to the front of the Mayor's office." They both directed their scopes towards the van and watched three people disembark.

"I don't mean to be racially profiling, but they don't look political enough to be going in there," Art commented. "Unit two, this is sniper two. If you're not busy, can you check something out?" Art radioed. "What do you have sniper two, I'll take anything you've got, I'm bored," Viola radioed. Viola was a hands-on type of leader. She worked at an upscale real estate office and loved moving around from estate to estate.

"We just spotted three suspicious characters entering the Mayor's office on Jefferson. We didn't see any weapons, but they could be concealing." Art informed. "We're right around the corner. We'll go look and see," Viola replied. "Okey, we see you now." Viola was driving her Jeep Humvee and slowly passed the building. "I don't see the guard that's usually there inside the window," Shubert Spero reported.

Shubert was Kentucky's militia combat trainer. They turned the corner and parked. The sidewalks were empty, so Viola got out, opened the tailgate, and opened a clothes bag. "I need to get into something more distracting," she said. So, she changed out of her pull-over sweater and cargo pants right there on the sidewalk.

Mayor's Office, 527 W. Jefferson Street, Louisville Kentucky

Now dressed in a white blouse, light blue short dress with matching shoes and purse, she placed her pistol and radio in her purse. "I'll enter first. I won't be able to hear you, but you'll be able to hear me.

I'll radio you when I'm in, and we'll go upstairs together. "Kevin, check out their van," Viola ordered. Let's try not to kill everybody," she directed and walked off.

Viola approached the entrance and as Shubert said, the guard was not there. She found him under his desk. He was gagged and tied. She spoke into her purse, "Front lobby is clear, the guard is down and alive. Get in here," she ordered.

Meanwhile, Kevin snuck up on the van and slid open the side door and found a shocked Lloyd Davis. Kevin stuck his pistol in his face and asked, "Can I join you?" and got in the van.

The others were just outside the building waiting, so they moved inside within seconds after Viola called. "Untie the guard and have him call 911. You all take the stairwell to the fourth floor, I'll be taking the elevator," she said. "Be careful boss," Shubert said. Master Sargent Leon Russel began to untie the guard and noticed the burn marks on the guard's jacket's chest area. "Viola, they stunned the guard!" he called as she was walking towards the elevator and threw him a thumbs-up signal.

When the elevator dinged on the fourth floor, thirty feet down the hall at the reception's desk Fred Lawrence straightened up and face towards the opening elevator door. Viola exited the elevator like she owned the place. As she approached Lawrence, she smiled and said "Your new here? I'm Gail, Greg's sister. I'm just visiting," as she walked closer. Focused on the cleavage of her low buttoned blouse, he replied, "Greg's in a really important meeting right now. Come back in an hour, he should be done by then," Fred replied. "Oh damn! Can I leave a message, you got a pen?"

Now she was an arm's length from Fred. He glanced down at the desk for a pen. When his eyes averted down, Viola smashed her knee up into his groin. When he doubled over, she slammed her fist down on the back of his neck knocking him out. She whispered into her purse "Hallway is clear." Her team was waiting down the hall in the stairwell. They entered the hallway and positioned on both sides of the Mayor's door.

Inside the Mayor's office, Don Lemmon and Dave Scully were warning Mayor Foster. "We have your wife and children and they are safe at this time, but you need to assure us that you will fire the

Attorney General Daniel Cammer and call a mistrial of the three pigs in the Taylor shooting," Don cautioned.

"Please, leave my family out of this! They have nothing to do with this," the Mayor pleaded. Dave slapped the Mayor on the side of his head. "You don't get it! Your family will not be safe until Cammer is looking for a new job," "Okey, I'll do what you asked, just leave my family alone," the Mayor relented.

A faint thump was heard outside in the receptionist lobby. "Dave, check Fred, make sure everything is alright," Don ordered. When Dave opened the door, he screamed as his body was hit with 50,000 volts from the stun gun, and Shubert Spero rushed in with his pistol pointed at Don's face. "HANDS!" Shubert shouted. "Who are you!" the Mayor asked. "Don't worry Mayor Foster, we're the good guys," Viola said as she entered the room with the stun gun electrodes still attached to Dave and stepping over his squirming body on the floor. "They have my family! They threatened to hurt my family if I didn't fire the Attorney General!"

Viola took the radio mouthpiece out of her purse and looked at Shubert, "What grid is the Mayor's house in?" Shubert took out his map which was marked up by grids, "Grid five," he answered. "Unit five, this is unit two over." "Go ahead unit two." "Get over to Mayor Greg Foster's home and confirm a possible hostage situation. Knock on the door as a relative or something. Call 911 if something seems fishy.

This could well be a hostage situation, call me back ASAP! Unit two out." Then she approached Don and said, "They're going to put you away for this. Attorney General Daniel Cammer is going to have a field day with your ass. Let us know right now if the Mayor's family are hostages and go easy on yourself," Viola offered. Don remained silent.

A few minutes later, "Unit two, unit five, the Mayor's house is clear. His family is frantic and wants to know if he's okay." "Tell them he's fine. He'll call his wife right now." Viola looked at the Mayor and nodded her head towards the desk phone, and he picked it up immediately.

Shubert slapped Don's head and snidely remarked, "You were bluffing the Mayor? Typical amateur." Shubert finished zip tying the perps as sirens could now be heard miles away in the distance. When the Mayor hung up with his wife, Viola touched his shoulder saying, "listen Greg, we're having a busy night and don't have the time to answer all kinds of police questions, so we'll be leaving now." "How can I thank you?" He asked. "Don't disband or defund the police," then she and Shubert left. When the Police arrived out front, they found the black van and inside a tied-up Lloyd and a tag on his computer with 'EVIDENCE' written on it.

2nd AM Center, Zero eight hundred hours, November 21st

After going through the buffet line and gathering their breakfast, John and Dutch sat at Viola's and Gail's table. "It is nice that your families take this Friday morning to prepare such a delightful meal," Dutch complimented. You've been with us two days dismantling ten Antifa attacks on businesses and civilians, one Distillery robbery, and a hostage situation of a high-end politician, it's the least we could do," Viola replied. "Do you see any missions in your future?" Viola asked. "I made a request to my boss that we get some time off to enjoy Thanksgiving and Christmas. We've been away a lot and some of the wives have been complaining. I don't want to be on their hit lists," Gail said laughing. John, Dutch, and Viola all laughed with the General.

"Have you heard about something not so funny? The Marxist half of the Democrat party are creating lists of supporters of President Travis. They will turn the list over to Antifa. They are calling them "Purge Lists" Once Antifa gets the lists, I'm sure they will begin to target and harras them," Viola said. "That sounds like what the Marxist leader did earlier in history. A Purge List was created by Joseph Stalin in 1936 and was officially used for the prosecution of people considered enemies of the state by the leader of the Soviet Union," John explained.

"ARE YOU KIDDING ME!! Are you sure Russians haven't infiltrated Antifa?" Dutch cried in disgust. "How do we know how much Russia influence has in America. Look how much influence China has on America!"

"China poses a greater national security threat to the U.S. than any other nation – economically, militarily, and technologically. That includes threats of election influence and interference," John added.

CHAPTER SIXTEEN

Militia Center, Monday, November 23rd

The ten units assigned to Louisville had returned to find their home relatively quiet. Protesters against police were still marching in Portland Maine even though there existed no cases of any police brutality or racial profiling in the city. But at the Militia Center, John and Dutch arrived at the same time to find General Lipton in the Communication Center reading a newspaper, the Portland Press Herald.

"What's up General, I thought you were taking today off?" John asked. "Yes, I was home and reading the paper when I came upon an interesting story," She replied. "It appears someone pulled a prank on the protesters Saturday and I thought we should question our people about it," the General suggested.

"General, Maine's a big State. What leads you to believe it was one of us?" Dutch asked. "Because, according to the article, witnesses reported seeing a drone carrying a large object hovering over the protesters and drop the object right on top of them," General Lipton reported. Both John and Dutch just starred at the general, hoping she would volunteer the answer to their question. When she didn't, Dutch asked. "What did the drone drop?" "A very large bee's nest, packed full of very angry bees. The drone drop was successful, scattering the protesters. Twenty-two went to the hospital with multiple stings and three stayed overnight because they were allergic," The General informed.

"I could be wrong, and I hope I am, but we need to speak with Ruth and Scott and hopefully clear them off the list of suspects," the General added. So, John made a couple of calls and both Ruth and Scott were standing tall in the office within thirty minutes.

The General read the article to them word for word. When Ruth started to laugh, the General stopped reading and gave her the evil eye which stopped Ruth's laughing immediately. When General Lipton finished the reading, she waited. It felt like an hour, but only thirty seconds went by when Scott relented.

"It was me," he said. "Can you explain why you would do something like that?" Dutch asked. "I know the owner of a bakery on Congress Street. He's fed up with the protests. He's also an avid hunter, goes out every season for Turkey, Deer, and Moose. He found the bee's nest one day and propositioned me that if he could deliver the nest safely, could I drop it over the protesters," Scott explained. The General stood, "Ruth, did you have anything to do with this?" "No, Ma'am!" Ruth answered. "Then you're dismissed," The General ordered.

When she was gone, the General turned back towards Scott, "This Militia has been at many protests and never have we EVER attacked a peaceful protester. When we did, they or Antifa was about to commit a crime of looting, destruction, or assault towards the police or became a threat to us. If Antifa did what you did to the police or an innocent, we would hunt them down and turn them in.

This REGULATED Militia UPHOLDS the Constitution of the United States, which includes the First Amendment, the right to assemble. You assaulted the protesters, and you violated their rights!" The General turned and took a seat. When she sat down, she looked deflated. "John, Dutch, and I will need to talk about this. Your dismissed," she said.

"I'm SO sorry General! I guess I didn't think it through. You don't need to talk about it. I'll turn myself in." Scott said. The General looked at Dutch and John and said, "wait downstairs Scott." When he left, Dutch spoke, "When we turn him in, I'll go with him Ma'am, he'll need some support." "No, Dutch, let me bring it to Kennebunk's Chief of Police first, he's more aware of our record. Scott was crucial in the rescue of Chuck Mason's hostages this year. Maybe that will be considered in Scott's favor," the General said. "John, go get Scott, I'll take him to Chief Cameron myself," the General requested.

Kennebunk Police Department

When they arrived at the police station, the Officer on Deck recognized the General and asked, "What can I do for you, Ma'am." "We need to see the Chief, it's important." A few minutes later, they went through a metal detector and were frisked. The Chief came out of his office and shook her hand, "General. What can I do for you?" The Chief offered. "We need to speak somewhere private." He led them to his office and the General explained their presence.

The Chief looked at Scott and yelled, "Sargent Wagner!" Sargent Wagner appeared, and the Chief ordered, "take this man to your desk and wait until I call you. You can poison him with that shit you call coffee!" "Yes sir," the Sargent responded. When they were gone the General explained, "the protesters owe your man a debt of thanks," he said "What? I'm a little confused," the General replied.

"The City of Portland was pissed! They had to turn a good portion of Congress Street into a crime scene, then they had to send in HazMat personnel to clear the bees. But then they found a backpack with a C4 bomb wired to a clock which was supposed to go off ten minutes after the crowd scattered from the bees. The bomber never hit the arm switch," the Chief explained.

The General was speechless. "What do you want to do with Scott?" The General asked. "Look General, if you turn your boy over to the Portland Police, those kids who got stung are going to sue your boy dry, especially with the losses from the pandemic. It doesn't matter they're still alive because of him. I may be taking Justice into my own hands on this and the way I see it, the whole incident is a wash. You want to reprimand him, have it your way, but don't throw him to the wolves," the Chief replied. "You want to say anything to him?" The General asked. The Chief chuckled, "if I know you, you already have." "Can we at least help the Portland Police find the bomber?" The General asked. "They know how to review the security cameras in the area, take your boy home and make sure he doesn't do it again.

Militia Communication Center, the next mission.

When the General got back, Rene, John, and Dutch were in a video conference with Admiral Palton. "Ah, General, good to see you! The report on Kentucky was outstanding. Viola Waite is an amazing soldier, don't you think?" The Admiral asked. "She is, we've made quite an impression with her too," Gail replied.

"I've been saving this question for you, and now that you're here, how would you like to take all your militia and their families on a two-week vacation to Jacksonville Florida, which includes flights to and from, with room and board?" The Admiral asked. "Admiral, so far every free ride you've given us was not a vacation. Excuse me if I'm a little skeptical when it comes to your vacations," the General replied. "Would you like me to explain?" The Admiral asked. "Most definitely," John answered.

"Well, it's not exactly Jacksonville, it's about fifteen miles due west of the city to Naval Air Station Cecil Field," He said. "Admiral, wasn't that base shut down during the Obama Administration?" John asked. "Yes, and currently the airfield is now an airport. The Navy still owns the base and President Travis is proposing to re-open the base and eventually buy back the airfield. A lot of updates have been made to the officer's quarters, barracks, and galleys, which is where you and your families will be staying." "Why are you making this offer? Surely, you're not really sending us on a vacation to a Naval base," the General asked.

"I want to assemble ten militia companies, that's about three thousand men and women, from throughout the country and send them to the base for the purpose of training for the Inauguration Day of the President of the United States on January, 20." "What type of training?" Dutch asked. "Combat training, baton, and crowd control. We have thirty Israelite volunteers to teach Krav Maga combat. It's been working very well for our militia so far. Look, the President may not have won as expected, and whoever is inaugurated, Antifa will still be there."

"Why not just send the Israelites to each militia's states and train there?" Dutch asked. "You should know that the best fighting force is one that acts together, in one accord. This mission is going to take more than three thousand men and women being proficient combat fighters, together," The Admiral answered.

"Excuse me General, I thought if Joe Black wins, Antifa wins," Richard asked. "The election isn't over. Antifa and BPM are angry the Travis Administration is still in the fight with the discovery of all the fraud cases. And remember all the cell phones we took off Antifa in Connecticut? I've had NSA monitoring cell phone contacts and internet traffic. They've hit a treasure trove of chatter about attacking the White House. Looks like Antifa's revolution will continue. Antifa and BPM want a no police Marxist government, and President Travis is still in the way." The Admiral reported.

"Do they really believe they can succeed in implementing a Marxist state?" John asked. "If they can wear down the country or take out the President, Vice President, and a few Republican Senators, they'll be on their way with President Nancy Jezebel," the Admiral replied.

"The Federal Police and Secret Service will typically be there. I spoke with the President and he wants the National Guard there but not visible," Admiral reported. "Who are you putting in charge of all this training?" The General asked. "You and General Errol Flynn, an outstanding tactician, plus you've got Dutch, John, Reggie Austin, and all the unit leaders." "General Flynn will be there?" The General asked. "You've heard of him Gail?" "Absolutely! It would be a pleasure to work with him!"

"This whole thing is Top Secret. Your families will have to sign disclosure statements of secrecy. Every militia family member will have to read a response to a question that will be asked by the town of Cecil Field as to why the influx of base personnel.

I also want Gunny Ann Wilson in charge of all Base Logistics. You MUST submit a roster of all you people including the children so her advanced team can assign their quarters. On November 30th, at zero seven hundred, the leaders will meet, set-up, and schedule training. You'll have two weeks to train. You need to assemble your company and gather your volunteers ASAP. Your flight leaves, wheels up from Portsmouth on the November 30th, thirteen hundred.

Arrival, Cecil Field Naval Air Station, November 30th

The Maine Militia under General Gail Lipton had mustered up ten unit leaders, plus one-hundred and five troops. Adding the family members, they totaled one-hundred and eighty-two. Three thousand

and forty-two regular militia representing Maine, New Hampshire, Iowa, Kansas, Kentucky, Tennessee, Alabama, North & South Dakota, Arizona, Montana, Seattle, Arizona, New Mexico, and Texas accepted the assignment to train for the President.

The once ghost town of Cecil Field was now bustling with activity on that Monday. As their flights arrived, the militia was checked off rosters, assigned buses, and transported to their base quarters. Some folks who lived in the closer States like Alabama and Tennessee drove to the base.

To their advantage, they would have a car to get around in during their stay. Others had to take shuttles off the base and dropped off in town if they wanted to shop. Some rented cars so they could drive to Orlando's Disney World that Saturday. The Base had two galleys (mess halls) where personnel could dine for free or take the shuttle into town which had several restaurants.

Assembly, Base parking lot, December 1st zero seven hundred.
The massive central base parking lot was three hundred feet wide by nine hundred feet long. Ann Wilson and her advance team set up tall signs made from portable basketball stanchions with each militia State's name. So, at zero seven hundred that morning the militia's assembly was quick and organized. They were milling around in their groups when General Lipton and Flynn stepped up onto a newly constructed stage. Before them was a podium with microphones. The six speakers were evenly spread out in front of the troops on six-foot-tall bi-pods so the sound waves wouldn't be blocked by the troops upfront. On the right and left of the stage stood thirty Israeli, fifteen on each side

General Flynn moved to the microphone, "I am proud as I look out at Three thousand and forty-two patriots representing the United States of America. Thank you for volunteering for the militia and this critical assignment. In front of you to my right and left are thirty Israeli special forces combat soldiers who have traveled from their sovereign State of Israel by request of the President of United States! Join me with an awesome applause from America!"

General Lipton spoke next. "Our Israeli trainers have been assigned to each militia State and will train your State according to the schedules that were passed out earlier, later, all militia States will meet for full complement training to teach us in acting in one accord. Unit leaders will also be scheduled to meet with General Flynn and I to study strategies to protect the President and the National Mall. Finally, we will all study the ROE (Rules of Engagement). We WILL NOT tolerate any unnecessary deaths or abuse of power while representing the President!"

General Flynn took the podium, "With the exception of specially assigned and vetted snipers, only unit leaders will be armed on the National Mall. Everybody will be armed with combat batons so learn how to use them! We also provided you with maps of the base. This place is designed like a University Campus, everything is within walking distance, with a park, administration buildings two chow halls, the town is sending five assorted food vendor trucks and we have three empty aircraft hangers indicated on your map. You have access to all these facilities to study your welcome package. We meet back here at fourteen hundred to begin combat training, ensure you dress appropriately."

Earlier that month, Black People Matter Headquarters, Philadelphia

Patrisse Colon, the current leader of Black People Matter began her meeting with an update on Rasha Tossa's court hearings. "Rasha has one of the best lawyers in the business and they are trying to get the logbooks and C4 explosives thrown out of court on illegal search and seizure. They also are refuting the video and that it really wasn't Rasha. Their contending that the video was faked.

As for the really bad news, our top operative Don Lemmon was arrested on kidnapping charges of Mayor Greg Foster along with one of our best hackers. On the same night, several attempts by Antifa in looting and destruction in Louisville completely failed. The local militia must've had ESP because they were at every attempted event to block Antifa. Many were arrested, but because the courts are in our favor, they all walked out of jail the same night. Then again some didn't walk because THEIR F**KING LEGS WERE BROKEN!! We need to put out the word; find the militia's families and start terrorizing these white privileged supremacists' republicans!"

Eric Manning interrupted, "Calm down Patrisse, I've learned over decades that patience is very important when revenge is what you seek." Eric Manning, an eighty-six-year-old white man with thinning grey hair, and a wrinkled pocked mark face, who made millions buying and selling foreclosed homes created by the housing bubble of unregulated banks in 2007. A man who holds dear the radical Marxist-Leninist ideology.

"When we demonstrated for defunding the police, it happened in several cities. When we began tearing down historic statues, all our followers started tearing them down. When we began looting, everybody began looting, it's practically a fad now. We have been successful in intimidating the public, and right now, our biggest threat is overturning the election. If Travis remains the President for another term, it will damage our cause.

I suggest a mega-protest in D.C. Let's get everybody down there especially Antifa. I'll support travel. Put your people on the logistics. George and I will make it worth their while. I want Antifa to storm the capital. I want to personally handle Antifa. Get a face-to-face meeting the Antifa's best organizer.

We should attack and destroy as many fascist museums and government buildings at the Mall as possible. It will provide a distraction while a massive group storms the White House steps. The Senate will be in session on November 24. George will put a bounty of $10,000 on any Republican Senator, We must succeed!" Eric plotted. "Yes. And if we succeed, we could re-start the government. A Marxist ruled diversified government with more women and black leaders," George Soriss added, the Hungarian-born American billionaire investor and philanthropist. As of May 2020, he had a net worth of $8.3 billion, after having donated more than $32 billion to the Open Socialist Society Foundations said. "Eric and I will also fund travel, $1000.00 per participant and $2000.00 if they're arrested."

Crystal River Seafood, Sweetwater, Florida, Saturday, December 5th

The hostess led John, Leah, Richard, and Cheryl to their reserved table at the five-star seafood restaurant. The restaurant was seven miles outside the main gate of the Naval Air Base. "I think the base galley food is pretty good, but there's no replacement for fresh seafood," Cheryl commented. "Absolutely! And it's nice just to get off the base," Leah responded. "And the furnishings in our apartments are deplorable!" Cheryl protested. "I've never experienced back pain until sleeping on those beds!" Leah complained.

"I say the issues of comfort are worth it! The Israelis are teaching us some Krav Maga moves I've never seen before. I mean, there's a move for every act of aggression. And I realize their system of repetitiveness is turning the moves into natural memory," Richard admitted. "The Israelis have updated Krav Maga since Elijah studied it when he was in the Mossad. And how about the strategy Generals Flynn and Lipton came up with! It's so simple yet incredibly effective!" John added. "Yeah, we will counteract anything Antifa throws at us!" Richard replied.

"Boys! Can we try and have a normal dinner and stop talking about your upcoming war?" Leah asked. The waitress showed up with menus and water. When she asked if she could get the couples a drink, she also asked if they were from the base. Annoyed, Richard answered, "yes." "What exactly are you doing there?" She asked. John spoke up, "We are advance teams with special professions to make the base ready for a major inspection that might result in its re-opening," He answered. That was the answer every militia was to give when asked by the locals. "Changing the subject, John and Richard stuck with water and the women chose wine, then they ordered

Before the meals arrived, Cheryl asked, "I don't get it, why can't America see how much the Democratic Party is moving towards a big government socialist party?" "I think It all began in 1962 when the United States Supreme Court decided prayer in schools violated the First Amendment. The following year, the Court found Bible readings in public schools also in violation of the First Amendment." John answered. "Yeah and in 1973 Roe versus Wade made abortion legal," Richard added. "These three landmark Supreme Court decisions started the war against God Himself. It became legal for Americans to sacrifice their babies on the altar of the god of selfishness, and it is absolutely stated in the Bible that God is against that practice!" John added.

Leah spoke next, "Did you watch Hannity last night? The White House press secretary Kayleigh McEnany presented 234 pages of affidavits she claimed were proof that election fraud took place. She revealed that they have now received claims of 11,000 incidents of fraud from witnesses and have compiled 500 affidavits from these witnesses so far."

"That's why we're here training over three-thousand militia to combat an insurrection like never seen before. Antifa and BPM are all college-aged kids. They are learning how to hate America in school," John said.

When they finished dinner, Cheryl said, "I have a friend who is a teacher. She's upset because her Elementary School has implemented the 1619 Project. What exactly is that?" She asked. "The biggest red flag of the 1619 Project is, it was developed by one of the most liberal magazines in America, the New York Times.

The Project teaches that the United States is and always has been an evil country. The thesis of the 1619 Project is that the history of the United States didn't start in 1776 with the signing of the Declaration of Independence, rather, it started with the arrival of the first slaves to Jamestown in 1619. The Project is very misleading. It teaches, it is evil to be white and we should be ashamed of our country. Yet, the vast majority of US citizens never held slaves. Many were opposed to slavery. Our Country eventually went to war over slavery, and guess which Political Party was opposed to freeing the slaves....the Democrats," John explained.

"I believe I am the least racist person I know. Damn! I fought next to men of a different color skin and put my life in their hands. You know what I'm talking about John! One thing the military taught me was to know your enemy and I'm not sure who is more dangerous BPM, or the media. I did a little search last week and found just as many unnecessary police shootings of whites as blacks. The media don't care about people, it cares about ratings, the mighty dollar. It's sickening!" Richard spouted.

Leah asked, "So what can we do to fight schools from adopting the 1619 Project?" "We all need to start attending school board meetings, even if you're old and don't have kids in school. We need to push schools in adopting the alternate of the 1619 Project. We need to push The 1776 Unites Curriculum, which offers lesson plans, activities, reading guides , and other resources to illustrate what 1776 Unites calls a more complete and inspiring story of the history of African-Americans in the United States. The 1776 Unites maintains a special focus on stories that celebrate black excellence, rejects victimhood culture, and showcases African-

Americans who have prospered by embracing America's founding ideals," John explained.

"John, how do you know all about the 1619 Project and 1776 Unites?" Richard asked. "Fox News. You won't hear about any of this stuff by watching the liberal media, NBC, CNN, ABC, and CBS, they're all in bed with the Democrats!" John answered.

Naval Air Station Cecil Field Florida, December 11th

The two weeks of the militia training was almost over. General Lipton and Flynn met with all the unit leaders and agreed to a plan which added strategies into the training. They agreed that, at a minimum, antifa would attack federal buildings on the National Mall by either spray painting graffiti on the buildings or by storming and destroying the doors for access inside where they could cause billions of dollars of destruction.

So, they implemented training to fend off attacks on steps by combat fighting on football bleachers. This training honed their balance as they practiced using rubber batons against plastic bats. They practiced techniques of fighting down the bleachers and fighting up the bleachers.   Two months ago, President Travis got fed up with the tearing down of statues, so he signed an executive order making it a federal law protecting American monuments, memorials, and statues and threatened those who try to pull them down, including graffiti, with a five-year minimum prison term, and the toppling of statues stopped.

Every militia fighter would carry at least a dozen zip ties with them. The militia's strategy would employ large groups assigned to every federal building on the Mall including the National Monument with orders to protect the buildings. Each militia would be armed with combat batons and each unit leader of each group would be additionally armed with concealed back holstered pistols. Additional groups would be deployed at the Library of Congress and the Supreme Court building.

The militia's strategy concluded the expectations of a frontal attack of the Capitol around 2pm on the 24th of November was imminent. The best combat fighters would be deployed behind the police defense line beyond the Capitol Reflection Pool. They would represent the last combat fighting defense. Anyone who got past their lines would be considered a 'Clear and Present Danger' to the President of the United States and shot by the Secret Service snippers.

Their final strategy would deal with the position of the militia groups. The Generals concluded that the militia should attempt to blend in with the Capitol's visitors. While milling around within the crowd, they could seek out suspecting rioters before they attack and then wait and watch. The ROE (Rules of Engagement) would remain not to inflict harm unless threatened. At the end of the Florida training, the Generals sponsored a militia family day cookout including some of the local's best BBQ chefs. The Generals had given their final orders to all militia to take what they learned back to their home States and practice. General Lipton's closing speech was, "practice, practice, practice your training! Keep your head on a swivel and your eyes sharp at the National Mall. See you on November 24.

Library of Congress, November 24ᵗʰ thirteen-thirty
Adam Shifty and his small group of Antifa rebels were walking down Independence Avenue thirty minutes before the attack hour. "All we need to do is blow the Library's door and destroy the Declaration of Independence. Got it?" Shifty asked. He got okays from the five men with him. "We get in, start a book fire, we get out as fast as possible." As they approached the Library, they noticed three men sitting on the steps. The men stood up as they got closer.

"Take a hike," Adam said. "I'm sorry, but the Library is closed," Elijah Goffstien said. "It's a free country! Move or we will move you!" Adam demanded. "As you said, it's a free country and we're staying," Elijah replied. Adam took two steps closer to within four feet and whipped out a Sig Sauer P220 pistol and stuck it in Elijah's face. "Leave or lose your head!" Elijah grabbed Adam's wrist with his left-hand raising Adam's arm in the air. The gun fired into the sky. Elijah thrust his right hand's palm into Adam's jaw-breaking it with a crunch, then he kneed Adam in the groin as he was falling, As Adam was dropping, Elijah twisted his wrist with a snap taking the gun away, all within three seconds.

"Nobody else needs to get hurt. Just walk away and stay healthy," Elijah said. Looking up at his Antifa fighters, "don't you dear!" Adam growled as he laid on the sidewalk bleeding. "I will hunt you all down if you don't complete your mission!" He snarled. The militia observed one of the Antifa rebels ease their backpack down to the sidewalk and pulled out his knife. The others pulled out their knives but just stood there watching the militia remove their batons from the holsters. "TAKE THEM you assholes!" Adam shouted.

As the stalemate continued, the militia fanned out, so the rebels had to pick their opponents. The rebels were apprehensive to attack since Elijah had Adam's pistol, but it puzzled them when he threw the gun to the ground six feet away. "Last warning walk away now and you will be able to continue to enjoy the ability to walk," Elijah said.

The rebels charged the militia. They were swiping their knives back and forth and the militia was dodging and fainting one direction and cracking ribs and knees in the other direction.

When it was over the militia zip-tied their wrists and ankles. "Larry, check out that backpack. This idiot was too careful laying it down," Elijah asked. When Larry opened the pack, he found the bomb. Elijah looked at Adam tied up on the ground, "how many bombs on the Mall?" Elijah asked. Adam just spued a mixture of explicit metaphors. Elijah stepped on Adam's broken wrist and Adam screamed in pain, "Stop! Please! I'll tell you!" Adam yelled. "How many bombs are on the Mall or you'll need a prosthetic after today," Elijah threatened.

"six to ten, I'm not sure," Adam confessed. "What are the targets?" "I don't know, each cell has its own target, none of us know who has what." Larry was examining the backpack and looked up at Elijah, "looks like C4 attached to an alarm clock set for 2 pm." "Larry, call 911 and get EOD over here," but before Elijah finished giving the order, Larry removed the fuse from the C4 disarming the bomb.

Elijah radioed, "All mall units, this is Library unit, we took down rebels carrying a backpack bomb, repeat, backpack bomb. Rebel leader claims max ten more in the mall. Targets unspecified. Backpacks will contain C4 attached to a clock set for fifteen seconds after 2 pm."

Smithsonian National Museum of American History.

Larry Wetzel and his unit of ten militia heard the radio transmission from Elijah and immediately conveyed orders to his fighters. "Dispersed two by two in front of the Museum of History. Circle around, look for a small band of possible Antifa, and focus on backpacks." One of his unit's fighters named Robin, posing as a BPM protester infiltrated a small group of possible Antifa men, and asked, "how can I help cause some chaos?" They laughed and said "Stick around if you want to really have some fun. We're going to blow doors!" One of them said.

Laughing with them she moved around the group and got caught trying to peek into one of their backpacks. "What are you looking for bitch?" One asked. "I'm thirsty and was wondering if you've got something to drink. And don't call me bitch!" She said. "There's a food kiosk right over there, go get yourself a coke and greasy burger if you want, but stay away from my stuff," he told her. She didn't get a good look into the backpack, but why was someone else carrying 'his stuff?' She knew they were Antifa based on their conversations. She also had an excuse to leave the group and began walking towards the kiosk. As soon as she was safely buried into a group of Protesters, she circled around and found Larry. "I found a group of Antifa," and pointed their way.

Larry had to come up with a quick plan. The first thing was to call in his unit. "History unit, on me ASAP," he spoke into his throat mic. As they were forming up, he weighed the options, should he try and take them down now or wait for them to make a move first. Robin knew he was considering a plan and suggested, "Larry, they called me a bitch. Why don't you pose as my boyfriend and defend my honor," she said smiling. Smiling back and nodding his head as her plan played out in his mind said, "good call."

He turned to his unit, unhooked his baton holster, gave it to one of his men, and said, "without drawing attention, surround that group and watch our backs. I'm going to try to get an apology for my girlfriend," One of them laughed and said, "Does Priscilla know?" Larry laughed back and said, "it's complicated." Then Larry waited, giving the militia time to get into position. "Let's go honey," Larry joked. "Keep it up Larry, and I might tell your wife myself." They both approached the Antifa leader and Larry got in his face. "My girl says you called her a bitch," Larry said. "What's it to you!" "It's not politically correct, not nice, and you owe her an apology."

Larry was standing with his body balanced, his weight centered on the balls of his feet. He didn't look like he was in a fighting stance because Krav Maga is a non-threatening form of defense, but he was ready. Jake, the Antifa leader, was a bigger man, with a linebacker's body. His noses looked like it had been broken once. Without warning, Jack shot a sucker punch at Larry. Jake made the mistake of telegraphing the punch by winding up first allowing Larry to just leaned back and let Jake's fist fly by.

Larry put his hands up in surrender. "Look I don't want any trouble. I don't want to hurt you. Be a gentleman, apologize and we'll be on our way," Larry asked. "You're going to hurt me?" He looked around laughing while his group closed in. One of them said, "We outnumber you, six to one, I think if anybody gets hurt it will be you." "Try six to two," Robin warned.

Jake smiled and suddenly rushed Larry like a linebacker. Larry sidestepped the attack and as Jake passed by, Larry kick him in the butt causing his forward momentum to carry him into a stumbling fall, flat face into the ground. The man that was on Jake's left lunge at Larry and Robin kicked him in the groin before he could take two steps. When he bent over, she sent her knee into his chin. He fell on his back and curled up in a fetal position groaning. Jake was up as quickly as he went down in time to see one of his men laying on the ground.

Jake quickly walked back up to Larry and threw a straight-out punch at Larry's face which he dodged and swept away with his arm. Jake followed up with a low swing towards the sola plex which Larry stepped into making it miss behind around his back. Now Jake was danger close, so Larry sent an uppercut straight under the jaw. Jake's head snapped back, and he went down like a falling tree. This left four Antifa rebels to face Larry and Robin, but two of them had backpack bombs and didn't want to engage. They watched as the next two rebels stepped up to take on Larry and Robin.

Robin's size was not intimidating at all. She was thin and even looked Anorexic, but her body was wiry and stone solid. She was a marathon biker, but she was also a trained Krav Maga fighter. The two Antifa without backpacks pulled their knives and anticipated it would be enough to scare off Robin and Larry. It didn't. The militia watched on while standing behind the backpack carrying rebels who had no idea they were there.

The Antifa who chose to fight Robin lunged at her with a swipe of his knife. He must have survived being an aggressor by weapon intimidation because he telegraphed his attack more than Jake. To her, it was like slow motion. She just dodged and waited for the swipe to pass the strike zone, stepped in, and like a rattlesnake thrust the palm of her hand into the nose of the Antifa. With a crunch, he dropped like a sack of dirt.

By now, a crowd had circled the fight. BPM supporters were enjoying the entertainment but weren't sure about cheering for the two outnumbered fighters. The crowd had no idea they were militia.

The two backpackers attempted to slink away but when they turned, they were faced with four men. "Relax and you won't get hurt," one of the militia fighters said. The final Antifa fighter kept his knife out in front of him making short quick swipes with his knife. It was a better defensive and offensive position, but his stance was all wrong. Both legs were under his shoulders instead of one leg forward. The Antifa rebel was surprised and watched Larry drop to the ground under the knives swipe zone landing on his left side.

Larry kicked out in a stomp motion aimed at the Antifa's knee, and connected directly pushing the knee in the direction it was not meant to go. As the Antifa dropped forward, Larry rolled away expecting Antifa to aim his knife as he fell. When the Antifa hit the ground, his knife struck dirt. Larry was on his feet. The defeat of the four Antifa rebels took less than three minutes.

Larry approached the bomb carriers. One of them said, "You can't legally search our backpacks!" "If you haven't noticed yet, we're not cops." Larry put his hands up in surrender. "Hey, if you want to sit here till the cops arrive in fifteen minutes, fine with me. We'll just give you some room." NO WAIT!" okay, please disarm the bombs!" "Whatever you say." Larry opened the backpacks and pulled the fuses. "they won't need to search because your backpacks will be opened to public sight and still attached to your bodies. You're going away for a long, long time, but if you answer only two questions, we'll remove the backpacks, and you can take your chances on possession charges during your criminal court hearing. One, who's the bomb-maker and Two, what other Federal buildings will be targeted?" Larry asked.

"I swear! I don't know who the bomb-maker is. I don't know what other buildings are targeted, but I do know the attacks on the Federal Buildings are a distraction for an attack on the Capitol. That's all I know, I swear!" Larry ordered one of the militia to remove the rebel's backpack and to another to call 911 and request EOD.

He turned to the other rebel and asked, "what about you, you want to be wearing that when the real cops arrive?" Almost sobbing, the rebel answered, "He's telling the truth. I was told to throw the backpack at the History Museum's door and duck. I know the Capitol attackers will have guns." "Take off his backpack, remove their cellphones and knives and display them with the backpacks for the police," Larry commanded and then he radioed his discoveries to the rest of the militia.

White House Roof, thirteen fifty

John Colton and the Secret Service were on the same frequency as the Mall militia. They heard about the bomb and radioed the Police Commissioner on a different frequency. The Commissioner held up a walkie talkie and informed the commander of the police line in front of the Capitol steps. Next to John, Dutch was watching with binoculars, he checked his watch and radioed, "All units, at our command, move to the steps of your buildings. Be prepared to repel attackers. Priority Antifa carrying backpacks and watch for small arms." Fourteen hundred hours was approaching quickly, and John turned to his militia's leader Captain Dutch Swanson who spoke into his throat mic. "All elements, prepare to execute."

The Antifa rebels were able to establish key positions near the Capitol's steps in front of the police defense lines. Some were gathered around the Peace Monument at the Capitol's front left, others were ready on the right at the Garfield Monument, the main force was gathered around the Ulysses S. Grant Memorial. They weren't using communication devices, but they would all attack the Federal Buildings and the White House at exactly 2 pm.

Part of Antifa's plan was the humiliation that the President was not able to protect any Federal Building, especially the Library of Congress where the Declaration of Independence was displayed and he couldn't protect himself if they were successful in this coup. With one minute to spare, Dutch spoke into his mic, "ALL ELEMENTS EXECUTE!"

National Mall Federal Buildings

All the Mall defenders moved to the steps of their objective buildings upon Captain Dutch's command. When the Antifa groups also moved, they were ambushed by teams of militia with batons. Militia fighters were taking down the rebels three to one. Backpacks were disarmed while still worn by the wounded rebels.

Suddenly, one of the bombs got through and exploded on the steps of the National Museum of Art. Thousands of peaceful protesters heard the explosion and dropped their signs and began screaming and running in every direction away from the sound. Antifa rebels who were taken down by the militia were trampled over by the panicked protesters. Bodies of people began to quickly pile up from tripping over a trampled body.

At this point, it was easy to determine who the Antifa were. They stayed to fight for a cash bounty. One of the unit leaders, Leslie Cunningham was fighting an experienced rebel street fighter. She was about to get the upper hand when a panicked protester unintentionally crashed into her, sending both her and the protester to the ground.

Leslie's opponent now stood over her and removed a small twenty-two caliber pistol from his front pants pocket. After connecting punches to her body in their fight, he knew she was wearing Kevlar, so he aimed for her head. A shot fired from her left dropping the armed Antifa dead. Leslie looked over and saw another unit leader Dick Vinaldo crouched with his pistol extended.

Luke Morgan had just taken down an Antifa with a backpack. He flipped the cover and pulled out the fuse. In his peripheral vision he noticed a rebel drawing down on him. Luke went for his gun, but he wasn't a unit leader and was only armed with a baton. All Luke could do was yell "GUN!" Unit leader Ronald Brown heard Luke and drew his weapon before he spotted the armed rebel. A quick snapshot wounded the rebel a second before the rebel fired. The rebel's aim was knocked off and his stray bullet hit a fleeing protester in the leg, and they tumbled to the ground.

The rebel still had the gun and rested his sights on Luke and fired. Ronald Brown fire at the same time killing the rebel, then ran over to Luke to find him holding his chest and coughing. He ripped open

Luke's jacket to find the Kevlar vest with a half inch indent where the bullet hit. "Elijah was right! You need eyes in the back of your head!" Luke said between coughs

Another Antifa rebel was able to toss their bomb above the militias defense line and onto the front platform of the Air and Space Museum. It slid up near to the wall. One of the militia fighters saw the backpack flying in the air and yelled "BOMB!" and all the militia dove to the ground.

Mike Ackroff saw the flying backpack and without thinking about his own safety ran after the bomb, instead of away from it. When he reached the backpack, he yanked open the flap, found the fuse, and pulled it out of the C4. He looked at the clock, he gasped, only two seconds left before exploding. Mike walked back down the steps, looked up and down the mall, and couldn't see any more active brawls. Most of the protesters were evacuating and now the militia was running around rendering aid to the injured. The militia had succeeded. He found the zip-tied rebel who threw the backpack sitting on the steps and wanted to kick a 100-yard field goal with his head.

Ulysses S. Grant Memorial, thirteen fifty-nine

Kentucky Militia Captain Viola Waite was on a knee below the steps and left of the Capitol just beyond the Reflection Pool. On a knee next to her was Ruth Taylor, whose portable drone hovered over the area. On the other side of the Reflection Pool was Sargent Richard Bloomer and Scott Hamlin, also at the controls of another drone.

Ruth had already observed a suspicious group milling around the Peace Monument. Nobody in that group was wearing backpacks, but Ruth's drone was able to zoom in on unusual bulges in some of their pockets. Viola had dispatched one of her units to shadow them.

Ruth also noticed a clump of fighting aged males in front of the Ulysses S. Grant Memorial. Viola ordered Master Sargent Leon Russel's unit to inconspicuously infiltrate the group and wait for Antifa's attack signal before engaging.

Freddy Booker was a stringy looking white crack addict with shoulder-length oily hair. Even in a crowd of hoodlums he looked out of place in baggy denim cargo pants and a black hoodie sweatshirt. His group of Antifa rebels were in position near the Grant Monument and was wondering why the attack hadn't started on the Federal Buildings in the mall yet, there were no explosions. His cell phone call to Adam Shifty failed and he was supposed to hear explosions!

He checked his watch again and took a couple of steps forward so he could see past the monument he was standing in front of. He saw several pockets of disturbances. *"Who are they fighting? What the hell?* Then he heard an explosion. It was time to attack. He turned to go back to his group and call the charge when he literally bumped into Master Sargent Leon Russel. Looking up at the six-four two hundred eighty-pound black man, who said. "I think your plan has gone sideways. Give me your gun and you'll walk into jail instead of being carried into a hospital."

Without thinking, Freddy shot his hand into his hoodie's front pocket and grabbed the gun. Both of Leon's fists dropped down onto Freddy's collarbones, his legs buckled like an accordion and he crumbled as his gun fired into the ground next to him. When Freddy's group of rebels saw what happened, some pulled their weapons and others began running towards the Capitol steps, they could be rewarded more if arrested inside.

Those who chose to draw their weapons, as soon as the pistols cleared their pockets, they experienced extreme pain in their wrists or arms when met with lead tipped batons of their shadowing militia. The twenty who charged joined with twenty more charging from the Peace Monument attackers. The pursuing militia caught up to the attacking rebels leaving behind crippled squirming bodies. The police hammered any rebel who got that far. The slower militia cleaned up the pistols dropped by those rebels who fallen.

The Garfield Monument

Richard expected that Antifa probably had a group on his side of the Reflection Pool near the Garfield Monument. He dispatched his protest sign carrying units to seek them out. Scott directed his drone's search to the area and sure enough, his drone's zoom was picking up some shady suspects. Richard alerted his units and ordered them to casually get in front of the rebels to block their charge.

When the explosion was heard out on the National Mall, the rebels charged forward and ran into a curtain of militia defenders.

Richard's unit were not so merciful and wheeled their batons at the rebel's heads. None of the rebels had a chance to grab a weapon. None of them were left squirming on the ground.

John and the Secret Service watched on, pivoting their rifles from one attack to another, to the left and another to the right, never firing a shot. John didn't hear anybody call, man down, but that didn't mean no militia had been shot. When things began to civilize, John radioed, "unit leaders, sitrep." Each unit leader responded according to their numbers. One man, Luke, was hit but alive.

Inside the Capitol General Flynn and Federal Police were standing outside the Senate and General Lipton and Federal Police were outside Congress monitoring the battle and finally received the call, "The Capitol is Clear!"

Two hours after the Insurrection

Admiral Patton walked up to John Colton and pat him on the back.

"The militia did a mighty fine job John. Numbers are coming in and so far, ninety-eight arrests were made, two dead, ten backpack bombs recovered, one exploded, which didn't do a lot of damage. It did crack one of the Museum's pillars. Fifty-three guns were confiscated and only five shots fired," the Admiral reported. "You know Admiral, even in the absence of promotions and medals in the Navy, I believe the last eight months have been more rewarding," John replied. They both laughed.

"John, you know it's not over. There are still people out there who are not happy with the results of this election on both sides. Freedom of speech is being threatened with Antifa still running around. I hope you're not thinking about retiring again," the Admiral said. "That little training exercise you arranged in Florida was pretty sophisticated. I don't know how you did it, but I'm impressed. We didn't get that kind of support in the Gulf and we're just militia."

"Not JUST a militia John, you're a Regulated Militia whose job is to protect the U.S. Constitution! Both potential Presidents like knowing you're out there."

"So then, what's next Admiral?" John asked. "I'd like to find out who's supplying the Antifa with C4. I'm organizing a small intelligence group with NSA support. We will be watching and listening." "Don't we already have that with the FBI and CIA?" John asked. "Yes, their operation and domestic and international terrorism, but Antifa, the proud boys or even the KKK is not on their radar. I've given General Lipton her orders. Get back to Maine, continue to train, and stay sharp. I'll call when I have something."

THE END

ABOUT THE AUTHOR

Living in Southern Maine with his wife Leah, John Pattanawick, a retired Navy Aviation Veteran has traveled around the world. He enjoys talking about current affairs with other retired associates from the CIA, Homeland Security and Gulf War. He has read hundreds of books in various genre and next to the Bible, his favorites have been about patriotic Black Ops. Special Forces, fiction and non-fiction. Learning the common objective of the lowest ranking Grunt to the highest-ranking General is to know your enemy. After decades of studying the Bible, John has concluded that enemy identification also applies in the Spiritual realm around us. John enjoys writing about the battles of both realms in life.

9 781636 610474